The Unimaginable

The Unimaginable

DINA SILVER

LAKE UNION
PUBLISHING

Text copyright © 2014 Dina Silver

Published by Lake Union Publishing, Seattle
www.apub.com

Amazon, the Amazon logo, and Lake Union Publishing are trademarks of Amazon.com, Inc., or its affiliates.

Cover design by Cyanotype Book Architects

ISBN-13: 9781477824962
ISBN-10: 1477824960

Library of Congress Control Number: 2014905955

Printed in the United States of America

Prologue

'll never forget the smell. It was jarring in many ways, but memorable because I'd never been afraid of a scent before. I closed my eyes and breathed through my mouth as I waited my turn.

They came for me third.

I stood and was blindfolded—loosely and without much care—and then led upstairs. There was no waking up from the nightmare, but once the fresh air hit my face it gave me hope. I nearly cried with relief when the ocean breeze filtered through me. The dank, salty air was my freedom, and, I thought to myself, if I could just get into the water, everything would be okay. But there was no easy passage to safety. No crack in the system that was designed to keep me in place. I was there for one reason and one reason only. A bargaining chip.

My legs were cramped and weak, and without my sight, my bearings were off. As soon as I was free of their grasp, I spun around, unaware of which way to go at first, and then got my footing and ran up the narrow path headed for the bow. The smell of the water got so strong that I could almost feel it on my skin. *Just get to the edge and jump. Don't hesitate, don't look back, don't think.* The water would cover me and keep me safe.

I had to reach my target. They were counting on me below, and I refused to go back down there. My feet were as determined as my mind, and eventually I knew exactly where I was. The blindfold slid down and restored my sight as soon as I rounded the corner, and I could see that I only had two more strides until the edge.

I almost made it . . .

Chapter 1

Six months earlier

The only reason I cried at my mother's funeral was because I hated seeing my sister Caroline so upset. Yet there she was again, ripe with sorrow, only on account of me this time. The date was August 3, 2010, and it was two months after my mom died, forty-five days after I lost my teaching job, and fifteen years after I first dreamt of leaving Indiana. And I was boarding a flight to Thailand.

It was the only airplane I'd ever been on.

Caroline, who was twenty-two years older than me, had driven me to the airport in silence, wiping her tears most of the way. Leaving her would be the hardest thing for me to do.

We stood for a moment at the curb.

"Thank you for taking me," I said.

She crossed her arms and forced a nod.

"I know you can't understand why I'm doing this, but I appreciate you being here. I could never leave without saying good-bye to you." I swallowed. "I only wish I had your blessing too."

She looked away. "I just think this is a little extreme. I could've helped you find another job here, Jessica."

"What would you know about extreme?" I snapped. "You've never done anything extreme, let alone considered it."

She glared at me.

I took a deep breath. "I'm sorry, but look at me." I paused and tugged at my thick blond hair. It'd been the same chin-length bob since I was twelve. My mother forbid long hair when I was young, and even as an independent adult I felt guilty every time it inched closer to my shoulders, so I'd lop it back off. "I'm twenty-eight years old, and I'm still wearing my hair like she wanted me to."

"I'm not going to speak ill of her. Not now."

Not ever, I thought to myself.

"This is an opportunity for me to make a difference." I paused to meet her eyes, but she looked away. "I don't want another job here—you know that. I want a change of scenery, something different . . . I need something different. The only thing keeping me here is you. And I'm not saying that's not enough—"

She put her hand up to silence me. "I know it's not enough for you, but I tried my best, I really did."

"I know you did," I said, and we hugged.

I always felt like I was born into the wrong family in the wrong town, and my mom did nothing to dispute those feelings. Following the status quo and the word of the Lord was all I was ever allowed to do. Go to school. Go to church. Get a job. Meet a good man. Learn to bake apple pie. Quit said job and start having children. Join the church auxiliary. Bake more pie. Cherry, maybe.

Caroline was my rock. She sang me to sleep when I was little, she dried my tears when I suffered through a broken teenage heart, and as far as I understood, she was the only person who ever loved me. But a sister just isn't a mother, no matter how hard she tries or how much she believes it to be.

Caroline was a teacher, so I became a teacher. I attended the same community college as her and graduated with a job as a second grade teacher at Milford Elementary School in Wolcottville, Indiana. In my free time I could be found at the library, sifting through DVDs. I used to sit around for hours watching American films and foreign films made in exotic locations, all the while dreaming about the challenges of living without strip malls and sports bars. Photocopied images of white sand beaches and *palapas* and sailboats and grass-covered mountains littered the walls above my bed, so that every morning I'd wake up to pictures of everywhere I'd rather be.

"You wouldn't last a day," Caroline used to say to me.

"You're right," I'd tell her. "I'd last a lifetime."

I loved Caroline more than anyone in the world and, sadly, more than she loved herself. She got married very young, right out of college, and when her husband learned that she was unable to bear children, he divorced her soon after.

I was all she had.

She desperately wanted me to share the same dreams as her, and for a while I tried really hard to appease her. But deep down I envied those who'd broken free from the monotony of LaGrange County. And with my mother gone, now it was my turn.

We stood for a final moment, before Caroline broke the awkward silence.

"I want to show you something." She reached into a brown paper bag that she'd brought with her and pulled out a photo album bound with a long, thin leather cord. "Take a look at this."

I took the book and unwound the cord. Inside, the pages were worn and filled with photographs—some color, some black and white—of a beautiful young woman posing all over the streets of New York City and sporting the biggest, brightest smile I'd ever seen. I barely recognized her, but she looked just like me. Petite in stature, with a slim figure, blue eyes, and blond hair—only hers was long. There were pictures of her wearing miniskirts and go-go boots in front of the Statue of Liberty, bell-bottoms and tight sweaters atop the Empire State Building, and blue jeans on the Brooklyn Bridge.

"It's Mom," Caroline told me as I turned the pages. "On her honeymoon. Back when she was a bit of a dreamer, just like you."

I brought my hand to my mouth.

"I found it when I was cleaning out her closet," she said with a small shrug. "Looks like you may have been more like her than you think."

I closed the book and held it close to my chest. "Thank you," I whispered.

It was with a heavy heart and high hopes that I turned and walked away.

Chapter 2

Twenty-four hours later I was a mess when I landed at Phuket International Airport. Mostly because I'd spilled an entire can of tomato juice down the front of my white shirt thirty minutes into the daylong flight. I didn't sleep very well, and my hair looked like I had brushed it with a whisk. Mrs. Smythe from the local travel agency in Wolcottville had helped me locate a place to live near Tall Trees Academy, where I'd been assigned to work, so once I made it safely through customs and had my passport stamped for the first time, I went to hail a taxi that would deliver me to my new home.

It was late Saturday afternoon, and the taxi line, like the customs line, was complete pandemonium. People pushing and waving their arms and yelling commands to each other in a language I couldn't understand. I kept checking my passport and my belongings, certain I was forgetting to do something, but there was so much activity that it was hard to focus. As soon as I thought I was next in line, no less than five people would walk in front of me and grab the next cab with no regard for the fact that I'd been waiting. I had so many bags—three large duffels, one small rolling bag, my backpack, laptop case, and a small purse—that I was afraid to step away from them for even a second.

"You go, witch!" a man said, startling me. He stood disturbingly close.

I gasped. "I'm sorry, what did you say?"

The heat was stifling, yet he was wearing a red velvet tracksuit, five gold chains, and enough cologne to sedate a horse. He carried a small leather portfolio in his right hand and cigarette in the other, and had we met anywhere else in the world I would have run. But something about his face, and the fact that he recognized it was I who looked painfully out of place, not him, made me want to trust him. At least long enough to get my bags off that curb and into a cab.

"You go which way?" He waved at the line of taxis.

"Oh, yes! I'm going . . ." I paused and fumbled through my back-pack for the piece of paper with my new address on it and showed it to him.

He nodded and then yelled to a man at the front of the line. I didn't understand a word of what he said, but the man came and grabbed my bags and threw them into the trunk of a car.

"Um . . . thank you." I extended my hand.

"I am Niran. I am born in Phuket," he said as we shook hands. "Maybe you know me?"

I shook my head.

"Everybody know me. You coming to Phuket before?"

"No, this is my first time."

"First time!" he rejoiced, and shouted something else to the driver before reaching in his pocket and handing me his card. "You coming to see me. This is my place. You coming there. You like vodka?"

I glanced down at the card. It read, "Niran [no last name], Owner, The Islander Bar & Grill." Underneath the address it said, "Come up and see me sometime." I could not contain my smile.

"Thank you, Niran. I promise to come see you sometime."

He took a puff of his cigarette, tilted his head while checking me out head to toe, then blew the smoke toward the sky. "You on vaca-tion or you need job?"

"I'm moving here to work at one of the local schools. I'm a teacher. An English teacher."

"So you need job." He took another puff and then stamped the butt out on the sidewalk. "I see you," he said, and walked away.

"Thank you!" I shouted after him, and then darted over to my cab.

About twenty minutes later we arrived in the town of Koh Kaew. The streets were crowded and narrow, and my driver swerved around an overturned bus like it was an orange traffic cone. People stood on the side of the road having conversations with little or no concern for the vehicles speeding past them.

I craned my neck out the open rear window and let the sun warm my face as I spied the ocean off to my left. The water was mostly calm with the occasional whitecap and flanked by enormous moss-covered rocks the size of small buildings. It was the most glorious and intimidating sight I'd ever seen. A moment later the cab made a sharp turn, and we pulled down a street filled with houses that all looked the same—boxy two-story homes, each with a small patio—until we stopped in front of a gray one. There was a waist-high metal gate surrounding the property, and a small square yard with freshly trimmed grass in the front. I hesitated before exiting the car.

The driver unloaded my things onto the sidewalk and lit a cigarette as he waited for me to get out and pay him. It was then I realized I'd forgotten to convert my dollars to baht at the airport, but thankfully he accepted American money.

The first thing I noticed when I emerged from the cab was the scent in the air. A wild combination of cumin, ginger, and hibiscus, infused with diesel fumes from the motorbikes and tuk-tuks whizzing by on the busy cross streets.

"Thank you," I said to him, and heard the front door of the house open behind me. A woman nicely dressed in white Capri pants and sandals came running out. Her grayish-brown hair was in a pixie cut, and her smile made me relax for the first time in two days.

"You must be Jessica," she said.

"Yes, hello. Mrs. Knight?" I extended my hand.

"Lovely to meet you. Now, bring your things inside, and I will show you to your room and introduce you to my husband," she said, and walked back into the house.

Soon after I'd lost my job in Indiana, I signed up for a teacher exchange program that matches qualified educators with needy schools around the world. Once I was accepted, I'd been paired up with Mr. and Mrs. Knight through Tall Trees Academy. Certain families—Thai, British, and American—took part in the program and offered rooms for rent to people like me. The Knights were a retired American couple in their early seventies who split their time between Phuket and their native city of Houston, Texas. That was all I knew about them at that point.

The house was very nice-looking from the outside, and I was pleased with the neighborhood as well. Many of the houses in Phuket are stilt houses, built elevated back in the day to prevent flooding and keep out unwanted animals. With most of the stilt houses, the terrace is the largest part of the home, and there is often no indoor plumbing. Luckily for me, I was able to find residence in a more modernized area of the city only about twenty minutes by bicycle, my only means of transport, from the school. Bottom line, it was a far cry from the farm I grew up on.

Once inside, I placed all of my bags in the front foyer and nearly fell asleep waiting for Mrs. Knight to return. My body was reeling from culture shock, jet lag, sleep deprivation, and living my dream.

"In here, dear!"

I followed her voice to a small family room with a covered terrace. Her husband was outside reading a book and struggled to get out of his chair. He was a heavyset man with wire-rimmed glasses who smiled and waved enthusiastically when I rounded the corner.

"Why, hello there," he said. "Aren't you a lovely young thing?"

I hurried to him. "Thank you, I'm such a mess. I'm Jessica Gregory. It's wonderful to meet you. I really appreciate you both so much for having me."

"Bob Knight. Please have a seat." He gestured to one of the chairs.

"Thank you."

"I'll fetch us some tea," Mrs. Knight said.

Bob slowly sat back down and glanced at the red stain on my shirt. "So, Jessica, tell me about yourself. Agnes mentioned you're from Indiana."

I thought of my life up until that moment and struggled to come up with what to say. The most interesting thing I'd ever done in my twenty-eight years was getting on that plane to Phuket. I folded my hands in my lap.

"Yes, I'm from Wolcottville. It's about an hour east of South Bend. I went to college near there and graduated with a degree in education, and then I moved back home, where I worked as a second grade teacher," I told him. But what I wanted to say was, "Despite the fact that I'm from a zero-stoplight town, covered in dried tomato juice, forgot to convert my money at the airport, and can't see straight because I couldn't sleep on a plane—having never flown on one before—I promise I'm not a complete fool!"

"Is this your first time in Thailand?"

"It is."

"And your parents, are they still in Indiana?"

"My mom passed away a couple months ago, but yes, my father and some of my siblings are still there." I paused and thought how little I spoke to any of them besides Caroline. My entire family could be standing at a bus stop together and would have almost nothing to say except for pleasantries.

"I'm sorry to hear that about your mother. Was she ill?"

I shook my head. "She had a heart attack."

He made a tsk sound. "Well, isn't that a terrible thing? I'm very sorry."

"Thank you," I said. I'd talked to people more about my mother in the past two months than I had in my lifetime. As the youngest of nine kids, I suffered the greatest distance from my mom, both in years and in emotional attachment. She was a strict, unemotional woman, a firm disciplinarian and a stringent Catholic who kept a ruler within reach at all times. She'd had too much sex to be a nun, so she ruled our home like a monastery instead. I glanced down at my hands and thought how much she would've hated the bright blue nail polish I was wearing.

Mrs. Knight brought in a tray of tea.

"Thank you so much," I said as she filled our cups. "You have such a lovely yard. I see you've started some tomato plants out back. Do you garden?"

She looked out the window behind her husband. "Not so much anymore," she said.

"I used to grow vegetables at home, so I'd be happy to help if you like."

Mrs. Knight smiled at me. "I would like that very much."

Her husband took a sip. "So what made you decide to leave your job in . . . where did you say?"

I laughed. "Wolcottville. I was let go. I was one of the younger teachers on staff, and they had to make some budget cuts. My principal was actually the person who gave me the idea of teaching abroad. He'd done it himself many years ago." I smiled when I recalled the conversation. Nothing had ever given me such clarity as talking with him about uprooting my entire existence to teach kids on the other side of the world. "Anyway, the schools in Phuket, as I'm sure you know, were so profoundly affected by the tsunami that this is one of the areas that still needs the most help. Even after all these years."

"Well, it's a good thing you're doing."

"Perhaps you'd like to see your room. You must be tired," Mrs. Knight added.

I sighed gratefully. "Thank you. I would love to unpack and lie down."

My room was toward the back of the house, just behind the kitchen. The walls were painted a pale coral color, and there was a woven pink and green throw rug in the center of the wood floor. There was no closet, only a removable bookshelf-like feature and chest of drawers. It was simple yet cheerful.

"There's a red Schwinn out back that is yours to use as long as you're here. We don't allow our guests to use the washer and dryer in the house, but there is a coin laundry up the road, and you may borrow the car once a week to go there. I would, however, be happy to wash your shirt for you if you'd like."

I looked down. "That's very nice of you but not necessary. I've sort of accepted defeat on this one."

"When you're ready, I'll show you the space in the refrigerator and pantry that you may use. We ask that you be respectful of our things and our space and use only what is yours. You are expected to buy your own food and household items."

"Yes, ma'am, of course. Thank you."

She smiled, and we stared at each other for a moment.

"It's lovely to meet you, Jessica. We always enjoy having company," she said, and closed the door behind her.

Once I was alone, I opened my computer and found the Knights' Wi-Fi signal. I made a mental note to set up password protection for them, and then sent a quick e-mail to Caroline as promised:

Caroline,

I made it! The plane ride was not as bad as I thought it would be, but I was awake for most of it. Thank you for the snacks. They were a lifesaver. My hosts, Mr. and Mrs. Knight, seem like wonderful people and made me feel very welcome. I have my own little room in the back of the house, and it over-looks a beautiful garden.

I have so much to do and will admit to being a little nervous about finding my way around here, but I'm mostly excited. Once I get some rest, I'll have a better handle on things.

Lastly, I'm sorry about how we left things. You don't have to come to terms with anything. I've come to realize that despite your years of best efforts, there was never anything you could've done to make Mom proud of me. We never had anything in common and never would. But you are the kindest, most selfless person in our family, and we'd all be lost without you. My whole life you were my biggest cheerleader and support system, and it's because of you that I was able to find the courage to leave. Maybe one day you'll understand why I needed to get out of Indiana, and maybe you won't. Either way, I love you more than anything, and I know you love me too.

I'll write again soon.

Jess

I could hardly grasp my own reality. There I was, lying on the floor with my head on a duffel bag miles from where I grew up, in a country where I couldn't speak the language or hang an article of clothing, but I was home.

This was my home now.

I couldn't help but wonder whether I'd made the right decision. Even with weeks of planning and anticipation, nothing could prepare me for closing the door to that coral room and lying there alone. A wave of fear rippled through me, like the one you experience when you step onto a roller coaster for the first time—or an airplane. Your heart beats a little faster, and your head is spinning from trying to calculate the safest amount of risk. I closed my eyes, but my nerves had gotten the best of me. I was afraid, yes, but in the best possible way. Afraid of what my life would've become had I not taken a leap of faith.

Thanks to the time difference, I awoke, wide-eyed and full of energy, at three o'clock in the morning. I was hesitant to traipse around the house at that hour, so I turned the light on and unpacked some of my things. At the crack of dawn, I opened my door and walked out. The house was quiet, and the streets were empty and calm. I tiptoed outside to the backyard and surveyed the neglected garden. While the veggies were not so impressive, the flowers were spectacular. I was unfamiliar with the different types, but they were everywhere, showing off their vibrant colors, almost daring me not to marvel at them.

There was a small shed near a rear fence, where I found some hand tools. Mrs. Knight had done a decent job of getting the tomato plants to where they needed to be in the ground, but I could tell they were too crowded and not planted deep enough. An hour later I'd replanted them, drenched them with water, and swept the back patio.

After a quick shower, I rummaged through my backpack, looking for the letters. Before I left, I'd asked some of my old students back in Indiana to write notes to the kids in Phuket and promised to start a pen pal program. I sat on the floor of my room and read through some of them. Their desire to share their favorite foods and colors and video games and questions like "Do you have McDonald's in Tie Land?" made me miss them more than I already did.

"Is everything all right, dear?"

I heard Mrs. Knight's voice from the door to my bedroom. I looked up at her and hadn't even realized I was crying.

Chapter 3

Monday afternoon I rode the bicycle to Tall Trees Academy and introduced myself to the director. Her name was Skylar Brown, and she was from London. Skylar was tall and slim and wore little silk scarves around her neck almost every day, like a stewardess. She'd been at the school three years and was the woman I'd been e-mailing with when I was arranging my plans back in Indiana.

"We have two classrooms." She pointed left and right. "Two morning classes and two afternoon classes. As I mentioned in my correspondence, the children are anywhere from six to ten years old, and most are on the same level as far as their English is concerned. They are mostly local children. Some have families that are financially better off than others, but for the most part they come from the lower-income spectrum in Phuket. I expect you to be here by seven thirty, ready to go when the children arrive at eight, and you'll need to sweep the floors every morning. There's always so much sand."

She was all business. I nodded.

Once we were through with the short tour, I went to familiarize myself with what would be my classroom.

"Hello, darling," I heard behind me. "I'm Sophie. I teach the afternoon class. It's bloody wonderful to finally see you. I've been doing double shifts for two weeks now," she said in a similar accent to Skylar's. "Where you from, mate?"

"I'm Jessica, from the States. Indiana, actually. How about you?"

"Born in Sydney, raised in London. Skylar's me aunt. I've been here a year already. Good to have ya 'round." She began to undress. "Don't mind me. Just changing for work. Me other work." She changed into footless fishnet tights, a denim skirt, a black halter-top, and flip-flops. "No more kids where I'm going," she said.

—◆◆►

"I can't believe some of the prices at the market. I was thinking I might need another job myself. Grocery shopping yesterday already dented my budget for the month."

"You ever waitress before?"

"Back in college I did."

"We're looking for another girl at the bar. It's The Islander Bar & Grill, at the marina. Come by over the weekend, and I'll introduce you to Niran." She looked me over. "He will love you."

My face lit up. "Niran?"

She nodded. "Yeah, he's the owner. Everybody knows Niran."

—◆◆►

My first day of teaching I arrived on time, eager to meet my students. I was given a list of their names, ages, and any pertinent characteristics. Things like "shy," "can't read very well," "troublemaker," "class clown." Not much different than kids in any other elementary school around the world.

I placed my backpack next to the teacher's desk and stood by the window as the bus pulled up. They were all in uniform—white T-shirts and khaki shorts—except for one little boy, who was wearing red slacks three inches too short for him.

Skylar walked in with them and instructed the kids to take their seats. Some had backpacks, some didn't, but the ones that did hung them on the coat hooks near the door.

"Good morning, class," she greeted them.

About a third of the kids mumbled a response.

"Alak, where is your uniform?" she asked, and all heads turned to the little boy in the red pants.

He shrugged, clearly uncomfortable with the attention.

"Please have your proper clothes tomorrow."

He nodded.

"I would like to introduce you to Miss Jessica. She is from the United States and will be joining us here at Tall Trees. Can we all give her a nice warm welcome?" she asked, and started applauding.

The same third that greeted her quietly clapped their hands.

I waved and smiled. "Thank you so much. It's wonderful to be here. I'm really looking forward to getting to know all of you."

Skylar patted me on the shoulder and walked out.

Alak came to school the next day with red pants.

I took him aside as he was walking into the room, and he just shrugged when I asked him about his uniform. I decided to let it slide . . . for the next four days.

My first week was a success. The kids were enthusiastic and sweet as could be, and I looked forward to being there every day. Each one of them grinned and laughed and reveled in being at school. The contrast between how little they had versus how big their smiles were was a beautiful thing. I couldn't wait to get to know them better and give them the letters from their American counterparts. Being there was a dream, but it was also a gift. To think that I, Jessica Gregory, from Wolcottville, Indiana, could leave a mark on this world and these kids was not something I took in stride. And this was just the beginning.

I'd arranged with Sophie to come by The Islander on Saturday night to meet Niran and apply for a part-time position. He kept me waiting an hour, so I sat with her as she tended bar and waited tables.

His arrival was nothing short of celebratory. It was like Peyton Manning walking into a sports bar back home in Indiana. Sophie let the dust settle and then brought him over to me. I smiled when I saw him. He was wearing a black linen dress shirt paired with white linen slacks, accented by a glistening assortment of gold rings and chains. On his head was a black knit beanie.

"First time!" he said, recognizing me.

"That's me, first timer. It's so nice to see you again."

"You know me now."

I nodded. "And I couldn't be happier about it. I feel as though I've passed the Phuket initiation."

He smiled at Sophie, not sure what I meant. "You need job?"

"Yes, in fact Sophie has told me all about The Islander. She and I work together at Tall Trees during the week, but I would love—"

"You hire! You start now, First Time."

I glanced at Sophie, and she laughed. "Told you."

Niran handed me an apron and started to rattle off instructions at lightning speed.

Sophie patted him atop the head to interrupt. "I've got her, darling. You go and do your thing. And her name is Jessica."

He waved her off, gave me a hug, and disappeared.

"Thank you, Sophie, I really appreciate it. Hope you don't get sick of me."

"Never. Glad to have the help. You're good to stay on tonight, eh?"

"Good as gold."

I trailed Sophie for a few hours, clearing tables and running food and drink orders back and forth from the bar. Once I was done, she let me go, and I walked down the hill to the marina entrance and strolled along the docks. It was a beautiful, contemporary harbor.

There was a bulletin board against the wall next to the marina office, where boaters had posted various flyers. Some were trying to sell things; others were looking for temporary crew members or boat maintenance. One person was giving away kittens. After I'd walked up and down the piers, marveling at the many different yachts, I headed home, well past one o'clock in the morning.

Sleep was the one thing giving me the most trouble. So when I woke up wide-eyed after only a few hours of rest, I decided to get up and head to the twenty-four-hour coin laundry. It was only 6 a.m., and I wasn't about to wake Mrs. Knight to borrow the car, so I filled my backpack with underwear, pajamas, shorts, and T-shirts. The sun was just coming up, but the heat was already ever present. Beads of perspiration decorated my forehead before I even hopped on the bike, but the morning ride was magnificent.

Without the traffic, the warm breeze carried the scent of tropical flowers through the air at every turn, leaving me grateful and bewildered at the same time. That morning I went out of my way so that I could ride past the ocean. There was a small cliff where I pulled over and could see for miles. The water was the loudest thing in that moment. Waves thrashing against the rocks beneath were like an aquatic symphony—and like nothing I'd ever heard before.

As I turned the corner onto Krabi Road, I saw something that brought my bike to a halt. Gravel crackled beneath my feet as I placed them on the ground and watched a young boy in a white shirt and red pants cross the street alone, balancing three brown grocery bags in his arms.

Sunday morning at the crack of dawn, and Alak was still wearing his improper uniform.

Chapter 4

"Skylar, do you have a second?" I asked her the next morning.

She looked up from her desk in the office. "I'm leaving for an appointment in a moment," she said, and took a rushed sip of her coffee as she stood.

I walked toward her and lowered my voice. "I saw one of my students, Alak, over the weekend, and he was wearing his uniform. Well, he was wearing his makeshift uniform with the red pants."

"And?"

"And—well, it was very early Sunday morning. It made me think he might not have anything else to wear."

"He probably doesn't."

I just stared at her until she read my face and sighed. "Look, some of these children come from unfortunate situations and have very little. It's quite sad I know, but our job is to see to them when they're here at school. They get our undivided attention, snack and lunch, and that is all we can afford to give them. If you become too attached to any one of the children and their life outside of school, it will consume you." She paused. "Trust me."

I nodded. "You're right. I understand. But we can't very well ask him to wear his uniform if he doesn't have one."

"He has one. He just likes the color red," she said, grabbing her purse. "It was his mum's favorite color. Poor thing lost his entire family in the tsunami when he was two. He lives with an aunt and uncle. I've tried reaching out to them in the past to no avail. There's only so much we can do."

She shrugged and walked out.

I went to my classroom and began sweeping the floor with a heavy heart. Perhaps he wore red in homage to his mother. I could certainly understand a child wanting to hold on to what little memory he had of her. I completely understood what it was like to be robbed of that critical motherly bond. I went through the same thing, yet my mother passed away when I was twenty-eight. I couldn't even recall if she had had a favorite color. Or maybe Alak was just being purposefully defiant. If so, then I liked him even more.

I would heed Skylar's advice and not get too attached, but the least I could do was find out more about him and see if there was any way I could help. If nothing else, just to get his uniform squared away.

"Alak." I pulled him aside after class. "Can I ask you about your uniform?"

He looked at the floor.

"I know Miss Skylar mentioned last week that you need to have your khaki shorts. Have you lost them?"

He shook his head, and I knelt beside him.

"Do you know where they are?"

He shrugged.

I gently reached for his wrist. "I want you to know that you're not in trouble and I just want to help you, because the rules are that you need to have your uniform. Will you let me help you find your uniform?"

He nodded.

"Okay, great. So you haven't lost them, but you don't know where they are. Is that correct?"

He nodded again.

"Does your aunt know where they are?"

"No."

"Can you try to think back to the last time you had them?"

"I know the last time I had them."

"Great. When was that?" I clasped my hands together and waited.

"They were taken from the Laundromat," he said quietly.

I glanced downward and thought that must've been where he was coming from when I saw him at sunrise the other day, carrying three bags of clean clothes. I looked into his big brown eyes.

"Do you do the laundry for your family?"

He nodded.

"And do you sometimes have to leave clothes behind because you can't carry it all?"

He nodded again, his expression filled with hope and gratitude.

"I have an idea! I know an extra pair of shorts can be expensive, so I'm going to get you a pair to borrow. Maybe you could even leave them at school and change when you get here. That way you can have your proper uniform, and you won't have to worry about someone taking them. How does that sound?"

He stared at me for a moment. "Where would I change?"

"In the bathroom, I guess. And we could keep the shorts in your cubby."

Alak thought about it. He crinkled his eight-year-old brow and scratched his little chin, then leapt forward and hugged me, nearly knocking me to the ground.

I laughed. "Looks like we have a plan."

Once he was on the bus, I purchased a pair of shorts for him from the school office and wrote his name in the hem with permanent marker. Later that evening, I borrowed the Knights' car and went to the mall to buy Alak a wagon—red, of course—so he could easily transport his clean laundry from then on.

Chapter 5

I planted roots in Phuket, grew my hair long, and managed to create a new life for myself. But it wasn't always easy. I worked a lot but saved little money, and even though I'd made some close friends, I spent many nights alone in my room or roaming the docks and beaches near the marina by myself.

Phuket is an easy place to meet people, just a tricky place to form relationships, because everyone is so transient. But I never questioned my decision, and I certainly never looked back. Devising my next leap of faith was always my top priority.

But despite any early misgivings I might have had, I became truly happy in ways I'd never *imagined*. I laughed more, I walked taller, I shed the skin I was uncomfortable in and grew into my true self through and through. The Knights became like surrogate parents to me, and when they were out of town I looked after the house and took care of anything they ever needed or couldn't do themselves. I loved my closet-less rented room and my two jobs, and with the help of the Knights and some of their local friends, I created a foundation called The Red Thread that provided school uniforms to local students free of charge.

After four months at Tall Trees Academy, I was made assistant director. Caroline had not been out to visit me and didn't have any plans to do so, but we'd Skype once a week and correspond through e-mail almost every other day.

Everything about Thailand fulfilled me. The friendly people, the white sand beaches, the spicy foods, the vibrantly colored buildings, the laid-back atmosphere, and the flowers. Wow, the flowers. Every street in every neighborhood was brimming with plants and greenery and flowers in the most disarmingly bright colors I'd ever seen. All of these things that once hung in one-dimensional posters over my bed in Wolcottville were not only tangible to me now but commonplace. Part of my everyday life.

But I couldn't allow myself to become complacent again by slipping into the same routine with just a better view. When Skylar informed me that I'd accrued four weeks of vacation time, I made a decision that would uproot me once again—and nearly cost me my life.

—◆◆—

It was an early morning in December, just past sunrise, when I rode my borrowed bike down to the marina and posted a flyer on the bulletin board. It read:

Crew Member Available

I'm a 28-year-old American living in Phuket and looking to join a boat on a passage from Thailand to the Med. I'm willing to clean, take night watch, and perform basic boat maintenance. I'm also a decent cook. I have an exceptional work ethic and can provide references if needed. My schedule is somewhat flexible.

Please contact me at jgregory1872@talltrees.edu.

J. Gregory

I stood for a moment and scanned some of the other similar notices tacked on the board. The water beneath me was calm and gently lapping against the hulls of the boats. There were two flyers posted by boaters looking for temporary crews, so I snapped a picture of both of them with my cell phone and then headed to school.

"Excuse me."

My thoughts were elsewhere when I heard a man's voice and then looked up from the dustpan to see him standing at my classroom door. His voice was strong and captivating, much like the rest of him.

"Can I help you?" I asked, and we locked eyes. His smile made me catch my breath.

"Sorry to interrupt. I would like to make a donation to the school."

I brushed some loose hairs out of my eyes. "How are you with a broom?"

"Horrible." He looked around. "But I'm a great storyteller." He was older than me, late thirties maybe, with rugged good looks. I guessed it'd been at least two days since he had shaved. But he was tall and strikingly handsome, and his comment piqued my interest.

"Maybe you'd like to come to one of my classes and share your stories."

He cocked his head and rubbed the back of his neck, then nodded. "Okay, you're on."

My face lit up. "Really? I didn't think you'd actually say yes."

"Then why'd you ask?"

I let out a small laugh.

He took a couple steps closer. "You look familiar," he said with a knowing glance.

"I do?"

"Yes." He crossed his arms. "I just said you did."

I shrugged and then leaned the broom against the desk and extended my hand. "I'm Jessica. I'm a teacher here, and also the assistant director."

He shook my hand, and I felt it in my heart.

"Grant Flynn. Nice to meet you, Jessica. You're American?"

"I sure am. Sounds like you are as well."

He nodded. "How long have you been in Thailand?"

"About four months."

"Have you been with the school the whole time?" he asked.

"I have. It's been a wonderful experience."

He crossed his arms again and studied me. "I see," he said, not taking his eyes off of me. "Are you the right person to talk to about making a donation? I'd like to leave a check if that's all right."

"Of course, yes."

He grabbed his checkbook from his front pocket and pulled a pen from behind his ear. His presence put my nerves on high alert, and the irony that I was behaving like a giddy schoolgirl was not lost on me either.

"Thank you, Mr. Flynn. This is very kind of you."

Many visitors to Phuket would come by the local schools and leave donations. It was sort of a ritual for some, a way to leave their mark, a gesture of kindness for many boaters to visit the schools and bring supplies or leave a small contribution of a hundred dollars or so.

"Please call me Grant," he said as he wrote.

I stood behind him dusting myself off when Sophie walked in.

"Hey, mate, what are you doing here?" she asked.

Both Grant and I looked at her, but he answered.

"Told you I was going to come by this week."

"Right. You met my girl, Jess, did ya?"

He turned to me. "I did. She was helping me decide whether my donation should be manual labor or monetary, but I'm going to stick with my original plan."

He tore the check out and handed it to me.

"You two know each other?" I asked.

"Grant's been coming in to The Islander all week," she said.

He pointed at me. "That's where I know you from."

I nodded. "Thank you," I said, taking the check from him. "I'll see that our director gets this today, and I look forward to hearing your stories."

I glanced down and nearly gasped when I saw the check was for five thousand dollars.

"I appreciate it." He touched my shoulder. "See you later," he said to Sophie, then waved his hand over his head and walked out, allowing me to breathe freely once again.

Sophie and I went to the window and watched as he got into his rental car.

"You know him from the bar?" I asked.

"He and his mate have been coming in every night. I'm surprised you haven't seen them. They're docked at the marina, both Americans."

"Niran had me on lunches last week."

"He's a charmer, eh?"

I nodded. "And quite generous."

"How generous?" she asked.

"Five thousand dollars generous."

"Shit, no," she said, and whisked the check from my grip. "Skylar's going to freak. You working tonight?"

"Nope. Not until Saturday."

"All right then. See you later," she said, and left.

I picked the broom up and saw the bus arrive, but all I could think about was Grant Flynn.

—◆◆—

When I came to school the next morning there was a package at the front door with my name on it. Inside were two DustBusters and a note that read:

These are more my speed. I'll see you in class tomorrow morning.

Grant

Chapter 6

Grant arrived at school about fifteen minutes before the children. He wore a royal blue polo shirt with white cargo shorts and flip-flops. His sunglasses were buried somewhere in his mop of hair.

"Good morning, Miss Jessica."

I waved. "Good morning. Thank you so much for doing this."

He nodded.

I pointed to the small bookcase against the wall. "You can choose from any one of those if you'd like."

He looked bemused and walked over to the shelves, then turned back to me. "I was going to tell my own stories. Talk about my travels." He raised an eyebrow. "If that's all right."

My lips curled into a wide grin. "That's wonderful, of course. They will love that."

"Good."

"What sort of travels have you had?"

"Are you sure you wouldn't rather be wowed along with the children?"

I laughed. "Fair enough."

The kids filtered in and paused one by one like stunned, suspicious little robots, as they did every time there was a stranger in the classroom. Their eyes were glued to Grant while they quietly put their things away and took their seats.

"Class, I would like to introduce Mr. Flynn. He's visiting Thailand from the United States, like me, and has generously offered to spend some time telling us about his journey. Can we all welcome him?"

A few of the kids mumbled a nearly unintelligible "Welcome, Mr. Flynn" salutation while I pulled up a chair for him in the front of the class. His legs were way too long for it, but it was all we had.

For the next thirty minutes, he engaged them with his tales of traveling the world. He was a boater—a cruiser as they were called in the community—and was sailing around the world on his sailboat with just one other crewman. He painted his picture in broad strokes, so it was easy for the kids to understand and enjoy. He talked of elephants and dragons and orangutans. He told them about how he was caught in a terrible rainstorm once, and how he and his crew survived the rough waters. He told them about fishing and swimming and being chased by dolphins.

I looked around the room, and all the kids were seated with their heads in their hands, elbows on their desks. Some had even come to the front of the class and sat cross-legged at his ankles.

By the time he was through, he'd captivated every single one of us.

I took a deep breath when he'd concluded his presentation and looked over at me. The applause was deafening.

"Thank you so much," I said as the kids were chanting for him to come back.

"It's my pleasure." He waved at them and a few, including Alak, ran over and hugged him around the waist.

"I'm going to walk Mr. Flynn out, so please take your seats and sit quietly until I return."

Grant and I stepped outside.

"Thank you again."

"You're very welcome."

"It seems like you've done this before."

"I have."

"Well, you really made their day. I don't think I've ever seen them so intrigued."

He placed his hands in his pockets. "I think your expressions were my favorite of all."

I blushed. I had been equally enthralled. "I guess you could say I've always been interested in seeing the world."

He pursed his lips into a smile. "Glad I could help." He touched my shoulder and then walked away. I was still staring at him when he turned back around and stopped. "I'll see you around," he said.

Chapter 7

Four days later I received an e-mail from someone who'd seen my note at the marina and was looking to bring on a third crew member for a three-week passage sometime in January. His name was Quinn, and we arranged to meet at his boat after I finished work that afternoon.

I locked up my bike and checked his e-mail for his location. He said he was on J Dock, Slip 46, and his boat was named *Imagine*. Once I reached his pier, I turned and scanned the boat names until I found the one I was looking for. It was a sailboat, and a beautiful one at that. A young, good-looking guy was lounging on the stern, peeling an orange. He winked at me and said hello and was a little surprised when I stopped.

"Hi, are you Quinn?"

He was even more surprised when I knew his name.

"I am," he said and stood.

"I'm Jessica."

He just stared at me.

I lifted a finger and then pulled his e-mail out of my backpack. "I'm so sorry. I hope I don't have my days messed up—"

"You're J. Gregory?" he asked.

"Yes, Jessica Gregory."

He let out a laugh and rubbed his forehead.

I put the paper back in my backpack and hiked the bag up on my shoulder. "Can I come aboard?"

"Why not?"

He placed the orange down, then reached for my hand and helped me onto the boat.

I smiled. "Thank you for reaching out to me. I really appreciate the opportunity. Can you give me an idea of what you're looking for, how long the passage will be, and where you're headed?"

He smiled and shook his head. "I wasn't expecting a girl."

My shoulders dropped forward. "I see."

He sat but kept his eye on me. "No offense, of course."

"Of course."

"But it's just me and one other guy, and, you know, I was thinking we'd find another . . . guy."

I nodded. "Well, you should have considered all of your options then, because I can do the job just as well, I promise you," I said, and saw Quinn's attention diverted to something else. I turned to follow his gaze and nearly lost my footing when I saw Grant Flynn standing behind me.

"Well, hello again," Grant said, leaning against the small doorframe that led to the rooms below deck.

I smiled with every inch of my body.

Quinn stood and cleared his throat. "This here's the *guy* I told you about," he said to Grant.

Grant smiled at me. "The one who loves to cook?"

"Yeah," Quinn said, placing a toothpick in his mouth. "Wait . . . you know her?"

I stood straight and adjusted the strap on my shoulder. "This is a pleasant surprise," I said, waiting for Grant to agree with or expand on my comment, but he didn't. I continued. "Look, you two obviously were expecting something—or someone—a lot more masculine than me. I get that. But I'm the one that put that flyer up there. I volunteered for this opportunity, and I promise you I can do the job as well as anyone. It's not like I'm inventing the notion of a female crew member."

Grant and Quinn exchanged looks, and then Grant shrugged. "It's your decision," he said to Quinn.

"Since when is it my decision?"

Grant let out a small laugh and disappeared below deck without answering either of Quinn's questions.

"Have a seat," Quinn said.

I looked back at where Grant had been standing and then sat down.

"Here's the deal: we're trying to fill a temporary third crew position to go from here to Sri Lanka and then across the Indian Ocean through the Gulf of Aden, up the Red Sea, and into Egypt." He paused. "How long have you been in Thailand?"

"Four months."

"So I'm sure you're aware that it's a treacherous passage, and we need a third guy—er, person—because we need to have someone on watch twenty-four hours a day during that leg of the trip." He thought for a moment. "I don't know what your schedule is, but we're not planning on leaving here until the first or second week of January. I don't have a date yet, but it's mostly dependent on the weather. Everything is."

I took a deep breath. "I'm not offended that you were expecting a man, nor am I going to leave without at least trying to convince you that I can do the job. I've seen many people over these past few months post classifieds to those boards, both men and women— some with experience, some without. I realize that as a woman with no prior sailing experience, I'm the least desirable choice. But as I mentioned, I'm a hard worker, a decent cook, a neat freak, a bit of an adventure seeker, and would be grateful for the opportunity. I hope you at least give me a second thought."

He clasped his hands together and gave me a nod. "I promise we will. And despite what the ol' man says, it's ultimately not my decision."

I looked over his shoulder, hoping to see Grant reappear, but he didn't.

"Thanks, Quinn." I stood and extended my hand.

"You're welcome."

He shook my hand before I turned and hopped off the boat.

"So how do you know the ol' man anyway?" he shouted.

"I teach at one of the local schools, and he came by last week to leave a donation and tell the kids about his trip."

He snapped his fingers as if what I'd just said gave him an epiphany. "Ohhhh, you're the girl from the bar."

Chapter 8

'd never met anyone named Grant before, and I loved the sound of it. It made him seem mature and self-assured—and he was. I knew very little about him other than his name, that he'd donated five thousand dollars to our school, he was traveling around the world on a boat named *Imagine*, and he was a master storyteller. Which I also loved.

I was filling the salt and pepper shakers when I spotted him. Grant had captivated me from the moment I laid eyes on him. He was handsome, yes, but there was something else in the way he carried himself with a relaxed confidence and a peculiar smile, unable to be flustered even by a room full of giddy, chanting schoolchildren that made me want to know more about him.

The Islander Bar & Grill was a less than a mile away from Royal Phuket Marina, where the guys—and most of our clientele—had their boat docked, and only a few blocks from where I lived. Living and working in a transient boating community, I never knew how long people would be around before they'd head off to their next destination and their next blond expat waitress. I hoped for some time to get to know him better and for the chance to crew on *Imagine*.

It'd been two weeks since he came by the school and left both his donation and his indelible impression on me. Since then I'd seen Quinn a few times already and formed a bit of a friendship with him. He'd been into the bar during three of my lunch shifts, alone, and as Sophie had warned was quite the charmer.

I placed the tray of salt and peppers shakers on the bar when I saw them choose a table near the water's edge. Quinn waved me over a moment later. Quinn was yin to Grant's yang. Within minutes of meeting him, he was your best friend, your cruise director, your "good-time" guy. He carried himself like a celebrity who won't leave a restaurant unless the paparazzi are waiting out front. Chin up, shoulders back, chest out. Nine times out of ten he had a toothpick in his mouth.

Quinn was the life of the party, even when there was no party. He was always waving at somebody while high-fiving someone else, and his chatting knew no bounds. Neither did his flirting. He was young, with a boyish charm to his handsome face, and looked like a typical boater. Blond windswept hair, tanned skin, calloused hands. I never saw him without a smile.

I hurried over with menus even though I knew what they were going to order—Sophie told me they had the same meal every night. She'd also told me that Grant said very little to her other than placing his order, but that he was polite and tipped her well. I watched as he sank into his chair, placed a leather-bound book on the table in front of him, and folded his hands in his lap.

"Hi, guys. Two Singha drafts?" I asked.

"Sounds perfect," Quinn answered, and then gave me a high five. "Is Niran here tonight? He owes me five hundred baht," he said, emphasizing the *t*.

"He's at a wedding but should be here soon."

In addition to being a local celebrity, bar owner, and man-about-town, Niran was an ordained minister. "You never know when somebody want to get marry," he'd say.

Niran was notorious in the cruising community for two things: quickie seaside wedding ceremonies and playing cards with the local boaters. And when he wasn't tending bar, marrying people, or shaking hands, he could be found dealing hands of poker. Sadly, he was also notorious for losing.

"I guess your drinks are on him then." I shrugged my shoulders. "I was hoping I would see you guys tonight," I said.

"How is that different from any other night?" Quinn winked.

I rolled my eyes but couldn't help but smile.

"We got caught up with some of the other cruisers," he told me. "We were supposed to head out for a ride over to the east side but had to order a part for the engine, which should take another week or two. You're not quite rid of us yet."

I smiled, relieved. "Grant, I wanted to thank you again for your contributions to Tall Trees. Both the DustBusters and the funds have been put to good use. And the kids haven't stopped talking about the monkey who spanked you in Indonesia."

Quinn gave him a curious glance before Grant looked up at me with a subtle grin. "You're very welcome. I'm happy to help. Really."

Grant was the taller of the two. He had longish brown hair and blue eyes, while his face seemed to be permanently covered with stubble. His physique was muscular but slim, and his mood was perpetually kind and polite. But oddly, where Quinn's cheerful enthusiasm was a magnet for most people, Grant's reserved demeanor drew me to him instead.

After getting their drinks and dropping a check at another table, I approached Quinn and Grant, carrying a bar tray with two draft beers and a basket of wasabi peas.

"What's it going to be tonight? Let me guess. A cheeseburger for Quinn?" I said, then followed with, "And a lobster club for you, Grant?," posing the question to him personally, but they both had their heads buried in a pile of printed pages. Upon closer look, I could see that they were studying a bunch of e-mails from MARLO, the Maritime Liaison Office, which sent sailing reports to boaters looking to cross the Indian Ocean from Thailand to Oman. A lot of our customers would come to The Islander to use the free Wi-Fi, check the weather and sailing conditions, and grab a burger. No one ever ordered Thai food. I was always cleaning up tables with pages of MARLO reports left behind.

I stood there awaiting an answer from Grant when Quinn finally turned toward me.

"Thanks for the beers, Jess," he said. "The usual for both of us, please."

I nodded and walked back toward the bar, where Niran entered their order into the computer."Hi, Niran. Quinn's looking for you," I said.

"Ya, ya."

I shook my head at him. "Says you owe him money."

"Ya, he beat me, but I go double or nothing later. You give bill to the other man," he said.

"To Grant?" I asked as I walked out from behind the bar and wiped down the stools.

"Yes."

"So poor Grant has to pay for your poker habit."

"He not poor. Quinn tell me." Niran grabbed a tumbler from underneath and poured himself a scotch and soda. "You like him. Niran knows." He tapped his forehead.

"Who? Grant?"

"Sophie tell me you been looking for him. You hot for him?" he asked.

I smiled. "No, I'm not hot for him."

"You the worst flirt I ever see."

I rolled my eyes. "You pay for your flirts, so what would you know?"

He smiled proudly.

"Besides, I'm not trying to flirt with anyone, I'm just being friendly, trying to get to know them better. Client relations, Niran. Just doing my job." I winked. "I do think it's a little odd that they've been here every night for a couple weeks and he has yet to have a conversation with any of us. Don't you think that's weird? Quinn doesn't shut up, and Sophie tells me that Grant barely says a word."

"He speak to me," Niran said, wiping a beer tumbler with a rag, then holding it up to the small light over his head. "Goddamn the lady lipstick," he mumbled.

"He did?"

He nodded. "He tell me you annoying, and you stare at him too much."

I tossed my pen at Niran, hitting him on the shoulder. "What did he say?"

"He say you ask too many question."

I glared at him. "I'd give you a smack if you weren't my boss."

"You love Niran too much for that."

"That is very true."

"That guy Grant come here himself one afternoon for lunch and left his book behind. I never clear the table."

"Of course you didn't," I added. Niran never cleared the tables.

"So he come back an hour or so later looking for it. He very worry, but naturally it was right where he'd left it." He smiled. "Good thing I never clean up."

Grant seemed to have that book with him at all times, or at least when he came to the bar. I assumed it was some sort of a journal. Too small to chart maps or anything, but maybe he was a writer. The thought made me eager to hear more of his stories.

He and Quinn were deep in conversation when I brought them their food, so I left them alone and refrained from asking if they needed anything else. I didn't want to prove Niran right.

Chapter 9

The next day Quinn came alone and sat at the bar.

"Hey, you," I said as I placed a coaster in front of him. "One draft?"

"I'll take a Belvedere on ice."

"Lime?"

He shook his head.

I poured his drink and placed it in front of him as he was scrolling through his phone, grinning.

"You get some lucky girl's phone number last night?" I inquired.

He gave me a look like I was out of my mind and shook his head emphatically. "Not me. I got the most beautiful girl in the world waiting for me back in Miami. I'm the lucky one."

I smiled, a little surprised to hear he had a girlfriend, thinking Sophie was going to be disappointed. "Well, well, well, I had no idea. Good for you, Quinn. What's her name?"

He reached for his phone and showed me her picture. "Bridget."

I looked at the screen and saw a beautiful young woman with long, dark hair and dark eyes. It was a close-up of her face—looked like she snapped it herself—and she was smiling coyly.

"She's beautiful," I said.

He smiled. "We've been together since our freshman year of college, so almost seven years now."

"I never would have guessed."

"She knows I'm a flirt, but I never cross the line." He winked.

"Seven years. That's a long time to be dating someone. Are you two going to get married?"

"I plan on proposing as soon as I get back to the States."

I slapped my hands on the bar. "Well, you're likely to break a few hearts around the world first, aren't you?" I winked back. "Congratulations on your impending engagement," I said, and lifted my glass of pineapple juice to toast him. "Was that a text from her that got you so giddy?"

He nodded.

"Good for you, Quinn. You seem like a real sweetheart, and it makes me happy to know there are guys like you still out there."

He cocked an eyebrow. "Uh-oh. Woman scorned?"

"No, just you know . . . not as lucky in love as you yet."

"A cute blond American chick who brings beers to weary sailors when they're parched? Love will find you in no time."

"Thanks." I rolled my eyes and walked over to the register.

"Where you from?"

"Indiana."

"No one waiting on you back there?"

I turned around and leaned against the counter. I'd had a few boyfriends growing up, but nothing serious. When I was in college, I dated a guy named Greg Van Der Heide for a little more than a year, but Greg was like everything else in my life at that time: representative of everything that was expected of me, yet nothing that defined me.

He was born and raised in Indiana with no intention of leaving, and his idea of travel was anywhere that had a football stadium. Every suggestion I made to venture outside the Midwest was quickly sacked. But don't get me wrong, I wanted to be in love. The sweaty palms, the racing heartbeat, the anticipation, the excitement, the passion. I longed for someone who when he'd walk in a room would make me catch my breath. Someone who could read my thoughts without me saying a word. Someone who held my happiness and well-being in great esteem—as I would theirs. Someone I could surrender myself and my dreams to. Someone I could love in ways I had never been allowed to before.

He was out there. He just wasn't Greg Van Der Heide.

The worst part was that Caroline loved him as a potential husband for me. Or if not him, the idea of him. She literally prayed for him to propose to me, and when I told her I'd broken up with him, she didn't speak to me for ten days. She was always looking for someone or something to ground me at home.

My stomach sank when I realized I hadn't e-mailed her in three days.

I looked up from the floor at Quinn, who was awaiting a reply. "Nope, no one is waiting on me."

Quinn took another swig of his drink and then his eyes widened as though he'd gotten an idea. "Hey, Grant and I and a couple friends are heading up to Bangkok for a couple days. Why don't you and your friend Sophie join us? Think you could get the time off?"

I blinked and considered his offer. "When are you going? I'll have to check with my school," I said.

"We're flying out on Friday and spending a few days there. How many jobs do you have to ask for time off from?" he asked with a smirk.

"Two, smartass." I tossed a wet rag at him. "I would love to go, but I'm not sure I can afford the flight. Just paid my rent last week, and I don't get another check until a week from Monday."

"Grant's chartering a plane, so don't worry about it," he said.

"He's chartering a plane? An entire plane?"

"Not a 747, you freak. A small charter jet. The old man travels in style, if you know what I mean."

I didn't know exactly what he meant, but I certainly acted as though I did.

"So . . . what's Grant's deal? Does he have a 'Bridget' back home like you?" I asked, feigning indifference. "How come a nice guy like him isn't married?"

Quinn looked as though he was about to answer me and divulge the details I was looking for, but then he just shrugged and shook his head.

I debated asking Quinn more about Grant's personal life, then decided against it. Better to find out on my own than have him report back to Grant that I was being nosy.

"Let me see what I can do. The kids I teach are actually on holiday, so it will be up to Niran whether he'll let both Sophie and I desert the bar. Thanks so much for the invite, though. It sounds like fun. I'll let you know."

"Sure thing." He stood and left his money on the counter.

"Does Grant know you're handing out seats aboard his plane?" I asked before he walked away.

"He doesn't care."

"Where is he tonight?"

"He's meeting with some people about the next phase of the trip. Trying to map out the best course."

I nodded. "Have you guys made any decisions about your crew yet?"

He glanced down at his cell phone before responding. "Not yet, sorry. Still have a couple more people to interview and some scheduling issues to work out. As soon as we cross the Indian Ocean and make our way into Egypt, it looks like I may be heading back to the States. Grant's planning on meeting up with some people and a new crew dude in the Mediterranean.

"It's all a bit up in the air at the moment. But most of the cruisers are trying to figure out the best route from Sri Lanka through the Gulf of Aden and on to the Red Sea. There's a lot to coordinate. Whether or not we should sail straight through like we'd planned or take some other course. A couple other cruisers that are part of a

rally are forming convoys to sail the"—he quoted with his fingers—
"'danger zones' together. So we might try and get in on one of those,
but we need to secure our third crewman first."

From what I'd learned from living and working in a boating
community in Thailand, Somalian pirates had plagued the Gulf of
Aden between the Indian Ocean and the Red Sea in recent years,
although most of the local chatter indicated the pirates were interested in capturing large commercial vessels with large crews that
would in turn command large ransoms, not sailboats.

He continued. "Like I mentioned, we'll probably be here through
the New Year and head out sometime in January, so it looks like
you're stuck with the Quinnster for a little while longer." He stood
and placed his phone in his pocket. "See if you can get some time off
to join us next week. We're only going for a day or two," he said, and
then walked away, singing "One Night in Bangkok."

I wanted to join them, but most of all I wanted to crew for
Imagine. I'd spent my whole life waiting for signs and chances and
timing. Going to church and praying for things that I was told were
frivolous. Wishing that opportunities would present themselves to
me so that I could finally do what I wanted, not just what I was told.
If I hadn't lost my job back in Indiana, maybe I wouldn't be lying on
a twin bed in Thailand, contemplating this next challenge. Crewing
for Grant seemed like the perfect opportunity to once again grab life
by the horns—or the sails, as it were—and nothing pleased me more
than a little adventure.

And although this "perfect opportunity" obviously wasn't my
decision to make, I still read it as a sign worth following. Tall Trees
was extremely flexible, other teachers were always coming and
going, and Niran would hold my job for me—I knew he would.
How long could it take? A couple weeks? A month? I'd saved enough
money to pay my rent, so that wouldn't be a problem. I knew I could
do it. I wanted to do it, and I was determined to make it happen.

After dinner, I took a quick shower and rode down to the marina. Once my bike was locked up, I walked around back to the docks. The air was breezy and infused with the scent of marine life. The sky was dark, but each dock was lit by a row of antique streetlamps. Almost like little runways for boats. I was walking from one end to the other, enjoying the quiet air and mesmerizing sounds of the water lapping against the boats, when I saw him.

Grant was sitting on the edge of one of the piers, about ten yards away, leaning against a wooden post and smoking a cigar, his leather-bound book beside him. I stopped and stared. His right hand was resting on his bent knee, while his other leg hung over the edge. A good two minutes passed before he felt my eyes on him. I waved when he turned and noticed me.

Although it felt like an eternity, he stood after a few seconds and walked toward where I was standing. My heart beat a little faster as he approached, but I maintained my composure. I hadn't gone there looking for him—consciously, anyway—but I reveled in the chance encounter.

"Hello," he said, narrowing the gap between us.

"Hi, Grant."

"Please call me Mr. Flynn," he joked. "What brings you down here at this hour?"

I rubbed my neck. "Just getting some air. I used to ride my bike down here all the time when I first moved to Thailand, and something just made me want to do it again tonight."

"I see."

"I didn't mean to disturb you." I gestured to his cigar.

"You didn't."

My mouth was dry, so I took a sip from my water bottle. "Did Quinn mention that he invited Sophie and me to go to Bangkok with you?"

He nodded.

"It sounds like it would be a lot of fun, and if I can get the time off, I would love to join you. Believe it or not, I've never been there."

He took a puff of his cigar and placed his other hand in his front pocket. "Let us know if you can make it work." His voice vibrated through me. "Quinn tells me you're from Indiana."

"I am."

"So what brought you all the way out here?"

I looked away for a second and pondered his question. "A lot of things . . . and nothing in particular, to be honest. I grew up in a very small farm community and always wanted a reason to leave." I paused. "It sounds selfish when I say it out loud."

"It sounds brave to me."

I lifted my eyes to his and smiled. "Thank you."

He opened his mouth as if to speak but nodded instead.

"I'm glad I ran into you."

"Was that your intention?" he challenged me.

I looked closely at his expression. "Maybe it was." I shrugged and matched his devilish grin with my own. "I guess I should be heading back," I said.

"Good to see you, Jessica. Have a nice evening."

"You too," I said, then turned and walked away and could feel his eyes on my back.

Maybe I hadn't come there to find Grant, but I was glad that I did. I'd wanted to be close to the boats and to the water and to see if my urge to travel with Grant and Quinn was a blip of insanity or a legitimate desire. After being there I had my answer.

Chapter 10

As soon as I arrived at work the next day, I asked Niran for some time off to go to Bangkok.

"If you cover your shifts, you can go."

"Sophie said she'd cover for me, because her cousin is flying in to stay with her, and she wouldn't be able to make the trip anyway."

"You don't have sex with him."

I snorted out a laugh and stared at him. "Is that a question or a prediction?"

He shrugged and batted his eyes, then placed his hands on my shoulders. "You are my good girl."

"I am?"

He nodded emphatically and placed his hand on his chest. "You have good heart, and I see that the first time we meet. Niran knows."

I leaned forward and squeezed him. "It takes one good heart to spot another."

He patted me on the head. "Maybe you can have sex," he said, and walked away. But not before grabbing a deck of cards.

When I saw the guys come in for dinner that night, I couldn't wait to tell them I was free to join them in Bangkok, but I hesitated until Grant was alone and Quinn had gone to greet some people at the bar before heading over to their table.

"Hi, Grant," I said.

He was huddled over his phone and briefly glanced up before responding. "Hi, Jessica."

I cleared my throat and made sure Quinn was still at the bar. "I just wanted to say that I was able to get the time off to join you and Quinn next week."

He placed his phone in front of him and looked up at me again. "That's great news. It should be a good time," he said, then turned his attention back to the pages of notes and charts spread on the table in front of him.

"Do you think you'll have made a decision about your crew by then?" I let my words hang for a moment. He turned in my direction and arched an eyebrow. I shoved my hands in the back pockets of my denim shorts to try and suppress my nerves.

For the first time, Grant took a moment to actually notice me. A moment that made me tuck my hair behind my ear and rub the back of my neck. His face was sympathetic, and he kept his lips together as he smiled, before commenting, "You're very persistent."

"Well, I just want to know if I should put my flyer back on the board or not. I'm sure you can understand. The demand for inexperienced female crew members is at its peak."

He smiled. "I can *imagine*."

He began to turn away from me, so I placed my fingertips on his shoulder for a second.

"Quinn told me he had no real prior sailing experience before you took him on in Miami. And—"

He was shaking his head before I could finish my sentence. "I'm thinking it's way too dangerous. Trust me, I've been receiving some concerning reports from MARLO, and it's no place for a beautiful young girl like yourself."

I basked in his comment, shifting my weight to one leg and folding my hands in front of me. Offhanded as it was, he'd just called me beautiful, and hell if I wasn't going to take the compliment. He also called me young.

"I'm the same age as Quinn," I noted.

"You are?"

"Yes, I am," I said, and then thought about it. "Well, okay, he's two years older than me. But it's close enough, and what does age have to do with it anyway?"

"Age has nothing to do with it. It's just not the place for someone like you. I didn't mean to imply you're too young. I apologize."

I pulled one of the metal chairs away from the table. "May I?"

He gestured for me to take a seat.

I took a deep breath before starting. "I know I'm a stranger to you, but I'm not a stranger to taking risks, or adventure, or whatever you want to call it."

"I called it dangerous, not adventurous," he reminded me.

I let out a determined breath. "My mom died a few months ago, just before I moved out here." I paused and looked away for a second. Grant folded his hands in his lap and sat back in his chair but left his eyes on mine.

"And soon after her funeral, I felt something change inside of me. We weren't very close, she and I, but for some reason I felt cut loose when she passed. Like I was being given the permission to do the things I'd never been allowed to do. That's why I'm here in Thailand, thousands of miles from the mediocrity that haunted me back in Indiana." He studied my face as I continued. "When Quinn e-mailed me to interview, I had that same feeling. Like this is something I'm meant to do." I paused to gauge how crazy I sounded from the look in his eyes.

He ran his hand through his hair and then stared at me for a good long time before answering, "I can appreciate that."

"Just think about it."

We locked eyes, and I felt as though he was trying to figure me out. His chiseled features were naturally twice as captivating and distracting up close.

"You have the darkest eyelashes," I said. The words just came out, cementing me as a lunatic in his eyes if I hadn't already.

He let out a small laugh and looked away for a moment. "Okay. I'll think about it."

"Thank you!" I squealed like the naïve young girl I'd just assured him I wasn't, and then tamed my enthusiasm. "Thanks, Grant. That's all I ask."

"I don't exactly know how long the passage will take. Will you be able to keep your job here? I'm not one for schedules."

"It's really more the school that I'm worried about, but I have four weeks' vacation, and I will talk to my director. That is, of course, if you decide to bring me along."

"I thought you were the director?" he asked.

"Assistant director, but I spend most of my time in the classroom, teaching English."

"Is that right?" He sat up. "I noticed the children seemed to be all different ages."

"There is a bit of an age range, but they're all on the same reading level. Our school doesn't have a ton of money, like some of the American schools here, so we sort of work with what we have. There are a decent number of books, as you may have noticed, but things like basic school supplies are, well . . . in short supply. Pencils, note pads, scissors. Those sorts of things. The other staff and I buy what we can when we have some extra money or receive donations."

Grant smiled at me. "I can tell you love what you're doing."

"Thank you. I really enjoy it."

Quinn walked up a moment later. "How you gonna get my beer with your ass in my chair?" he asked, tousling my hair with his hand.

I stood and smoothed my hair down. "I'm going to Bangkok with you."

He lifted his arm for a high five.

Chapter 11

Okay, everybody!" I said, clapping my hands and trying to get my students' attention. "It's time to clean up. Please put all the markers back in the bin, bring me your drawings, then line up against the wall."

The kids quickly did what I asked—all except for Alak, who was always in his own world, and still drawing when I walked over to the table where he was seated.

"Alak, sweetie, it's time to clean up."

He looked up at me and flashed me a toothless grin.

"You lost another one?" I laughed and pointed to the hole in his mouth.

He nodded enthusiastically, then stuck his tongue through the space.

"You better grow those back quickly, or you'll have to drink milkshakes forever!"

His eyes lit up, and he leapt into my arms. Alak was a hugger, and I loved that about him, so I let him hang on for a second or two before pulling away and taking his drawing. He'd become like family to me. We'd meet on Sunday mornings and do our laundry together, and I'd bring food for him to feed the numerous stray cats and kittens that lived near the Laundromat. He called them Laundry Kitties. He loved cats, but his aunt forbade any pets in the house.

"This is beautiful," I said slowly. "Beau-ti-ful! You draw the best flowers, you know that?"

"Yes," he said, and hugged me again.

"Okay, sweetie, go ahead and catch up with the other kids, all right?"

"Yes," he repeated, and ran after the others as they left for the day, single file.

When I stood, I saw Grant leaning against the doorway with a backpack on his shoulder and a smile on his face.

"Grant, hi. What a nice surprise." I placed Alak's drawing on my desk. "What are you doing here?"

He walked into the classroom, absorbing every inch of the room with his eyes, then placed the backpack on the teacher's desk. He was wearing long board shorts, sunglasses on his head, and a white cotton T-shirt that nicely accentuated his tanned skin.

"I brought you some supplies."

I shook my head in disbelief. "You . . . wow, thank you. That was so nice of you. But you've already done so much."

"I figured you all could use a few extra things. It's no big deal. I sent Quinn to the mall. There are ten more backpacks filled with stuff over there in the entryway."

I was grinning, but my mouth was wide open. "Oh my gosh." I couldn't contain my astonishment. "I don't know what to say. Thanks so much."

He shrugged. "Happy to help," he said, then slipped his hands into his front pockets and walked over to the blackboard, where most of the kids' drawings and schoolwork hung around the perimeter. He studied their work and even lifted a few of the overlapping pieces to see what was underneath.

I stood silently and watched him glide about the room. He was in my space again, and I could feel him. He'd crossed the barrier between our two worlds and was getting to know me better whether he'd intended to or not. I was so intrigued and surprised by his gesture, I didn't know how to properly express my gratitude in that moment. Gushing didn't seem like the right thing to do, so I did my best to just keep him where he was.

"Can I get you anything?" I offered. "Wait, let me rephrase that. Would you like a Dixie cup of warm water?"

He sniffed. "I'm good," he said, and slid into one of the desk chairs. "Maybe you can entertain me with a story about you this time."

I crossed my arms. "I haven't been anywhere but here."

"Then tell me about where you come from."

I leaned against my desk. Not many people were eager to know anything about my hometown. I cringed while I thought about how to make it seem even remotely exciting.

"Let's see. Well, I led a relatively simple life back in Wolcottville. Population eight hundred. Traffic signals none. If you ever did happen to meet anyone at an intersection, you'd both just wave until the politer of the two held out, then you could proceed . . . with the guilt of knowing that you made the other person wait. There is a large Amish community there as well, so oftentimes you might encounter a horse and carriage, in which case you'd naturally give them the right of way, since horses tend to roll their eyes at niceties."

He laughed.

"Your typical small town where church dinners and high school football games are the main source of entertainment. That and the 4-H Fair every summer."

"4-H?"

"It's a youth organization, and stands for Head, Hands, Heart, and Health. Some kids would show sheep and pigs and offer them for auction. Others would do baking or clothes making, both of which I tried and failed at due to 'lack of enthusiasm for the craft' I was told, so I showed horses. All summer long I'd ride every day once my indoor chores were done. Then I'd head out to clean the stalls, brush the horses, feed the horses, and exercise them. If I had a dollar for every time my dad told me to 'practice my riding,' I'd have had enough to hire someone to practice for me."

"Sounds wonderful."

"Which part?"

"The whole thing. A little slice of Americana," he said with a wistful look.

"Are you feeling homesick?"

He took a moment before answering, "Not in the slightest." He stood. "I really need to get back to the boat. I'm having some work done on the generator."

I glanced at the floor, then threw my arms up. "Can I at least give you a hug?" I asked, briskly walking toward him. "I'm a hugger," I told him. Who can resist a hugger? I know I couldn't.

He turned to face me, and I stood on my toes and wrapped my arms around his neck and shoulders. He gently patted my back as I inhaled the scent of him. He smelled regal and damp and solid. Like Poseidon, king of the sea.

I began talking as he slowly released his grip. "Well, I can't tell you how much this will mean to the kids. Especially when they hear it's from you." I rested my weight back down on my heels but kept my head up to look him in the eyes.

"It's my pleasure. Thank you for telling me about yourself."

I nodded. "Thank you for asking."

"I'll see you around," he said, and turned to leave.

"Grant?" I didn't want him to leave.

He stopped and looked at me over his left shoulder.

"Have you made any decisions about your crew yet?"

He smiled with his eyes. "I have," he said, and walked out.

Chapter 12

I was working the lunch shift the following Saturday when Quinn sidled up to the bar in his signature Nike visor that read "Just Do It Me."

"Morning, Jess."

I glanced at the clock. "It's almost two o'clock," I said, and leaned my elbows on the bar, crossing my arms.

"So you're really serious about this crew position? Grant tells me you're relentless."

I stood straighter. "I am."

"Have you ever sailed before?" he asked, grabbing a toothpick and placing it in his mouth.

"No."

"Ever been on a boat before?"

"Many times."

He nodded. "Ever get seasick?"

"Nope."

"You like whiskey?"

"Nope."

"You mind moldy bath towels and clogged toilets?" he said, grinning.

"Nope."

"Now I know you're lying," he said.

I put a glass of ice water in front of him. "I think it would be an unbelievable experience, and I will do the best job I can possibly do. I promise I'm not just looking for a vacation."

"Good, because it will be anything but. We basically need a third person so that we can split up the lookout shifts between us and allow each other to get some sleep."

"I can do that," I said. "And I require very little sleep as it is. Most nights I'm up reading until past midnight, and then I get up at six to teach."

He patted the countertop of the bar and stood up. "Well, I told Grant it was a great idea. It's only a couple of weeks, and the threats are the same each year. Grant's on top of it, so there's nothing to worry about." He smiled. "And, hey, *Imagine* could use a woman's touch."

I was elated to hear he was on my side.

"I'm only concerned about one thing," I said.

"What's that?" he asked.

"It's Grant. I can't get a read on him. I don't think he likes me very much."

Quinn rolled his eyes. "Who, the old man of the sea? He likes you a lot. In fact, he likes everybody. He's just a hard nut to crack."

I shook my head. "No, no, I'm sure he does. That sounded stupid. I just mean that he doesn't say much, and I'm sure we'd have to communicate on the boat."

"He'll talk to you plenty. He's just . . ." Quinn paused and glanced over his shoulder before continuing. I waited for him to elaborate, but he didn't. "It's nothing. He'll be fine, and I think you'd do a great job."

I was curious about what he'd left out, but I didn't want to pry. "Well, I'm glad you're on my side. I hope it works out."

"He needs to make a decision soon because I have to get back to the States by early March."

"Well, I hope I get the chance to join you."

"Me too, but let's focus on Bangkok first. You own any short skirts?"

I tossed an olive at him.

—◆◆—

That Friday I took a cab to the back entrance of Phuket International Airport, where they have the runway for private jets. I paid my driver, then walked through the gate of a chain-link fence toward a sleek, petite white plane fit for a movie star. Its ladder was folded down to the ground, and there was a golf cart parked at the bottom of the steps, where two men were discussing some paperwork.

I began walking toward the plane when Quinn appeared at the top of the steps, stuck two fingers in his mouth, and whistled at me.

"Let's go, woman!"

I strapped my backpack onto both shoulders and ran with a small, wheeled carry-on trailing behind me. The two Thai men at the bottom of the steps greeted me with smiles as I boarded. Quinn reached for my bag and told me to quickly find a seat. I scanned the five rows for Grant and saw him in the back, talking with a man and a woman.

"Yo, Angela and Adam, this here is Jessica," Quinn shouted to them.

"Nice to meet you," Angela said with a warm smile, and waved.

Quinn leaned in to me. "They're from New Zealand. Grant met them when he was there, and we're planning on meeting up with them and their boat, *Destiny*, in Sri Lanka."

I nodded and let my eyes wander to Grant. He was wearing a white linen dress shirt with the sleeves rolled up, khaki shorts, and a chunky metal watch on his wrist that kept sliding around as he moved his arms during the conversation. The watch was catching the sunlight and was as pleasingly distracting as Grace Kelly's charm bracelet in *Rear Window*. So much so that I hadn't realized he'd waved hello to me until Quinn tapped me on the shoulder.

"Good morning." I smiled and waved to him and his friends, then took an open seat in the second row.

Quinn was in front of me and leaning over the back of his seat like a little kid who refuses to sit down.

"Do you know where we're staying?" I asked. Quinn had told me not to book a room, that Grant had taken care of the accommodations for everyone. I wasn't very comfortable with him paying my way, so I brought some extra money in hopes that he would let me contribute or, at the very least, treat him to lunch.

"The old man booked a couple suites at the Mandarin Oriental. You and I have to share a room, though." He winked. "Just kidding," he said, and aggressively squeezed my shoulder. "What? You don't want to bunk with the Quinnster? Better get used to it if you're going to be my shipmate."

"I feel like a mooch," I whispered, "weaseling my way onto this gorgeous miniature plane and into his hotel suite."

Quinn lifted a hand to silence me. "He's well connected and has worked for, like, ten years in the hotel industry. Doesn't say much about it. I think his family owns a few properties in the States and maybe Great Britain. I'm sure he's on some sort of investor stipend. Trust me, he's happy to do it." He gave a singular nod. "So just relax. You excited?"

"I am," I said, catching my breath. "How long is the flight?"

"Little over an hour," he said, then lifted a bottle of rum over his head. "Thirsty?"

I wasn't afraid of flying necessarily, since I'd only done it once before. But after running to catch my second flight ever—and climbing into what resembled more of a minivan than an aircraft— I was thrilled to see Quinn's bottle of rum. Even if it was only 8 a.m.

Chapter 13

We landed in Bangkok, and the five of us cheered as we taxied to the gate. Once off the plane, we were met by oppressive heat and a town car sent from the hotel. During the drive, I had my first real glimpse of the capital of Thailand. Bangkok is an enormous modern city that is rich in ancient history, but with that comes all the pluses and minuses of that reality. Traffic congestion was atrocious, and poor urban planning had left rice paddies next to skyscrapers. But despite a few minor nuisances, the city was throbbing with culture and excitement.

I stared out the car window and felt like we were driving through a pinball machine. Horns and bells and flashing lights emanated from every inch of the metropolitan downtown area. There were more neon signs than I could count, and open-air buses were fighting for space on the roads with motorcycles, cars, trucks, cabs, even pedestrians, all caught up in the same hypnotic traffic jam.

When we arrived at the hotel, located near the river, I stepped out of the car into what felt like a sauna but was simply the heavy, humid Bangkok air. After grabbing our bags from the trunk, we were quickly welcomed by the perfumed, air-conditioned lobby of the hotel, and I did my best to keep my astonishment to myself as we all walked through the vast reception area and surrounding gardens. The scent of lilies and tea leaves filled the room as two staff members, who greeted us in their native tongue, bowed first, then placed a small garland of orchids on Angela's wrists and mine. Floor-to-ceiling windows exposed the greenery from outdoors, and birdcage-like light fixtures hung from way overhead. The indoor foliage was bright and lush and peppered with fuchsia flower buds.

En route to our rooms, we were taken through what was called the Author's Lounge, one of the most breathtaking spaces I've ever seen. The large white room had an expansive ceiling, and in the center was a large imperial staircase with a curtained passageway underneath the divided flights of stairs. Oversized white wicker loveseats and high-back chairs were scattered about the room. Impeccably dressed Thai women went from table to table dispensing tea service. I paused for a moment to take it all in. I could have stood there forever. It was like an Asian *Casablanca*.

A hand on my shoulder awoke me from my daydream.

"You coming?"

I looked up into Humphrey Bogart's eyes.

"It's beautiful, isn't it?" Grant said.

"Yes."

"Why don't we meet down here for tea service after we see our rooms?"

I stared at him. "Yes."

He tapped my shoulder again. "Come on," he said, and I followed.

We all unpacked our things, and Quinn announced he'd be at the pool with Adam and Angela and insisted I join them in a bikini. As I was hanging the last of my things in the closet, I got a text from Grant.

Ready for tea? it read.

Always, I texted back.

I need to make a call first. Meet me in the Author's Lounge in 20, he wrote.

Consider it done, I confirmed.

I took those twenty minutes to jump in the shower and reapply my mascara and lip gloss. I hadn't brought many outfits with me, since we were only going to be there for a couple days, so I put my bathing suit on and then a white sleeveless sundress over it. I placed my hair in a ponytail and stole a pink flower from the arrangement in the hallway of the suite and tucked it into the rubber band.

Grant was sitting alone on one of the many loveseats when I arrived, so I pulled up a chair next to him.

"Mind if I join you?"

"Please." He stood. "You look lovely," he said, and then waved to one of the waitresses. Each of them was more stunningly exotic and gorgeous than the next.

A woman waltzed over, bowed ever so slightly, and smiled.

"Tea service for two, please," Grant said.

She nodded and left.

I placed my palms on my thighs. "Thank you so much for letting me tag along. I feel like a complete mooch so far but am shamelessly loving every minute of it."

He lifted a hand. "Don't mention it. It's my pleasure. It was worth a king's fortune just to see the expression on your face when you walked in here."

"Can I at least treat you to tea?"

"No, you cannot treat me to anything."

I nodded. "Well, thank you again."

"You're welcome."

Our tea service arrived on a silver tray, along with homemade lemongrass scones, finger sandwiches filled with Thai spiced tuna, steamed pumpkin custard, and warm washcloths to wipe our hands. Grant served us both. I marveled at the way he controlled the situation with such little effort. He poured us both a cup of tea and sat back into the plush cushion of his loveseat, which was decorated with bright green palm leaves and was responsible for some of the only color in the grand foyer.

"So how long have you been at sea?" I asked, then carefully tested my drink with a tiny sip.

"Just over two years."

My eyes went wide. "That's incredible."

"Yes, it's been quite incredible."

"And you don't miss being home at all?" I asked, eager for more details about his life back in the States.

"Nope."

"Where is home for you anyway?"

"I'm originally from Chicago, but I sold my place before buying the boat, so I haven't quite decided where to call home yet. I guess *Imagine* is my home. Looks like we're two homeless Midwesterners," he said.

"Cheers to that." We tapped our cups, and I braved another sip of the scorching liquid. "So has it been just you and Quinn the whole time?"

"No. He's my third crew. I spent six months in New Zealand on my own, and he met me there. Flew over from Miami when I was ready to leave. I can't sail *Imagine* alone. It's too much work without help. I always like to have at least one crew on board."

"Six months in New Zealand by yourself? Why so much time in one place?"

"Mostly to wait out the cyclone season."

"Did you have any friends or family come out and see you while you were there?"

He adjusted his posture in his seat and thought about something or someone for a moment. "A few of my friends flew out for a couple of weeks here and there. The Kiwis and the boating community there are quite embracing, so I was never really alone."

I smiled. "A lot of the American boaters I've met set sail from Miami or Key Biscayne. Is that where you began your journey?"

He shook his head. "No, we started in Chicago. Set out right from Monroe Harbor smack-dab in the middle of the city. That first year me and my crew at the time, a guy named Jeff who used to work for me, sailed close to fifteen thousand miles from the States to New Zealand." He paused. "Chicago seems like a world away."

Grant crossed his legs and leaned back into his chair. I loved how he crossed his legs, exhibiting such poise in that one move. I fidgeted with the thin shoulder strap of my dress as we sat silent for a moment before he continued.

"From Chicago we sailed through the Great Lakes to the Hudson River and made our way down to New York City. He and I met up with a few people we knew and spent about three nights off the boat in Manhattan just hanging out."

"Do you mind me asking what sort of job gives you two years off to sail the globe?"

"Not many that I know of." He smiled. "I'm sort of an independent contractor. My family is in the hospitality business and has been for many years. I have a company that books very exclusive vacations for people who can afford a priceless travel experience."

"I'm guessing priceless does not refer to the *price*?"

"Correct."

"How are you able to maintain the business from so many miles away?"

"I've hired good people to run it for me, and they only bother me if absolutely necessary. I have a few clients who like to deal with me personally, so I check in with them on a need-be basis."

"I've always wanted to go to New York," I said, and thought of my mom. "It's like the brass ring of the States for me."

"You would love it. It's not unlike Bangkok in a lot of ways. Very urban and maybe not as global, but certainly as culturally diverse. Once we were back on board, we left New York and headed down the coast to the Chesapeake and stayed in Annapolis for a little while. Jeff's brother and wife live there." He leaned forward and grabbed a sandwich. "Then we went to Hampton, Virginia, where we prepared for our trip to the Caribbean. That was an amazing leg." He shook his head and smiled. "One of my favorite stops was Dominica. I mentioned it to your class." He finished chewing.

"I remember."

"It's a tiny speck of an island often referred to as the only island Columbus would still recognize. No cruise ships and not many tourists, until one of the *Pirates of the Caribbean* movies was filmed there. It's a very poor island but has some of the nicest people—and the highest percentage of Bob Marley look-alikes per capita I've ever seen. Jeff and I called it the incredible edible island. We went on a tour, and our guide would just stop his car and pull a branch off a tree and tell us to eat it. One was peppermint, another was spearmint."

"It sounds like paradise," I added, ripe with admiration; I could hardly take it all in. "You must tell me more. I'm in heaven listening to all of this," I said, and then craned my neck to look around the room and it's seemingly endless ceiling. "Come to think of it, I may be in heaven right now."

He smiled. "Well, Jeff left me once we got through the Panama Canal, and two of my nephews met up with me. I have an older stepsister, and she has two sons in their early twenties, who were chomping at the bit to come along for the ride." He paused to sip his tea. Not many men could make sipping tea and sitting cross-legged look as manly as he did. "So once we left Panama, we sailed to the Galápagos and then made a twenty-day passage across the South Pacific to the Marquesas and enjoyed the French Polynesian islands for three months."

His lips and the words emanating from them were an aphrodisiac. He'd traveled the world. He'd been places I'd only read about or seen on film. His toes had been covered in white sand from beaches in the middle of the South Pacific. My heart was racing at the thought of experiencing these things with him. I hung on every detail and became more enamored with every story.

"Please, don't stop."

"You sure?" he asked.

I nodded.

He sat back in his chair and tilted his head to the side. "I love seeing how interested you are in my trip. To be honest, I haven't really bored anyone with all the details, since most of the people I spend time with are other boaters."

"You can count on me as a captive audience."

"Good to know." He folded his hands in his lap.

"What would you and your nephews do all day? Did you ever get bored?"

He shook his head. "Never. We did a ton of fishing, swimming, snorkeling. Caught and ate fresh fish every day. Visited the local schools everywhere we went, like we did yours." He paused and thought. "Watched a lot of sunsets."

How romantic, I thought to myself. Poor guy stuck watching sunsets with his twenty-year-old nephews.

"See, you need a woman around," I said.

He smiled. "I'm selling the dream, but the reality is that we're fixing the boat all the time and spending a lot of our days with constant maintenance and upkeep. Repairs, cleaning, et cetera. A sailor's work is never done. Trust me."

"That's wonderful. What you do for the schools."

"It's really the best way to get to know a place and its people. There is such a mutual admiration between us travelers and the kids and their families or teachers." He gestured to me. "There's really nothing more gratifying than being able to contribute to the communities we visit."

I smiled.

"Anyway," he continued, "from there we sailed to Auckland, New Zealand, and the boys flew home, and I stayed there for about six months, like I said. That's when I met Angela and Adam and some other really great people from all over the world. Toward the end of my stay there, Quinn flew over and met up with me, and then he and I left and went straight to Fiji. That was the start of my second year at sea."

I could hardly remember enjoying myself more than I was in that moment. "I've heard Fiji is one of the most beautiful places on earth," I said.

"You heard right."

"How did you end up in Phuket?"

"Once we left Fiji, we stopped at a group of islands called Vanuatu, then from there we sailed over the top of Australia, stopped in Darwin for a couple of weeks, then sailed to Singapore and Malaysia. After about a week in both of those places, we went from Malaysia to Phuket." He nodded toward me. "Where we had the pleasure of meeting you."

I grinned and sat up straight. "No doubt a trip highlight."

"Indeed." He let out a small laugh and then reached for his tea. He was about to take a sip when he looked over at me instead, brow furrowed. "Look, Jess, I know you really want to make this next leg of the trip with us, and I admire you for volunteering. I really do. It says a lot about you."

"But . . ."

He sighed. "But I've given the job to someone else."

My heart sank.

"Please don't be disappointed," he said.

I inched forward to the edge of my seat. "Just sitting here listening to you recount your journey, my hands are sweating and my heart is pounding. I've wanted to travel the world my whole life, but until I came to Thailand, I'd never made it anywhere besides my aunt's condo in Florida when I was six years old." I gestured around the room with my hand. "This is what I've always wanted. Not fancy hotels—although that doesn't suck—but just to experience the world. I promise you that I would not have taken advantage of the opportunity, but I respect your decision."

Grant took a deep breath. "It's not that I don't think you're capable of pulling your weight and helping us out. The boat is very self-sufficient."

"Then what's your hesitation?"

"My hesitation is that this leg of the journey is where we have to be the most cautious."

"In regards to the piracy threats?"

"Yes, and while there hasn't been an attack on a private yacht in over two years—and even then they were close to Madagascar—I'm not so bold to think we're invincible or immune to the dangers. We won't be anywhere near where that attack took place, but it is a real threat, and we all need to be aware of it." He shrugged. "Look, it's a vast ocean, and hundreds of private boats make this passage safely every season. I just need to be as prepared as possible."

I nodded. "I understand that, and I've lived here long enough to know that's a concern, for sure. From what I hear, hijacking ships with large crews and large cargo means more bargaining power."

"Yes, but it's not about the people . . . There's no bargaining power with people. The US and many countries will not negotiate with pirates. Period. It's the companies that own the ships that end up paying large ransoms to get their cargo back. They pay for the cargo, not for the people. I just feel better having someone on board with a little more experience."

"The person you gave it to, is it a man?"

He nodded. "He is a man."

I sat back in my chair and folded my hands in my lap. "I understand." And I did. I couldn't fault him for wanting someone with a little more experience and testosterone. "What more can I say? I'll just have to dust off my thumbtacks and get my flyer back up on the board." I said.

"I wish you wouldn't do that."

"You said yourself that hundreds of boats make this crossing each season without incident. There've been crew notices posted on that bulletin board for as long as I've lived here."

"Yes, I did say that."

We locked eyes for a moment before he looked away and checked the time on his phone.

"I'm sorry I won't get a chance to sail *Imagine*."

"Maybe when we get back you'd like to come aboard and check her out."

"I would love that," I said. "By the way, I keep meaning to tell you how much I love that name, *Imagine*. It's such a fantastic name for a boat. How did you think of it? Are you a John Lennon fan?"

He shook his head, then fixed his eyes on the floor for a second, lost in thought. "It just sort of came to me," he said after a long pause.

"Well, it's lovely." I smiled but was disappointed. Yes, I could post my notice back on the board at the marina, but my desires had changed. I wanted to sail with him. "So when are you planning on leaving Thailand?" I asked.

"We'll probably stay in Phuket another few weeks or so and head out mid-January."

Just then Grant got a text and checked his cell phone. "Quinn wants to know where we are," he said, and then looked up with a crooked smile. "And if you're wearing a bikini."

I let out a laugh. "Tell him yes, and that we're on our way."

Grant and I reached the pool deck to find Quinn in the water surrounded by a group of Swedish women. He waved us over.

"Should we crash his party?" I asked Grant as we placed our towels on two pool chairs.

"I can't see why not." Grant lifted his shirt over his head. His tan, muscular arms glowed in the bright sun, and I could hear my mother's voice telling me not to stare. He tossed the shirt on the chair and looked up at me just as my eyes were making their way back to his face.

I cleared my throat. "I'll meet you over there."

"I'm in no hurry."

Glancing away from him, I made a slight turn with my body and reached to untie my sundress.

"Allow me," I heard him say as he stepped behind me.

My spine tingled as his fingers brushed against the base of my neck. For a second I could feel the warmth of his breath on my skin as the straps tumbled off my shoulders. I placed my hand on my chest to catch them. "Thank you."

"My pleasure." He walked back around as I quickly stepped out of the dress and pulled the rubber band out of my hair.

I watched his eyes go from my face to my hair and then back again. "You look beautiful."

"Thank you again." I blushed and loosely crossed my arms.

"Shall we?" He extended his hand.

Chapter 14

The next day we all woke up with different agendas.

"I went online before we left and made sure to print out the top ten things to do in Bangkok," I told Grant and Quinn as we were sitting on the veranda having coffee.

Quinn gave me a blank stare.

"What?" I said.

"We're here on vacation, to relax and hit the pool, not to don fanny packs and snap pictures," he responded.

I rolled my eyes. "I'm here to explore." I paused and looked over in Grant's direction. He was refilling his mug. "Grant, would you care to join me?"

"I'd love to," he said without hesitation. "What did you have in mind?"

Quinn shook his head and stood. "See you two later. If you need me, I'll be sucking on complimentary frozen grapes in the deep end."

I folded my legs up on my chair and turned toward Grant with my piece of paper in hand. "Okay, well I admit to being a bit of a tourist. I'm not the type who likes to visit the back-road treasures that only the locals know about. I like the big, shiny, crowded 'you can't go there without seeing this' type of spots."

He leaned back and crossed his legs.

I continued. "According to TripAdvisor, the top three attractions in Bangkok are Wat Arun, also known as the Temple of Dawn—I'm sure you've seen pictures of it; it's one of the more recognizable structures in all of Southeast Asia—The Grand Palace, and Wat Pho, the house of the famous Reclining Buddha . . . Oh, and the Floating Market. I'm dying to see that. The first three are all near each other, by the river. Also, The Bridge on the River Kwai would be cool too, but that's a couple hours away." I placed the paper in my lap and looked up to catch him smiling at me.

"We'd better get a move on then," he said, and slapped the armrests on his chair.

Grant and I grabbed a taxi and headed first to The Grand Palace, which was about a twenty-minute ride from our hotel. The driver dropped us off on Na Phra Lan Road in the old city, close to the main entrance of the mammoth structure, where we stood and marveled while I read him some details about the palace from my printout and then grabbed my camera and began taking some pictures.

"Will you stand over there?" I asked Grant. "I like having people in my pictures."

He gave me a blank stare and folded his arms over his chest. "I'm not really one for posing," he said.

"No posing necessary. Feel free to stand there and look as grumpy and annoyed as you'd like. It's not like you're in Thailand walking around some of the world's most renowned—and shiny—architecture with the world's most charming tour guide . . . but whatever."

He dropped his arms to his side and positioned himself in front of my camera with The Grand Palace at his back.

"Say 'I'm cheesy'!" I yelled.

Grant lifted his arms up in a V formation and gave me a huge grin.

"Thank you very much; that was fantastic." And it was.

"I thought maybe if I did one good smile, I'd be given reprieve for the rest of the pictures. And besides, you're much more photogenic than I am. Let me take them of you instead."

"Deal. And by the way, it's the compliment just now that won you the reprieve, not your two-bit impression of the Cheshire cat," I said, and handed him my camera.

The air was balmy that day, not stifling like it had been before, but warm and humid. Much like summer in Indiana. We took a few pictures outside The Grand Palace, which is so much more than one royal temple. It's a series of buildings and pavilions boasting bright red and gold hues, with the traditional multitiered peaks atop the roofs made to look like hands in prayer formation, pointing toward the sky. Surrounding the palace were lush gardens and courtyards filled with people walking and resting and ogling.

We spent close to two hours there, with me reading to Grant from brochures and posing for pictures all over the place. From there, it was a short ten-minute walk to Wat Pho, the Temple of the Reclining Buddha, where we removed our shoes and went inside.

"I think I may refer to Quinn as the reclining Buddha from here on out," Grant said as soon as we approached the statue.

"Oh. My. God," I said. "It looks like an enormous gold Slip 'N Slide. I can't *imagine* how they got this thing in here. Maybe they built the building around it."

"It's incredible. How long is this thing, Jess-ipedia?"

I scrambled through my bag for the brochure. "Says here it's forty-six meters. Oh Lord, I'm terrible with metric conversion . . ."

"That's about a hundred fifty feet long."

"Holy cow, that's half the length of a football field," I said.

Grant turned to me, impressed. "But you can convert feet to yards? Either that or you're a football fan." He looked me over from head to toe. "Or former cheerleader maybe."

I rolled my eyes. "Ah, no and no. My ex-boyfriend played," I started as he was forming a smile.

He placed his hands in his pockets. "Go on."

"How about instead I tell you a little bit about this massive, golden, lounging Buddha? Says here that the Buddha is an impressive fifteen meters tall, forty-six meters long, and that his feet alone are five meters long and exquisitely decorated in mother-of-pearl."

"Thankfully, he can't wear shoes in here. He'd never find a pair sixteen feet long."

"Very true. It also says that there is a famous Thai massage school in the building. Maybe we should check that out."

Grant walked over, placed his hands on my shoulders, and squeezed. It was a simple gesture really, but I shivered when his palms met my bare skin. He kneaded my neck and arms for about twenty seconds—during which I nearly lost consciousness—and then stepped in front of me.

"There. How was that?" he asked.

My eyes were closed. "I'm going to need, like, fifty-nine more minutes to give you my honest opinion."

"Let's get out of here and find some spicy noodles and cold Thai beers to recline with," he said.

After a late lunch, we grabbed a cab and headed back to the hotel, where we met Quinn for a drink in the lobby.

"Have you told him?" I said to Grant.

"Told him what?" Grant asked.

"That you gave the crew job to someone else."

Quinn looked over at Grant and then at me. "Of course he told me. I guess the old man's not such a sucker for a pretty face after all."

Grant rolled his eyes.

"I'm teasing you." Quinn winked at me, indicating all was right in the world.

"Just out of curiosity," I started, "is that route you're taking—the one that seems to be giving everyone so much concern—the only way to get to the Mediterranean? I mean, if there's such a threat of danger, why not go around?"

Grant finished tapping out a message on his phone before answering. "There really isn't any other way into the Med from where we are, and it's always been part of the plan—my plan, anyway—to sail through there and make stops in Greece, Spain, and Italy. Otherwise, there are other options, like going south by way of Madagascar and circling down around Capetown. But that would add another year. Or we could forgo the Med altogether and head east toward Japan, but that would add more time and take me off course as well. Once you go that route, it's good-bye Europe, hello Alaska."

"*Brrrrr*," I said, shivering.

"Even colder with no one to warm you up at night," he said, smiling at me.

I blushed and noticed Quinn giving me a quizzical look as the waitress approached Grant. For a moment I was concerned that I might have misread Grant's comment, so I looked away.

After he ordered drinks for the table, Grant continued. "The dangers we and other boaters are facing have been prevalent for years now, with the highest risks being in the Gulf of Aden, a narrow passage between Somalia and Yemen that is highly populated with commercial traffic. It's at this point that these Somali gangs started to realize that owners and insurers of unarmed crews would sooner pay a large ransom than risk damage to their shipments or a delay in their business. But in recent years and months, these pirate gangs have been spreading out beyond the gulf and far into the Arabian Sea." He exchanged a glance with Quinn. "We're hoping that we can get to the western tip of Oman and then set up a convoy with some other boats so that we can sail the Gulf of Aden together."

After cocktail hour, we met up with Adam and Angela, and everyone got ready for dinner. As soon as we were dressed—me in a black cocktail dress and heels—we took the elevator up to the top floor of the hotel and entered an executive suite, where a dining table was set near a large window, treating us to views of the city. Grant had the hotel prepare a traditional Thai dinner for us with dishes like fried snowfish with garlic and red chili sauce, beef curry with sweet potato and onion, and stir-fried vegetables in oyster sauce. As soon as Grant took a seat, Quinn pulled out the chair next to Grant and offered it to me.

"I'm guessing you'd like to sit here," he whispered.

I looked into Quinn's eyes and narrowed mine ever so slightly.

"What?" he asked. "I figured you'd be thanking me."

Grant was talking with Angela as Quinn and I stood behind the chair. "Thank you," I said.

"Quinn knows all." He tapped his index finger to his forehead. "Quinn sees all too."

I rolled my eyes.

"Quinn know you hot for the old turkey." He snorted out a muffled snicker, and we both laughed as I gladly took the seat next to Grant.

The amount of pleasure brought on by hours of eating and drinking and laughing and storytelling was immense. I said very little during dinner because I was so keen on hearing about everyone else's journey at the table that night.

Adam and Angela had bought a home in Auckland about a year prior and were trying to start a family. Adam was a salesman for Coca-Cola, which he only drank when he had to, and they were going to be living in New Zealand for at least four years. Angela was a former ballet dancer and was hoping to start a dancing school for little girls. She wanted a daughter, she said, and was worried she was getting too old—at thirty-four—to have children.

I told her about my mom and how she had my twin brothers at age thirty-four and me at forty-two, and it brought tears to her eyes. She was a kind, thoughtful woman who reminded me of Caroline and looked every part the ballerina she was. Her hair was pulled into a tight bun, and her figure was slim and toned. She looked me in the eyes when we spoke, and I hoped that she would get the child she was wishing for.

There I was in one of the most exotic cities in the world, sipping expensive wine in one of the finest hotels and eating a buffet of custom delicacies. It was a moment of quiet consternation and conflicting emotions for me, where I actually was slightly uncomfortable in my own skin. I thought of Caroline's homemade mashed potatoes and saturated chicken salad, and even though I was immensely happy for the first time in a long time, I missed Indiana.

After a few hours and countless bottles of wine, the combination of missing my sister and feeling sorry for myself about losing the opportunity to sail with Grant was about all my alcohol-fueled emotions could handle. Just past midnight I excused myself from the table and headed back down to the suite. As I was getting undressed, there was a knock on my door.

"One sec," I said, fumbling to get out of my dress and into my nightshirt without falling off the edge of the bed.

Grant was standing there when I opened the door.

"Are you okay?"

I nodded.

"You sure?"

"I'm fine. I think I had a little too much to drink, and I was thinking about my sister and such, and I thought I was ready to turn things around . . . I mean in." My speech was slurred. "I mean it was time to turn in." I rubbed my forehead.

He let out a muffled laugh. "All right. You seemed a little quiet up there, so I just wanted to make sure you weren't upset or anything."

I lifted my chin and looked up at him. My inhibitions, along with my self-control, were nonexistent at that moment, and for some reason I burst into tears. I brought my hand to my face and walked away from him. He followed me to the bed, where I sat and wept into his shoulder as he ran his hand up and down my spine.

"I don't know why I'm crying," I said quietly.

"It's okay. Sometimes that's when it feels the best."

I took a deep breath and sat straight. "Talking with Angela about having kids made me think of my sister . . . and myself, I guess, and how . . ." I wiped my eyes. "How little I've focused on family and what's really important."

"Looks like there's your answer as to why you're crying."

I nodded. "I'm always so concerned with running away and finding something better."

"Is this about the crew position?"

I shook my head.

Grant placed his hand gently under my chin and turned my face to him. "I just went with my gut. It had nothing to do with you being a woman. I don't doubt for a second that you could do the job." He paused and scanned my eyes. "Nor do I doubt how much I'd enjoy having your company every day."

The room was dark, and my head was spinning. Staring into his eyes, feeling his breath on my skin, made me want him more than I'd ever wanted anyone or anything in my entire life. I kept my eyes focused on his face as he studied me. His expression changed from sympathy to desire in an instant. His head tilted, his lips parted, and his eyes narrowed as he leaned forward and placed his mouth on mine.

Before I had a second to enjoy the softness of his lips, he was standing in front of me, running his hand through his hair, and the words "I can't; my wife" were left hanging between us like a black fog.

Chapter 15

He was gone as quickly as he had appeared.

I ran into the foyer just as Quinn was walking through the front door.

"Nice jammies," he said.

I crossed my arms over my chest and looked over at Grant's room. His door was shut.

"Did I interrupt something?" Quinn asked.

I didn't answer.

"Is everything all right?"

I shook my head and then hurried back into my room. Quinn followed me and shut the door behind him.

"I'm such an idiot," I said, pacing. Hearing Grant mention his wife was more sobering than a cold shower.

"What happened?"

"Nothing," I said, and buried my head in my hands.

"Hey, come on. Sit down. Tell me what's wrong. Is this about Grant giving away the crew job?"

I laughed and rolled my eyes. "Thank God, he gave it to someone else. I just made a complete fool of myself."

He sat next to me. "Tell me what happened."

I took a deep breath. "I kissed him," I said, and tilted my head back. "We kissed each other, I think, or we were about to, and then he mentioned his *wife* and left." I threw my hands up and looked Quinn square in the eyes. "I had no idea he was married!"

Quinn let out a heavy sigh, glanced down at the floor between his feet, and placed his hand on my knee. After a beat or two, he turned back to face me. "Jess, his wife died four years ago."

The room went silent, and time stood still while I absorbed the gravity of his words.

"What?" I asked, exasperated. My lungs filled with air as Quinn's explanation left me speechless but brought me some clarity. "Oh my God," I whispered after a moment.

But before Quinn could respond, there was a rap on the door. "Can I come in?"

Quinn stood and patted Grant on the shoulder as he walked out. Grant bent his knees and crouched down in front of me. "I'm sorry."

I just stared at him, my heart aching for whatever he was going through. He'd had a wife, and I knew nothing about her. Yet there she was in the room, occupying both of our thoughts in that moment. I was sorry too. Sorry that I'd let myself fall so hard for a man whom I knew very little about.

"I mean it," he said, and took my hand in his.

"I appreciate the apology, but does that mean I'm not getting an explanation along with it?"

He lowered his eyes. "I'm just not ready."

After a second or two, he stood and walked out.

Not ready to kiss me? Not ready to give me an explanation? Not ready to talk about his past? Not ready to get close to someone? I threw myself back onto the bed and went to sleep.

At four o'clock in the morning, I woke up with a wicked headache and walked to the kitchenette for a glass of water. At the other end of the suite, Grant was sitting alone on the balcony with his leather-bound book on the table next to him. He was sitting too straight to be asleep. I took one step toward him and then changed my mind and returned to my room.

The next morning I awoke to a text from Grant. It read, *I'd still like to have you on the boat one day when we get back.*

To which I responded, *I'm ready when you are.*

Chapter 16

One week after our trip to Bangkok, I rode my bike to Royal Phuket Marina after the lunch shift at The Islander and boarded *Imagine* for the second time.

She was still breathtaking. A fifty-three-foot Hallberg-Rassy, built in Sweden, with golden teak decks, stainless steel accents, and a polished hull that sparkled like a diamond. Grant was her second owner. Quinn talked about the boat like it was his, though, proudly boasting of every modern amenity and gadget, including two bathrooms, dual zone heating and air conditioning, washer and dryer, water maker, electric winches, dual autopilots, and a complete "electronics package." The galley was equipped with a refrigerator, wine cooler, and gas oven.

"Ahoy!" Quinn shouted from the bow when he noticed me walking my bike down the dock. "You looking for a couple of sailors, young lady?"

"I sure am!" Grant had kept his word and invited me for a boat ride, but we had yet to discuss anything that happened between us in Bangkok. However, I wasn't about to carry a grudge or put any unnecessary pressure on him. All I could do was keep my feelings in check and move on. As much as I wanted an explanation from Grant, I didn't feel it was owed to me.

He extended his hand and helped me aboard. "Rubber soles, I hope," he cautioned me.

"I'm all good," I said, and pointed to my flip-flops.

"Have a seat." He gestured to one of the benches. "I have some news for you."

"Oh?"

"Our third crew fell through."

My eyes widened. "Are you playing with me?"

He shook his head. "Nope. Happens all the time. The guy we hired found someone leaving sooner. Didn't want to wait until January."

"You're not joking?"

"Nope."

"Are you offering me the job?"

"Yep."

I sat back and folded my arms. "How does Grant feel about it?"

"He told me to offer it to you, obviously. That is, if you still want it." He paused. "Well, do you?"

"I do." I smiled. "What changed his mind about me?"

Quinn thought for a second. "He never doubted you could handle the job. I think he just needed an extra push."

"Do I have you to thank for that?"

He winked at me, then clapped his hands together. "Well, I guess I better show you around then."

Quinn gave me a quick tour, pointing out Grant's master bedroom at the stern of the boat, with its own head (a.k.a. bathroom). Then he took us back through the salon area to the bow, where there was another bathroom, a teeny, tiny closet-like room with bunkbeds, and just past that a larger bedroom where Quinn slept.

"This is where I bunk," he told me. "And you'll get the room we just passed, next to the head."

I looked around his room, and my eyes landed on his bed. "What a lovely quilt," I said, noticing the folded blanket on the end of Quinn's bunk.

"My girl, Bridget, made it for me," he said, grinning.

"My mother used to quilt. May I?" I asked as I lifted it off the bed and gently unfolded it. There were University of Miami patches, patches representing different US states, like Georgia and Texas and Nevada, and other squares with colorful stripes and paisley patterns.

"Those are places we've been together, and Bridget's going to add patches for all the countries from this trip when I get home."

I folded it back up and gave it a quick pat once it was back on the bed. "I love that you're such a softie," I said to him.

"And I love that you're a real sweetheart. I mean it, Jess. I told Bridget all about you, and she can't wait to meet you one day."

"Thanks, Quinn. I can't wait to tell her what a lucky girl she is."

He raised his arms to his side. "As if she didn't know," he said as we walked back through the salon to find Grant.

"So what do you think? Manageable enough for you?" Grant asked me as we climbed the stairs into the cockpit just as he was coming aboard.

"She's beautiful," I said as he joined us, carrying two grocery bags.

And so was he. Captain of his ship. King of the sea. I couldn't help but marvel at both him and his boat.

"Thank you," he said.

"And I'd be honored to join the crew."

"Thank you again."

The cockpit was enclosed with glass windows to protect the wheel and the controls from the elements. Quinn and I took a seat behind Grant on the white padded benches that surrounded that part of the boat.

"I thought you might want to take a ride, if you have time. Nothing fancy. Just a quick turn out of the marina and up the coast a bit."

"I'd love to."

Quinn stood and took the bags from Grant and then paused. "Wait a minute. Does having Jess as part of the crew mean I'm off grocery duty?"

"No," Grant said.

"I'd be happy to take over grocery duty," I spoke up.

"I'm teasing you. Better get used to it," Quinn said, then leaned over and whispered in my ear. "And used to grocery duty." He cracked himself up, then went down the stairs with the bags.

Grant rolled his eyes at me. "Don't let him get to you."

"Never. I adore Quinn," I said. "And besides, I'm eager to carry my weight around here."

"Well, you can start by hopping off the boat and throwing the bowlines off so we can set sail."

"Aye, aye, captain!" I said with a salute, and leapt gingerly off the boat onto the dock, where I unhooked the ropes and tossed them on deck, freeing *Imagine* from her restraints.

"The marina has a long, shallow, and narrow channel that we have to exit through," Grant said to me as I got back on board while holding a thin metal rail and stretching my right leg out in front of me. "So I'm putting you in charge of reading the depth meter as we navigate our way out of here."

I looked at him like he was crazy.

He continued. "Don't worry. I'll show you what to do. Come here."

I sidled up to his side near the steering wheel.

"This here is the depth meter," he said, and pointed to something that looked like a small digital clock. "It gives us the measurement between the keel—which is the fin-shaped piece underneath the boat that ideally will prevent us from capsizing—and the ocean floor. Your job is going to be to tell me as the numbers drop so I know whether we're about to get stuck or not."

"What happens if we get stuck?"

"Then we crack a couple beers and wait for high tide."

"Doesn't sound too bad to me."

"Ready?" he asked.

I nodded and checked the display on the screen. "We're at ten feet," I told him.

"I don't need the reading until we're away from the dock and exiting the marina."

A few minutes later we were out of the slip, and Grant asked for a depth reading.

"Five feet!" I said, and kept him abreast of any changes.

Three feet.

Two feet.

One foot.

Crap. We were stuck. I could feel the boat come to a gentle stop.

"What the fuck?" Quinn yelled up from below.

Grant looked over at me as he reversed the motor and rolled his eyes.

I stifled a laugh before defending myself. "In all fairness, you didn't actually say at what depth we'd get stuck." I shrugged.

Once we were through the channel, Grant said the wind looked good and that he'd turn off the motor after the sails were up.

"I'm happy to hoist if you need me."

Quinn laughed as he emerged from the salon. "The old man doesn't hoist, Jess. Everything is on pussy pilot. Press a button and it's done."

I smiled. "My kind of boat."

Grant shook his head. "True, everything is automatic—we wouldn't want Quinn to break a nail either—but you can help put out the mainsail if you'd like to. The mainsail has what's called in-mast furling. The sail is wrapped up in there and will unravel when you're ready. Once it's up, we'll kill the motor."

"I would like to."

"As soon as I push the button that lets out the main, you grab the line and wrap it on the winch—Quinn will show you—and give it a good pull to tighten it. I'll take care of the rest. After that, we'll let the jib out."

"If you get tired of pushing buttons, I can get that one for you," Quinn shouted over his shoulder as he was tidying up the dock lines.

"I'm trying to teach her a few things, smartass."

I gave Quinn a playful shove, then shouted to Grant, "Just ignore him. I'm here to learn!"

Once the mainsail was out, we rejoined Grant in the cockpit.

"Can I let the jib out?" I asked Grant. "If it's truly as easy as pushing a button, then there's every indication I won't screw it up."

Sure. Just press the green button that says 'jib out,' and that will allow the sail to unfurl. Then this button over here controls the winch that will pull the jib sheet tight. Two steps and you're good to go.

Watching *Imagine* unfold her canvas wings was a magnificent sight.

The guys and I drifted at the mercy of the wind for just a little while and dropped anchor about a mile out from a little island called Ko Rang Yai. Quinn was laid out on the bow with a baseball hat over his face.

"You're a hugger; Quinn's a napper," Grant said, and I laughed.

"He seems like he knows what he's doing, though, no?"

"I'm just kidding. He's been my best crew yet. Never complains—other than to bust my balls—he's a hard worker, and people love him everywhere we go. He's been great to have with me. I might not have made it through the last leg without him."

"Why's that?"

Grant thought for a second. "By the time I was ready to leave New Zealand, I'd been there for a long time and sort of lost my motivation to move on. My goal was always to circumnavigate the globe, but after six months without sailing I just didn't feel like finishing."

"Did Quinn make you change your mind?" I asked.

"In his own way, he really did. I'd e-mailed him about two weeks before he was supposed to fly out, telling him kind of where I was in my head, and he literally flew out a week later . . . and eight days before we were supposed to set sail to Fiji."

"He surprised you? I thought you two had never met before?"

"We hadn't. He's a friend of a friend, and I guess he told her that he might not be taking the trip with me anymore, because I was throwing in the towel or whatever, and she asked him to change his flight and meet me earlier—to try and encourage me to finish my trip. As you can see, he can be quite convincing in person."

"That he is," I agreed.

"Anyway, I'm pretty grateful for him and what he did for me. Even though it's an unbelievable trip for anyone, he left a lot behind—with Bridget and all—and I want to make sure he has a great experience."

We sat in silence for a few minutes.

"Would you like something to eat?" he asked. "I picked up some cheeses and bread before we left."

"That was so nice of you. Maybe in a little bit," I said, and sat biting my tongue, wishing I could ask about his friends . . . and his wife, but it just didn't feel like the right time. Maybe there would never be a right time.

Grant removed himself from the helm and lay down on the bench across from me. The sun was behind us and shining brightly into the cockpit on its way down for the evening.

I sat up. "So tell me what you do for excitement."

He turned his head and arched a brow. "Excitement?"

"Yeah. What excites you out here? Is it the wind in your sails, the beers at dusk, meeting new people, seeing new places? What gets you the most excited when you're out here doing your thing?"

Grant propped himself up on one elbow and donned one of the biggest smiles I'd seen him wear thus far. He just stared at me and gave one singular nod before he spoke. "I'll let you know as soon as I find out."

Once Quinn woke up and joined us in the cockpit, I insisted on heading down to the galley and preparing a cheese tray for us. I sliced the baguette, placed the brie and aged cheddar on a plate, and carried it upstairs with three cold beers.

"To our new crew!" Quinn toasted, and we all clanked our bottles.

I caught Grant's eyes on me when I looked his way.

We spent the day on the island lying on the beach and playing volleyball. Grant and I against Quinn. Anytime I'd fall in the sand diving for the ball, which was often, Grant would offer his hand and help me up. After about an hour, I was covered in sand and sweat, so we all jumped into the water. Grant and I stayed close, while Quinn swam farther out. The water was tepid, and crystal clear near the edge of the sand. The sight of Grant diving under and shaking his hair as he emerged made me catch my breath. I had to force myself to look away.

"Come here," he said, moving the water with his hands.

I was no stranger to the charms of the many cruisers that passed through Phuket during my time there. I'd gone out with a few guys, slept with one or two, but never anything serious. I'd never even considered getting attached to any of them, because they were usually gone as quickly as they came. Pun not intended.

But with Grant, it was different. My primal instincts were awakened the first time I laid eyes on him, and I was determined more than ever to be around him for as long as possible. Maybe he had no interest in me. Maybe he had a girl in every port. Either way, I felt alive when I was with him, and I didn't care whether it was right or wrong. I just knew that my heart beat faster when he was close to me, and my insecurities hung over my head like a bright neon pub sign, flashing my vulnerabilities for the world to see. What was one more leap of faith?

I walked deeper into the ocean, letting the water come up to my chin. "This island is beautiful."

He looked toward the shore, then back at me. "It is."

Quinn swam up just as Grant had floated closer to me. "I'm starving," he announced.

There was a tiny hut of a sandwich shop that sold soft drinks in glass bottles and the most mouthwatering spicy peanut chicken skewers, of which we each devoured four.

On the sail back, Quinn fell asleep down below in the salon, and I sat with Grant at the helm. His eyes were comforting, more so than words. The way he emanated warmth and trust and tenderness with one glance, you could tell he'd had that gift all his life and had been the type of child people call an "old soul."

Later that night when we got back to the marina, I hugged the boys and hopped on my bike. My heart and head were full as I relished the chance to experience life on that beautiful boat, with that equally attractive man. My mind was in a spinning haze as I rode home.

It was nearly midnight when I crawled into bed and heard my phone chime. It was a text from Grant that read, *Having you on board gets me excited.*

Chapter 17

It was my first Christmas away from home, and no, I never did get used to celebrating the holidays without snow. A week earlier I'd sent gifts to Caroline and my dad, in which the postage cost more than the presents themselves. Christmas morning I awoke to a rarity: homemade breakfast by Mrs. Knight. She'd made pancakes and eggs and bacon, and she invited me to join them on the back patio. On the table was a small wrapped box with my name on it.

I placed my hand on my heart. "You didn't have to get me anything."

"Oh, honey, it's nothing. I promise. Just a little token of Thailand. I noticed you didn't have one in your room."

I unwrapped the package. "My very own Buddha!"

An enormous grin filled my face. Thailand is overwhelmingly Buddhist and wildly loyal to its royalty. You can't turn your head in either direction without seeing a Buddha statue or a picture of the king. In fact, the country's constitution makes it an offense to publicly insult the king, so I always warn island newbies to be careful about what they say in regards to the monarchy.

"Thank you so much. I've always wanted one but haven't found just the right belly yet. This one is perfection," I said, and lifted the polished gold statue to my sight line.

In Thailand, the Buddha is ever present and represented in hundreds of types of statues, each with its own symbolism. In one type of statue, representing simplicity and detachment from material things, Buddha is shown unclothed and without jewelry. His all-hearing and all-knowing aspects are indicated by another type, in which he has long ears and a bump on his head. The most common Buddha figures show him smiling or laughing and making various hand gestures, called mudras, that each have a different meaning. This particular one given to me by Mrs. Knight was giddy as ever with a large, scepter-like stick in his hand.

"He's holding a travel stick. To protect you from harm during long journeys," she told me. "We want you to be safe on your trip."

The Knights were not keen on me applying for a crew position, but they were supportive.

I nearly cried. "Thank you. I love him."

I gave them each a quick hug and then skipped back to my room and placed the little guy on my nightstand, all the while hoping Buddha wouldn't get seasick aboard *Imagine*.

—◆◆—

A week later, Niran, Sophie, and I joined Grant and Quinn aboard *Imagine* and prepared to sail around to the west-side beaches in Patong to ring in the New Year together. Watching Grant man his ship was intoxicating and left me feeling all light in the head like just after a glass or two of champagne. He shouted a few commands to Quinn and then guided *Imagine* into the wind and to Patong Bay.

Patong is a party town. Anything goes at any hour. Stripper poles in bars are as common as alcohol. Quinn described it as being like Bourbon Street on steroids and said that though prostitution is illegal, it's gladly tolerated.

"I'm thinking Jessica should man the helm, don't you think, old man?" he said to Grant, patting him on the shoulder. "Since she begged you for the job, why not test her skills at the wheel?"

Grant looked at me and nodded. "Agreed."

I leapt out of my seat and watched as Grant stood up from behind the wheel and offered it to me.

"If you want to make it to Patong, you might not want to leave me alone at the wheel quite yet," I said to him.

He leaned over me and pushed a couple buttons. His chest pressed against my shoulder for a moment, and I couldn't help note—or comment—that he smelled delicious.

"You smell like oranges," I said, and heard Niran snort out a laugh behind me.

Grant exchanged a glance with Niran that I didn't trust for a second. As soon as Grant was back tending to the controls, I glared at my boss, who only teased me with his "don't look at me" expression.

"We've got autopilot," Grant said. "So unless you spill your drink on this panel here, we should make it there with no problem." He stepped away and headed down below, but not before turning back to me as he reached the salon. "And there are fresh oranges down here if you want one."

New Year's Eve 2010. It was a beautiful day, and smooth sailing. The ride took about three hours, and Quinn called on Grant just as we were about to drop anchor in the bay in between dozens of other yachts gathered for the massive firework display. Grant came up and began to lower the dinghy as Quinn secured our position off the shore of the beach. The five of us grabbed our belongings for the night, boarded the smaller boat, and motored over to the beach, where we left the dinghy at a secure lockup spot. There is almost nothing more glorious than the beaches on the west coast of Thailand. White sand, crystal clear water the color of sea glass, mountains, and palm trees. Paradise in its purest form.

Walking up the beach that day, I found it hard to *imagine* that exactly six years before, in December of 2004, Patong Beach was one of many along the western coast of Phuket and Thailand that were pummeled by a tsunami, devastating most of the town and killing many of its people. It was, in fact, one of the worst affected areas, but had largely recovered since. You never would have known that New Year's Eve the extent of damage the town and its people had endured. No, this day would be a celebration and a night I would never forget.

Quinn, who we referred to as our cruise director, had mapped out the best clubs for us to go to before we'd end up back at a bonfire at the beach in time for the fireworks. As we followed his lead through the crowded streets, I thought of my sister Caroline and how much our lives were in contrast. I'd sent her an e-mail wishing her a happy New Year. Maybe her life was not what I wanted for myself, but I thought—and hoped—she was truly happy.

We squeezed our way into an outdoor beer garden, and thankfully Niran knew one of the managers there, so we were able to get a table. I took a seat in between Grant and Sophie. A woman wearing what looked like a diaper but instead was the tiniest pair of white leather shorts I'd ever seen, with a white bikini top and white platform heels, was gyrating on a pole behind us, mesmerizing Quinn for a good five minutes before he declared, "A round of shots! On the old man's dime, of course," and grabbed Grant by the cheeks and planted a kiss atop his head. Grant smiled, and we all cheered.

There was music and laughter and new people hanging on our table every half hour. Our server kept a constant flow of cocktails and beers and pitchers of spiked punches coming our way for hours.

The alcohol-fueled afternoon turned into evening in the blink of an eye, and once the bill was paid we headed back down to the beach, Quinn with his arm around Grant's shoulders, while Sophie and I locked elbows on either side of a stumbling Niran. I removed my flip-flops once we reached the welcoming sand, which was cool and soft as baking flour. Quinn and Niran walked off for a smoke and left Sophie with Grant and me at the bonfire, where the flames illuminated our faces under the black sky.

I'd had way too much to drink. I knew this for two reasons: one, I could barely stand, and two, Grant told me. Not in so many words, but he kept asking me if I was okay and encouraging me to drink some water. By the time I sat down on the sand, I nearly fell asleep from the warmth of the fire.

"What?" I heard him ask me.

"I didn't say anything."

"I know, but you're staring at me."

"I am?" I asked, blinking.

"Yes," he said, laughing.

"It's nice to see you laugh," I said, and cocked my head to one side.

"Thank you."

"How old are you, Grant? And don't say, 'How old do you think I am?' I hate when people say that."

"I wasn't going to say that. I'm thirty-seven."

I pulled my knees in and sat cross-legged, facing him. Everything about him drew me in. His voice, his demeanor, the way he ran his hand through his hair when he was thinking about something. The way his body relaxed when he crossed his legs. The way he looked and talked like a young Indiana fucking Jones.

Reflections of the flames were dancing in his eyes, making it hard for me to focus on anything else, but in the back of my mind I thought about the opportunity and responsibility he was giving me—to crew on *Imagine* with him—and I didn't want to do anything to jeopardize it. I looked down just before he spoke.

"I'm getting up there. Closer to forty than thirty," he sighed, and interrupted my thoughts.

"You're hardly getting up there."

I rolled my eyes, then glanced at his hands and thought of his wife. It made me sad to think of him losing her so young. I wondered if he thought about her every moment of every day. Did he picture her sitting next to him in front of the fire? Would he have ever come to Patong with her? Would he have needed to hire Quinn? Would I have ever met him?

Sophie excused herself to find a bathroom, leaving Grant and I to sit in silence for a few moments. Were he and I both thinking of the same person?

"I haven't seen you with your book in a while," I observed.

He turned away from me and continued to gaze into the crackling flames. His smile faded, and his lips pursed before he stood and said he was going for a walk.

"Grant?" I called after him. "Wait! Where are you going?"

Quinn and Niran plopped down with a bucket of beers just as Grant sauntered off.

"Where's he off to?" Quinn asked.

I buried my head in my hands. "I don't know what happened. I think I screwed up."

"Yes, you are," Niran added.

My head shot up. "No, I'm not screwed up—well, maybe I am a little—but I think I screwed things up with Grant. I think I may have upset him or something. We were both just sitting here, and he was all quiet, staring into the fire, when I asked him about his book."

"Why'd you ask him about the book?" Quinn asked.

"I don't even know why. I was just trying to make conversation when it dawned on me that he didn't have it with him. I'm so used to seeing him carry it around that I just made a comment about him not having it tonight."

Quinn sort of shook his head and reached for a beer. "He'll be fine."

"What is it with that book anyway?" I asked.

Quinn grabbed a bottle of beer, twisted the cap off, and took a long drink with his eyes closed before opening them and answering me. "I really don't know. I think it belonged to his wife. There's a piece of paper in there, always folded up. I've seen him take it out once or twice and glance at it when he didn't know I was looking. I don't know much else about it."

My heart sank. Grant was finally opening up to me—to all of us—just trying to enjoy himself for one moment without the sorrow that plagued him every day, and I refused to let him. I lowered my head at the thought of ruining yet another holiday for that man.

I placed my hand on Quinn's leg and pleaded with him. "Please can you go after him? I feel awful. Go get him and bring him back to the group."

"I promise you he's fine. He'll be back here in no time. Probably went to use the john."

Ten minutes later I spotted Grant's unmistakable stroll. I quickly stood and ran across the sand to meet him before he reached the bonfire. Standing before him in the sand with no shoes only exaggerated his height over me. I craned my neck to meet his eyes.

"I'm so sorry," I started. "I never meant to upset you by asking about your book."

He looked at me.

"Quinn told me it belonged to your wife. I had no idea. I never would have said anything."

His past was a mystery to me. I basically knew very little about his personal life other than that his wife had died. I didn't know when, I didn't know why, and I didn't know how much of it he still carried with him. But I did know that I cared about him, and the last thing I meant to do was to arouse his pain.

He took a step backward. "It's fine, but I think I've had enough for tonight. Maybe we should all head back to the boat soon, and you guys can watch the fireworks from there. I'm getting tired," he said, and walked away.

I stood with my arms at my sides and my head hung low as I watched him walk past the bonfire and disappear into the night. I followed a few paces behind.

"Grant suggested we head back to the boat," I told Quinn when I reached him and the rest of the group.

"What for?"

"He's not fine," I said.

"What?"

"You said he'd be fine about the book, and he's not. I upset him, and now he wants to leave."

Quinn sighed and loosely draped his arm around my shoulder. "Sorry, Jess. Whatever you said, he knows you didn't mean any harm. Maybe he's not fine now, but he will be," he assured me, and removed his arm.

"We're just in time!" Sophie leapt to her feet and squealed.

"For what?" I asked.

She pointed toward the water's edge. "The lanterns!"

I lifted my head to see over the circle of people seated around the fire and watched as a mob of children raced down the beach, holding paper lanterns, which looked more like paper balloons. One by one, they each lit a wick inside their lantern, filling it with hot air, and then released it upward toward the glow of the moon. Thousands of them floated through the air, peppering the dark sky with an almost otherworldly radiance, much like someone had strung the stars with Christmas lights. I shook my head in disbelief and caught Grant staring at the dazzling splendor from a distance.

After the light show, we listened to someone play the guitar for about ten minutes, and then the crowd on the beach started to grow in anticipation of the fireworks. Grant walked over to Quinn and said something before Quinn waved for us to leave.

Once we got back to the boat, Grant retreated to his cabin and never returned. There was an uncomfortable silence at first as Sophie, Niran, and I exchanged looks, but thankfully Quinn rescued the evening with noisemakers and party hats. There was nothing more I could do for Grant than apologize to him and give him his space, so the four of us rang in the New Year on the bow And once the fireworks started at midnight, they never stopped.

At about one thirty in the morning, Quinn—wearing nothing but his boxers and a party hat--lay snoring on top of his bed. Sophie was wrapped in a blanket on the couch below in the salon, Niran was passed out like a drunken sunbather on the bow, while I was curled up, half asleep, under a cardigan in the cockpit. I lifted my head and sat upright when I heard footsteps and saw Grant emerge from below.

"Hi," I whispered, and glanced at the dashboard clock with one eye open. "We missed you." I pulled my knees to my chest.

"Are you cold?" he asked.

"I'm okay. It's only a little chilly. Nothing like New Year's Eve back home, though, so no complaints."

He sat on the bench across from me, wearing shorts and a sweatshirt, and leaned back against the cushion, with his legs stretched in front of him, ankles crossed. "Come by me," he said, and rested his palm on the spot next to him.

I glanced at his hand, then made eye contact with him before walking over and sitting down. He reached into a storage drawer underneath the seat, grabbed a beach towel, then wrapped it around my shoulders and pulled me close to him. "Better?" he asked.

I nodded, staring down at my bare feet, my heart beating rapidly. He had me in an embrace with my cheek pressed against his chest. Yes, my body temperature was definitely warming, but it had nothing to do with the towel. I wanted to say something about what happened before, but maybe his departure meant that he just wanted to put it all behind him. The silence made me shiver.

His hand and fingers were slowly caressing my right arm just above the elbow, and every time he paused my heart would skip a beat. I swallowed the lump in my throat and tried to muster the strength to lift my head and look him in the eyes. I wanted to know that things were good between us and there were no hard feelings. His eyes would give me the answers. The eyes always say more than the mouth.

I shifted my body toward him ever so slightly, curling myself even further into his embrace. He tightened his grip on me and then continued to move his hand up and down, rubbing away the chills. I closed my eyes, counted to ten, then opened them and lifted my chin. He immediately looked down at me, stopped moving his hand, and squeezed hard, forcing the tips of his fingers into my arm. I froze. He studied my eyes and then looked away, loosening his grip.

My breathing intensified as I brought my hand to his cheek, brushing my thumb across his stubble and turning his face back to mine. He shifted his body, threaded his fingers through my hair, and rested them at the base of my neck. Just as I inhaled, he bent down and pressed his lips to mine. First, hard and firm, then soft and exploratory as he parted my lips with his tongue. My head went back, and my body fell forward into his arms as his hands tugged at my hair and the back of my shirt.

"Are you sure you want to do this?" I whispered.

"Yes," he said without a second thought.

He was lifting my legs up onto the bench under the weight of his body when we heard a cough.

Both our heads spun as Niran was gesturing to get past us to the bathroom. Grant sat up and smiled, and I did my best to threaten Niran with my wide eyes as he snickered and passed. He brushed me off with a wave of his hand, unconcerned, and accidentally woke Sophie when he bounded down the stairs.

"Remind me to smack him when he resurfaces," I said, my eyes ripe with disappointment.

Grant adjusted the towel on my shoulders and smiled. "That won't be the last time I kiss you."

I sat motionless, desperate to rewind and relive those last twenty minutes. I placed my hand over his as Sophie called my name from below. I stood and said good night, then walked down into the salon.

It was nearly 6 a.m. by the time the last of the fireworks fizzled out with the rising sun.

Chapter 18

The morning of January 22, 2011, my bags were packed and I was ready to set sail.

I wasn't certain of how often I'd be able to communicate with anyone, so before heading out I sent a quick e-mail to Caroline.

> *Hey you,*
>
> *My excursion/adventure/boat trip extravaganza starts today. Just wanted to touch base with you and let you know that I'll be aboard Imagine for a few weeks and likely only able to communicate through e-mails. I know what you're thinking, so here are my answers to all your questions:*
> *Yes, I'll be careful.*
> *Yes, I'll write as often as I can.*
> *Yes, I'm excited.*
> *Yes, I will have a great time, thank you.*
> *I love you too.*
>
> *Jess*

I said good-bye to Mr. and Mrs. Knight and told them to expect me back sometime toward the end of February. Sophie borrowed

Niran's car and gave me a ride to the marina, where Grant and Quinn were readying the boat for our departure.

"Have fun and be safe," she said, giving me a squeeze on the dock. "I'm going to miss having you around, so hurry back, right?"

"Will do." We hugged again. "I'll try to e-mail you and my sister with updates as often as I can."

"All right, take care, you," she said with her hands resting on my shoulders. "I'll be rooting for you, my darling."

She winked at me and gave me one last pat on the rear as I blew her a kiss good-bye.

I lifted a large duffel bag onto my shoulder and grabbed my backpack, then made my way down the dock to *Imagine*. A wave of contentment washed over me as Quinn hopped off the boat onto the dock and grabbed my bags.

"All hands on deck!" he shouted.

I stepped aboard and greeted them both with hugs, holding Grant for a beat or two longer than Quinn.

"You ready?" Grant asked.

I nodded, grinning from ear to ear.

Once aboard I unpacked what little I brought into the tiny closet in the bunkbed room and placed my traveling Buddha statue on a bookshelf in the salon. There was a working washer and dryer on the boat, and the guys told me to bring as little clothing as possible. A couple bathing suits, couple pairs of shorts, a few tops, underwear, pajamas, and my toiletries. I was perpetually tan those days, so the only makeup I brought along was some lip gloss and mascara. Quinn and I shared a bathroom, and all he had was a toothbrush, a bar of soap, and a razor.

After I'd unpacked, I found the guys up in the cockpit. Grant was starting the motor, and Quinn was logging our route.

"So," I began, "what's the plan?"

Grant looked over at me with a subtle smile. "We made the decision to sail back to Langkawi, Malaysia, before hitting the Indian

Ocean. It's only a day's sail, but we calculated that it would save us at least a thousand dollars. The prices for food, beer, wine, and fuel in Malaysia are kind of hard to beat, and we know we won't see those prices again for food and alcohol as we approach the Middle East and Med."

"Is there anything I can do to help?"

"How about a sandwich?" Quinn interjected.

"Screw off, Quinn," Grant said.

I smiled at Quinn. He was the type of man who needed a woman's touch, and I was happy to oblige. I lifted a hand to scold Grant for snapping at him. "Quinn, it would be my pleasure to make you a sandwich."

"I only asked because I know it'll taste better if you make it," he shouted after me.

I skipped down below and figured it was as good a time as any to familiarize myself with the galley. I knew my reason for being there was basically to let them sleep when they needed to, and not much else. The least I could do was feed those boys.

I could see why they wanted to load up on food and drink, because the fridge was nearly empty. It was located right next to the sink and resembled more of a chest-like freezer, where the lid lifts up and you have to dig through everything to find what you're looking for. Organizing the fridge was high on my list of priorities.

I leaned in and pushed a few things around and was able to find some wheat bread, American cheese, and butter. Above the sink were only two cabinets. One had plates and cups, the other had a couple pots and pans. Each had a latch to keep it from flying open while the boat was in motion. The stove was on a gimble, which meant that it moved with the boat to prevent a pot of boiling water from sliding off in turbulent waters. It was a tiny kitchen, but I had no doubt I could get used to cooking under those conditions. Like Quinn said, everything is better with a woman's touch.

I buttered the bread on both sides and then put about a tablespoon in the pan. Once it was warm, I placed four slices of cheese between the bread and slowly browned the sandwiches in the pan on both sides. My mouthwatering grilled cheeses were done in about five minutes, and Quinn referred to them as marriage material. He never made another sandwich again.

When we arrived in Langkawi to provision, we docked the boat, checked in to the country, and had to rent a car so that we could get to the local grocery.

"Target would kill it over here," I said to Grant.

Quinn came over and whispered to us, "I just asked about the bacon. Black market only."

Grant nodded that he understood.

"Wait," I said quietly. "What's going on?"

Quinn leaned in close and covert. "It's an Islamic country, so you can't get bacon at the supermarket. We gotta do deep underground to procure the pork, Jess. Deep!"

I laughed. "Do you really need bacon?"

He took two steps backward and pointed at me. "Everyone *needs* bacon."

After finding the perfect pork dealer at a Chinese black market about a mile from the grocer, we headed back to the marina and unloaded the car in about four separate trips. Each.

Once aboard, Quinn begged me for a grilled cheese and bacon sandwich.

After a couple of whirlwind days getting to and navigating through Malaysia, *Imagine* was filled to the brim with fifteen hundred liters of fuel, ten cases of beer, heaps of soda, juice, canned goods, cookies, Pringles, bacon, and plenty of wine. With our shopping done, we prepared to set off on an eight-day sail from Langkawi to Galle, Sri Lanka. And even though I would be returning to Phuket in about a month, it was with mixed emotions that I left that part of the world. First of all, I was saddened to leave my friends and makeshift family behind. Second, I was anxious to begin the long passage across the Indian Ocean and into the Red Sea. Although I desperately wanted to visit and enjoy Sri Lanka and the Maldives, the anticipation of the journey—and a bed as narrow as a bathtub—was starting to cause a few sleepless nights. Thank goodness for the wine.

Our second night leaving Malaysia was my first solo night watch. I'd sat up with Grant the previous night to get an idea of what was required of me, but there really wasn't much to it. Listen for unusual sounds. Look for any foreign movement in the water. Keep your eyes and binoculars peeled for any other lights or blips on the radar. Besides that I was free to read or watch movies on the portable DVD player.

But that first night I wanted to be free of any distractions. I was alone with only the sounds of the waves against the hull, and I was a little nervous. There was a significant responsibility with keeping watch, and I wanted to make certain I did right by *Imagine*. I was grateful that the moon was especially full that night, because the ocean looked like a brightly lit stage. I could see for miles thanks to its radiance. Periodically, I'd check the controls, and everything seemed to be as it should, until I noticed something odd on the depth meter. Since the meter didn't measure more than six hundred feet, there would be hash marks on the screen instead of numbers when we were out that far in the ocean—as we were that night. But suddenly the depth meter started to register numbers, and they were getting rapidly lower and lower.

Two hundred feet.

One hundred feet.

Fifty feet.

Ten feet!

My heart was beating out of my chest. The guys were asleep, so before I went to wake them up, I ran up the side of the boat to see if I could see anything. As I was leaning over, my hands tightly gripping the thin rail, a dolphin jumped out of the water next to the boat. I screamed and watched as it dove underneath and came out the other side. I fell to my knees, stunned. Two more appeared by the bow.

"Why, you little rascals," I said quietly, and then hurried back to the depth meter once they were out of sight. There were only hash marks on the screen.

—◆◆—

The next day, we were told by a few boaters that they were suffering through some pretty nasty storms ahead, so we had to hove our sails—put them in a fixed position so the boat wouldn't move—and we'd just float out there for a day before continuing on.

"Checking the weather is always the most important thing to do before any passage," Grant told me. "It looks okay tonight, not perfect, but we'll get on the SSB long-range radio to download the latest weather files in the morning and check in with some other boats that are ahead of us."

Unfortunately, we must have caught the tail end of one of the storms, because that night there was some rain and rough seas, which kept me up most of the night. At about midnight I ran to the bathroom and emptied my stomach.

"Thought I heard something. You okay?" I heard Grant ask from behind.

I leaned against the wall and nodded. "Dammit. I thought I was getting used to the movement."

"This one is particularly bad. I'll get you some water."

Grant returned with a bottle of water, steadying himself on the doorframe. "Come on," he said, extending his hand.

I stumbled to my feet and leaned on him as we walked back into my room.

"Thanks for looking out for me."

"The pleasure is all mine."

"Did I wake you?"

"Nope. I was up."

"But it's Quinn's watch."

"He's up there. I'm just not a great sleeper."

He took a short breath and looked at me as though he was going to elaborate, but didn't. I thought about the time in Bangkok when he was on the balcony alone in the middle of the night.

I ducked my head, crawled under the blanket, and curled up on the bottom bunk. "Am I green?" I asked.

Grant knelt beside me, our faces inches apart. "Yes. Is there anything else I can do for you?" he asked, and gently brushed some loose hairs off my face.

"Tell me a story."

He let out a small laugh. "A story?"

"About your trip. I love hearing about the great adventures of Grant Flynn."

"Let's see. Well, I told you about the edible island of Dominica, and some of the people we met there. Did I tell you about the orangutans and Komodo dragons in Indonesia?"

I shook my head.

Grant sat on the floor and kept his arm rested on the small of my back. "All right. Well, where do I begin? I met a man in Komodo who worked on a dragon conservation. He was a real character . . ."

I closed my eyes and smiled as he began to speak. The sound of his voice caused my natural breathing to resume, calming me from the inside out and easing the distress in my stomach, allowing me to fall back asleep.

—◆◆—

Bad weather delayed our arrival into Sri Lanka, but ten days after we left Langkawi, we arrived in Galle and were greeted by what Grant and Quinn agreed were the worst port conditions they'd seen. The harbor was nasty. Tall concrete docks that were built to accommodate commercial ships, not sailboats. Stray, pissed-off dogs everywhere, filthy run-down conditions, and no electricity on the dock. Which meant no air conditioning for us in the one-hundred-degree heat.

As soon as we pulled into the slip, we were greeted by a wonderful agent named Marlon who took care of our check-in formalities, as they do in most countries. Although in most countries the boaters only deal with the agent, and then the agent deals with the officials. Not in Sri Lanka. About an hour after Marlon left, two grumpy-looking Sri Lankan officials boarded *Imagine* for their "compliments."

"Their what?" I whispered to Quinn below in the salon as Grant was trying to talk with the two men in the cockpit.

"They want gifts. Bribes. Booze, cigarettes, whatever we have they'll take in exchange for letting us into their country. Corrupt bastards." He took a toothpick out of his mouth and leaned toward me. "You got anything our guests might like?" he said with a wink. "How much for the little girl?" he added, quoting a line from *The Blues Brothers*.

I smacked him on the arm, and he cracked up. "You're a creep, and you're lucky I like you. Do you guys have to do this everywhere?"

"Nope."

"What do they want exactly?"

"Free shit."

Grant came down the stairs, rolling his eyes. "Find something to give these mooches so I can get them off my boat."

"Maybe they like bacon?" I teased.

"Don't you dare, woman," Quinn said.

Quinn won them over with a bottle of rum and his infectious personality. About an hour later, the three of them were drunk, and Quinn escorted them off the boat. Since they drank their compliments, they never realized that they'd left empty handed.

Quinn returned from the port captain's office about an hour later, chewing on a piece beef jerky.

"I just ran into Angela and Adam," he said to Grant. "I guess they arrived a couple days ago. They said the *Drunken Sailor* is docked here too, and they were wondering if we wanted to convoy with both of them for a few days. Angela saw in the MARLO reports that a Russian supply ship was just captured."

Grant glanced downward in thought. "I guess we could do that, sure."

"Great," Quinn said, replacing the jerky with a toothpick. "I'll be back." He turned around to face us before hopping off. "I assume we want to leave this place as soon as possible? Couple days?"

"Couple days," Grant concurred.

Once Quinn was off the boat, Grant sat next to me on the cushioned bench in the cockpit. He smiled and placed his hand on my bare thigh. His touch sent chills through my body, and my arm lit up with goose bumps. Our eyes met, and I smiled as I did every time I held his attention.

"I know Sri Lanka isn't on your travel wish list, but I thought you might want to do some sightseeing."

"I would love that."

He patted my leg and stood. "I'll have Marlon set up a tour for us."

The next morning Marlon had arranged for us to go on a four-wheel-drive Jeep safari tour, and both our butts were sore after bouncing around looking for wildlife. At one point I was literally thrown into Grant's lap, and he wrapped his arms around me to keep me from falling out the other side.

"Are you going to turn green again?" he asked.

"Did you rent this particular car for that particular purpose? To see how many bumpy vessels cause me to lose my lunch?"

He smiled and glanced at my lips. I thought for sure he was going to kiss me, but he didn't. I scooted off his lap back into my seat.

"Two can play at your game," I said.

"What game is that?"

I squared my shoulders to him. "This flirty, teasy whatever-you-want-to-call-it. Yes, I'm waiting for you to kiss me. Yes, you know it. And yes, I can play hard to get too, so look out."

Grant's eyes lit up with the rest of his face. "Is that a challenge?"

"You're a challenge." I crossed my arms and faced forward.

He bent close to my ear. "When the time is right, Jess," he said, and then asked the driver to pull over for a minute. "Please look at me," he said once the car had come to a stop.

I turned toward him.

"Are you angry with me?"

I shook my head. "No, of course not."

"Good. Because I don't mean to be a tease. I don't want you to get that impression. That's not who I am at all, I promise you."

"I know."

"I would like to think that I'm too old for that, but clearly I'm too old for any of this, because I'm screwing it up so badly. He gently ran his fingers through the ends of my hair, causing my breath to still. "I like being with you a lot. You've managed to make me feel . . . like myself again, and I just don't want to rush anything. I just want to enjoy some time with you without any expectations."

I opened my mouth to speak, but the words didn't come. I wanted to be careful about what I said, so instead I closed my mouth.

"Is that selfish of me?" he asked.

I shook my head. "There's nothing selfish about you," I said. "I enjoy my time with you more than anything in the world. And to be fair to you, I get pure enjoyment out of the times when you flirt with me, so next time I'm going to keep my mouth shut."

"Well, to be fair to you, it's been a long time since I've wanted to kiss anyone this badly."

"I know the feeling."

Grant asked the driver to continue on what was one of the most harrowing car rides I'd ever endured. Sri Lanka is a very populous island, with cars everywhere. However, the roads are "island roads." Outdated, winding, and just plain terrifying. People drive fast and pass each other with reckless abandon. In fact, at one time we were in the middle of a line of five cars with everyone passing each other in different directions. I was white knuckled for most of the day.

"And you were worried about a little rainstorm," Grant shouted, clutching the handle above his head.

Our next stop was at an elephant orphanage that was really more of a zoo-type tourist attraction. It was quite enjoyable, though, to see so many elephants up close—about forty in all—and some as young as three months old bathing in the river and wandering about.

As we were turning to leave, Grant reached for my hand.

"This is not a tease . . ."

"Wait," I interrupted, and placed my other hand over his lips for a second. "If you want to hold my hand, please hold my hand. If you want to kiss me, please do so. And if you don't, I promise not to read into anything or accuse you of playing games or taunting me in any way. I also guarantee that I will be receptive, because I spend most of my days hoping you'll do at least one of those two things."

He smiled, and we held hands on our way back to the death Jeep.

I clutched Grant's hand and closed my eyes during most of the ride back to the marina. Once we reached our slip, I bent down and kissed *Imagine*.

"I will never leave you for four wheels again," I said aloud.

The next day we left the marina in Galle with little regret and were treated to a gorgeous three-day sail from Sri Lanka to the Maldives. Downwind sailing, smooth waters, clear, starry skies at night, and periodic flirting. What more could a girl ask for?

Chapter 19

About a week had passed since we left Sri Lanka, and I'd finally gotten my sea legs. I'd slept through the night and awoke with a new energy and infatuation with the water. I could smell that the coffee had been made and saw that Grant and Quinn were up top in the cockpit when I emerged from my bunk. But before I joined them, I made myself sit down and write an e-mail to Caroline. I knew she got terribly worried when she didn't hear from me.

February 11, 2011

Dear Caroline & Sophie,

I promise to be better about writing. Anyway, we just spent three restful days anchored off of the island of Uligan, in the Maldives.

Talk about picture-perfect. I have never seen such a beautiful place in my entire life. No, Caroline, not even Fort Myers. The oddest contrast is that it's a conservative Islamic country, so the women here are all in burkas, when they should be in bikinis. Very interesting. Also, the water is like glass and packed with fish. From our boat, we could snorkel amongst giant angelfish, triggerfish, and manta rays. And from the beach, we were entertained by over fifty spinner dolphins.

I wish you could see it one day, Caroline. I mean it. It's the most lovely, peaceful, picturesque place in the world.

Great place to fall in love. Just saying . . .

I could probably spend the rest of my life here braiding hair for money, but sadly we are leaving tomorrow, making our way over to Oman and then eventually the Red Sea. Grant says it will be a long trip—possibly nine days at sea. More on dreamy Captain Grant later.

We are now traveling with two other boats that we met in Galle in sort of a convoy situation so that we can look out for each other. The more eyes, the better. Strength in numbers, blah, blah, blah. Anyway, lots of love to you both. Miss you like crazy. I will e-mail again soon.

Jess

The day after we pulled anchor and left the Maldives, it was my turn to sit on the night watch, and the waters on this passage were the first that were beginning to be truly threatening. I took a late afternoon nap, and Quinn woke me at about half past midnight when his shift ended. By about one o'clock in the morning, both of the guys were asleep. I might have said a prayer or two. One for safe passage, and one for smooth sailing.

I sat for a while with the DVD player watching When *Harry Met Sally* for the fortieth time until I realized that I was on the verge of falling asleep. I switched it off, did a few stretches, and then opened a Diet Coke before going about organizing the cockpit, which was always left in disarray after Quinn's shift. I went to pick up some magazines off the dashboard when suddenly Grant's leather book dropped to the floor, and the folded note fell out of its secure resting place between the pages. My eyes darted toward the stairs to make sure no one was coming, but who would be coming at this hour? They were both sound asleep. Still, I paused for a moment, thinking the commotion might have woken Grant, before carefully lifting both the book and the note from the deck and checking the stairwell again. The coast was clear, but just in case, I tiptoed to the bow with the book and note in hand and sat down with my back to the cockpit.

For about five minutes I held them in my lap, debating what I wanted to do against what I should do.

> *Just slide the note back inside, and place the book where you found it.*
> *vs.*
> *They're both sound asleep; one little peek will satisfy your curiosity and do no harm.*

It was pitch-black outside, but I always had my flashlight with me when I was on watch, so I switched it on and opened the book.

Emma by Jane Austen.

I smiled, remembering it was one of Caroline's favorites. I read the first few lines aloud in a whisper.

"Emma Woodhouse, handsome, clever, and rich, with a comfortable home and happy disposition, seemed to unite some of the best blessings of existence; and had lived nearly twenty-one years in the world with very little to distress or vex her."

I took a deep breath. "Lucky girl, that Emma," I said quietly to myself, thinking Grant's wife must have considered herself lucky at one time too. I closed the book and placed it next to me before turning my attention to the folded piece of paper in my left hand. It was a standard white piece of printer paper. Quite worn around the edges and at the folds. I ran my thumb over the top of it, wondering how many times Grant had unfolded it and read it during the past couple of years. I wanted to read it—badly—but didn't want to betray him in any way. Had anyone else ever read the letter? Would it give me some insight into what kind of person he was, or would it only give insight into how intrusive I was?

I quickly grabbed the book and the folded note and headed back to the cockpit. I stood, poised to place the paper back in the book, and the book back where I found it, when instead I unfolded the note. It was typed, not handwritten as I was expecting, and I quickly began reading it, not daring to move any part of my body except for my eyes.

You're going to hate me for writing this letter, but I'm doing it anyway. I don't blame you for not wanting to talk about my illness, but there are a few things that need to be said, and if you won't listen, then maybe you can just read this when you're ready.

Despite how well you and everyone else are trying to pretend, I know I'm dying. Maybe you sense it too. I know you're praying for things to turn around, and for me to come home, but in my heart I know that's not going to happen. I feel the erosion inside of me. It's not always painful, but it's always present. My mind and my soul have made peace with it, and I'm not scared for myself anymore, only for you. My sweet, gentle Grant.

Who's going to scratch your back on that one spot near the center of your spine when it itches? Who's going to set the timer on the coffeepot, since you refuse to learn after six years? Who's going to buy you new socks when yours get holes in them? Who will bring you a bowl of rocky road every night? Who's going to sail around the world with you? Who's ever going to love you as much as I do?

As I lie here, watching time slip from my grasp, all I think about is you. You don't deserve this, and I'm so sorry for that, but I'm not sorry for being the center of your world . . . if only for a short time. All I can dare to hope is that you will be okay.

That my illness doesn't take two lives instead of one. And that you won't remember me this way. Please don't remember me like this. I know it will take you a long time to get over losing me, but I will never be at peace until I know you're happy again. I miss your smile already, because it's been months since I've seen it.

Please take the trip we dreamed about. Imagine me on board and I will be there. Imagine me with you every step of the way. Imagine me when you look into the water. Imagine me clapping and jumping and smiling and cheering you on. Imagine me at peace once you return home safely.

As for what you do afterward . . . I can only imagine.

My limbs went stiff as I held the paper in my hand, tears streaming down my cheeks. Finally, I slapped my hand over my mouth to muffle a loud, singular sob that could not be contained in my throat.

I quickly folded the letter back up and placed it between the pages of the book. Sniffling, I ran back to the bow and burst into tears. I'd never felt so many emotions in one moment. Sorrow, sympathy, shame. Tears were now spilling into my hands and onto my lap. It was the most beautiful and most awful thing I'd ever read, and I would never look at Grant the same way again. It'd be a miracle if I could look him in the eyes the next morning. He'd finally opened up to me in Sri Lanka and admitted to feeling like himself again. I hated myself for what I'd just done.

Once I caught my breath and dried my face with my hands, I went back to my post. I placed the magazines on top of *Emma* and swore never to distress or vex her again.

At 5 a.m. I tapped Grant on the shoulder a couple times until he stirred and awoke for his shift, then I retreated to my bunk, exhausted.

Chapter 20

When I woke up that afternoon, I found Grant at the wheel and Quinn with a bowl of soup on the bow.

"Good morning," he said.

"Sorry. I didn't mean to sleep so long."

"It's only noon."

I sat next to him in the cockpit and looked over our dailies. Each day we received fresh reports of any piracy attacks that had occurred over the last twenty-four hours.

Grant looked over at me as I was reading through them. "I got those pretty early this morning, and the trend is disconcerting. Several attacks occurred very close to the exact route we just crossed. One was actually in the same location they warned us about three days ago."

I looked up from the pages and tried to read his expression. "Are you really worried?"

"I have an uneasy feeling. She's so vulnerable," he said, referring to the boat. "I hate that."

Quinn made his way back to the cockpit when he saw I was there. "Morning, squirt. Don't let those pages drain the color from your face," he said, pointing to the reports with his elbow.

"We need to be on our toes, Quinn," Grant said.

Quinn nodded. "I know, and we are. Also, we've got our convoy for a few more days. All of those are commercial or military ships, so I think we should all be okay, don't you?"

I looked over at Grant, and he nodded in agreement.

That night we had an early dinner of grilled mahimahi and a caprese salad that I made with some fresh tomatoes we'd picked up at a street market in Uligan. After I cleaned up, Quinn laid down for a nap because it was his turn for the overnight shift, and Grant opened a bottle of wine. It was a perfect evening. Warm air, no wind, and the rhythmic sound of the water splashing against the boat. After what I'd done to Grant—albeit unbeknownst to him—I vowed to manage my expectations and stop putting any pressure on either of us. We sat together and talked and laughed, and I didn't hint or holler about anything that was going on between us.

"I see you've e-mailed your sister a few times. How is she do-ing?" he asked.

I shrugged. "As expected."

"What does that mean?"

"It means that she doesn't get out much. She'll be in Indiana forever, but she's happy there. Before I left, she began dating a guy who works at the bank."

"Not much of a dreamer, like you?"

I shook my head. If Caroline did have big dreams, I never knew about them.

"Any other siblings?"

"Nine of us in all."

He nearly gasped. "Wow, you're kidding me."

"Nope. And you're looking at number nine right here. The mis-take that keeps on . . . taking," I joked.

"You're the loveliest mistake I ever met."

"Thank you."

"I guess I shouldn't ask you too many questions. You might run out of surprises."

I didn't mind talking about myself, but there was so little to say in comparison to his stories. I didn't want to put him to sleep with tales of show ponies and high school football games. All I really wanted to hear were more stories about his trip around the world and, more importantly, what he had in store for himself once I departed *Imagine* and headed back to Phuket.

We talked for a couple hours, feet up, wine going down. Like I said, it was a perfect evening—until it wasn't.

Just after 10 p.m. we heard a frantic distress call over the radio.

"Mayday, mayday, mayday. This is the motor vessel *Libra*, our position is twelve degrees, nineteen minutes north, sixty-three degrees, thirty-five minutes east, and we are being attacked by two suspected pirate vessels. Need assistance. Any vessels in the area that can provide assistance, please help! Skiffs with multiple suspected pirates are firing weapons . . ." He paused. Grant and I kept our eyes glued to the radio. "Shots have been fired. Any military vessels in the area, please respond immediately and provide assistance!"

My stomach sank. Grant and I made eye contact that required no words, and seconds later we saw the first flare go up. The *Libra* was not far from us. Grant immediately grabbed the satellite phone.

"Get Quinn up," he said to me as he dialed.

I flew down the steps to the salon and into Quinn's stateroom.

"Hey," I whispered, gently shaking his shoulder. "Quinn, get up."

He rolled over and tried swatting me away like a fly.

"We just heard a distress call from a cargo ship, and Grant said to come get you."

He sat up straight and banged his head on the low overhang. "What?"

"There's an attack nearby, and we just saw the first flare. Grant needs you."

Quinn, with only one eye open, charged up the stairs to the cockpit, and I followed just as the second flare lit up the sky. Quinn and I listened to Grant's conversation with the officer at MARLO as he reported our coordinates.

He hung up the phone.

"He said the *Libra* is a US-flagged cargo ship, and they're taking evasive measures to deter the pirates," Grant told us, and then pointed at the radar.

"Like what?" I asked.

"Look here. You can see they're spinning and making erratic turns to deter them from hooking their ladders."

"What was the call?" Quinn asked Grant.

"They reported an attack by multiple skiffs with shots fired less than eight miles south of us."

Quinn grabbed the binoculars.

Grant continued. "I called UK Maritime Trade Operations on the sat phone to report the incident and give them our coordinates as well. The guy took down the information and basically said that was all he could do at this point."

"Did you call over to *Destiny* or *Drunken Sailor*?"

"Not yet."

"Did he confirm if there are any coalition forces close by?" Quinn asked.

"No." Grant shrugged his shoulders, but the expression on his face did not convey the same ease. "Looks like we're all on our own."

My throat tightened as I stared up into the black skies above us. The evening hour made the whole situation much more ominous than it would have been at daybreak. We were all basking in an eerie silence when one of the boats in our convoy hailed us on the VHF radio. It was Angela from the *Destiny*.

"This is *Imagine*," Grant responded into the microphone.

"Why do you have your red light on?" Her voice crackled through the static airwaves.

"We don't," he answered her.

"I'm looking across my bow and I can see a red light," she said.

The three of us exchanged glances and then turned our attention to the darkness. There was no red light on our boat, but sure enough, there it was on someone else's boat, heading toward us. Just off our stern was a tiny red light flickering like a firefly and coming at our eight-o'clock position at high speed.

Our eyes were glued to it when suddenly it went dark and the light disappeared.

"I don't like this at all," Grant said. "I'm calling MARLO."

Quinn placed a hand on my shoulder. "Relax, kid. It's going to be okay," he said.

Grant began to speak. "Hey, Chris, it's Grant Flynn from *Imagine*. We're only about eight miles from the USS *Libra*, which just put in a distress call, and our radar shows an unidentified vessel approaching us pretty aggressively."

Quinn and I waited, as we could only hear Grant's side of the conversation.

"Yeah," he said. "I can hold."

Grant looked at Quinn. "He's showing a US warship nearby. He's got me on hold while he tries to contact them."

"See that, Jess? A US warship. Nothing to worry about. The navy always saves the day," Quinn tried to reassure me, but my hands were shaking.

"I'm here," Grant said into the phone. "That's great. Yes. Thank you." Grant hung up the phone. "He spoke with the ship, the USS *Enterprise*, directly and said they're steaming toward our position and will put a helicopter in the air as soon as they can. He's given them our coordinates." He managed a closed-mouth grin.

Quinn placed the binoculars back down, took a seat on the bench next to Grant, and made a loud stretching noise. "Y'all woke me for nothing."

We'd lost visual of the red light and could see no sign of an approaching skiff. Grant set *Imagine*'s speed at maximum and tried to close in on the *Enterprise*, which was twenty miles away, doing thirty knots. We eventually made radio contact with the *Enterprise*, and they estimated that they would reach us in twenty minutes, which seemed like an eternity, but the mere fact that it was anywhere close was incredible.

"The cavalry is on its way," Quinn said.

"Did he say anything else?" I asked Grant. "The commander from MARLO?"

Grant nodded. "Just some last advice."

"Last advice?"

"In the event we're boarded. Do not resist, keep your hands up, et cetera."

My eyes widened.

"They obviously don't suggest fighting back, and there isn't much a private yacht can do other than put in a distress call and overwork the engines in hopes of stalling things until help arrives."

"It's game over at that point," Quinn said, and then burst into laughter. "I'm joking, kid. You should see the look on your face."

"Knock it off, Quinn," Grant said.

"Well, I ain't 'not resisting or holding my hands up,' I can tell you that. No fucking way I'm spending springtime in Somalia."

I knew Quinn was acting that way for my benefit. He would never admit to being worried, but more than that, I could tell he was putting on a brave face for me, and I loved him for it . . . I just wasn't buying it. About ten minutes later, the *Enterprise* hailed us on the VHF radio and said they had us and the two other boats in our convoy on their radar and that they had a helo in the air sweeping the area. The commander also asked if we wouldn't mind if they took up a position on our stern for an hour or so. We were all extremely grateful, and Grant jokingly asked if they wouldn't mind tagging along all the way to Egypt. In the background of our phone, we could hear some radio transmission from the helo to the *Enterprise* but could not determine if they'd found the suspicious skiff or not. The report came back that all was clear.

"Well, that's all I need to hear. I'm going to head back to my bunk. Thanks for the excitement," Quinn said, and retired below.

"Our convoy is breaking up in the morning, so I guess tonight was as good a time as any for this to happen." Grant looked at me. "I don't say this very often, but I could really use a drink," he said, shaking his head.

Chapter 21

I scurried down the stairs to the galley and grabbed two beers from the fridge, then rejoined Grant in the cockpit. It was just after midnight, and Grant said he'd wake Quinn at 2 a.m. instead to give him some extra sleep.

He took a long sip from his beer bottle and breathed an even longer sigh of relief.

"I gotta be honest. That really shook me," he said.

"Me too."

"I'm sorry to put you in that position. For all we know, it could have been fisherman screwing around—or simply in the vicinity—but it's better to be safe than sorry. I don't want you to be afraid."

"Do people fish at this hour?"

He cocked his head. "Not typically."

"I'm okay, really. It was a little intense, but I'm just glad it's all clear. Do you think everything is okay aboard the *Libra*?"

"I think so. I'm sure we would've heard if it wasn't. The helos cover a lot of area."

Grant went to set his beer down on the crowded console and accidentally knocked the stack of magazines and his beloved *Emma* onto the floor. My jaw dropped as the letter fell out again, as it had the other night when I was alone. Instinctively, I reached down to grab them for him, and he met my eyes when I placed the letter in his hand.

"Thanks," he said.

I couldn't take my focus or my thoughts off the letter.

"It's a letter from my late wife, Jane," he said matter-of-factly. Hearing her name for the first time made me catch my breath. "This was her book. I'm sure Quinn must have told you. It's his favorite thing to razz me about. He's always threatening to toss it overboard when I wake him up too early."

I smiled. "He hadn't mentioned the letter to me," I said. But I'd already read the letter. Quinn didn't need to divulge any secrets, because I'd already committed such an intrusion into Grant's life I could barely forgive myself and would expect he could never forgive me if he found out.

Grant took a breath and smiled sheepishly before placing the piece of printer paper back inside the book. "I can't quite let it go. Weird, right?"

"Absolutely not. No," I assured him.

"I'm taking the letter and the book around the world and then burning them."

I just stared blankly at him.

"Weird now?" he asked.

I let out a small, nervous laugh. "No, Grant, you're not weird at all. In fact, you're one of the kindest, smartest, strongest, most normal people I've ever met in my life, and I'm so sorry you lost your wife," I blurted out. "She . . . Jane . . . must have been something special to have found you."

"Thanks, Jess. She was."

I hated myself for being such a snoop. Why couldn't I just fly under the radar like Caroline used to tell me? I never learned.

"What was she like?" I asked. "If you don't mind me asking."

"I don't mind at all. Not many people ask me about her. I guess I give off a 'don't talk to me about it' vibe, but I really don't mind talking about her at all. Jane was just . . . a really good person. You know? Trustworthy, kind, generous. One of those people who no one could say a bad word about. She was on the quiet side at parties and such, mostly because she wasn't a fan of large groups of people, but one-on-one she could talk your ear off. She was happiest just being with me. She was very smart and was in nursing school when we got married. She found out she had breast cancer right after her graduation. Unfortunately, she'd caught it too late." He paused. "We did everything we could. Chemo, experimental drugs, holistic medicines, but she died about two years after being diagnosed."

I felt compelled to say something but was momentarily silent. After a beat or so, the words "I'm so sorry" escaped my lips in a tiny whisper.

He nodded. "Thank you. It was a pretty bad time, and I do still miss her, but she wouldn't want me to suffer for it, and I don't want to diminish what we had by sulking for the rest of eternity." He mustered a smile. "It's been almost four years now since she passed."

I wanted so badly to wrap my arms around him, squeeze away the pain, and never let go. The words he used to described Jane were exactly the words I would've used to describe him. I lowered my eyes, thinking of the letter and her beautiful words. I owed it to him to tell him, and just as I was about to lift my head and confess, my eyes welled with tears.

He gave me a funny look. "Jess? You okay?"

I shook my head and blinked, releasing droplets onto the front of my shirt.

Ever the gentleman, he gently lifted my chin with his finger, reached for a tissue, and then handed it to me.

"You're very sweet," he said. "But I'm fine now. Really."

I shook my head again and lifted my hand for a moment. "I've done something terribly wrong."

He sat back an inch or two and questioned me with his eyes.

"You may never forgive me," I said, and dabbed my cheeks.

"I'm sure that won't be the case."

"No, I mean it . . ."

"Jessica, what is it?"

I squared my jaw and gazed into his eyes—dark blue, like the water that carried us—so that he might sense a shred of the shame that was festering inside of me.

"I read the letter. Jane's letter. The one you just tucked back into the book."

He held my stare, then looked away, releasing a breath through his nose.

"The other night during my solo shift, I was trying to tidy things up, and the letter fell out of your book when I moved that stack of magazines. Just as it did a minute ago. Anyone with any sense of decorum would have put it right back, but I didn't." I paused. "You and I have become closer, and I care so much about you that I just I couldn't help myself . . . I mean, I could have, but I didn't. I'm so sorry, Grant."

He nodded, then stood after a beat. I watched as he walked up the side to the bow of the boat and leaned over the front rail with his elbows. I lowered my head. What more could I say? I did a terrible thing, but I was honest with him, and I couldn't take it back. I sat and waited as he processed what I'd done. The sound of the water lapping against the boat, while normally comforting, put me on edge. After about five minutes, Grant returned to where I was sitting.

"I'm so sorry," I repeated.

"What's done is done."

"I violated your privacy and your one remaining piece of intimacy with your wife, and you can't *imagine* how awful I feel about it."

He tapped the cover of the book, then placed it back up on the counter, tucked next to the console where it wouldn't be disturbed. "It is a sacred thing, that letter, and as much as it might seem like I guard it like the Holy Grail, it's just a letter. Believe it or not, it's one of many that Jane wrote to me right before she died. If you or anyone had ever asked to read it, I would have let you. But . . ." He shrugged.

"But most people with common decency know how to respect people's private property without being completely intrusive and inappropriate," I interjected.

"May I finish?" he asked.

I nodded.

"But . . . no one has ever dared to ask. For all I know, you're not the first to read it behind my back either. I've read that letter many times, and it's not an easy read, so don't think for a second I don't know how you feel. But please don't beat yourself up about it. It's over with," he said. "As I mentioned, I don't get the chance to talk about Jane much anymore, but when I do, I always feel so much better. So thank you for that."

He smiled at me, and our eyes locked. If he had leaned forward even one millimeter, I would have kissed him.

"Grant, only you would thank me after I've been so intrusive," I said, and then hugged him hard. I embraced him with every ounce of my being and with every bit of desire that I'd been holding on to for the past three months. He wrapped his arms around my back and buried his head into the base of my neck. "You're welcome," I whispered into his chest.

I pulled away slowly when he loosened his grip on me. We both paused as our faces were inches apart. I scanned his lips and his five-o'clock shadow and smiled, before sitting back in my seat. My heart was pounding as I watched him lean back into the cushions and cross his legs.

He draped his arm over the back of the seat. "Why don't you tell me something about you now?"

"Like what?"

"I don't know. Something personal about yourself. Then we'll be even."

I inhaled through my nose and stared at my bare feet. I was never very good at opening up about myself. Always more interested in learning about other people's issues than divulging my own. I turned toward him. His arms were now crossed in his lap, and there was a hint of a smile across his face. Did he really care to learn anything about me, or was he just being polite? I thought for a moment, trying to come up with something equally substantial, but everything about my life before Thailand seemed trivial. Except for one thing.

"I didn't cry when my mom died," I said, shaking my head slightly.

He tilted his head to one side. "When did she die?"

"About six months ago. Just before I left Indiana."

He looked at me and released a barely audible "hmm."

"Do you feel badly about it?" he asked.

I thought for a moment and dropped my gaze to the ground again before responding, "I guess I do."

He pursed his lips.

"She never understood me, and she never wanted me," I said.

"That's doubtful."

"No, really. I'm not even fishing for sympathy here. She was forty-two years old, and I was an unplanned pregnancy. I was mostly raised by my eldest sister, Caroline, who by the way was a sobbing wreck at the funeral." I paused. "Church was Mom's life, and what with God, nine kids, and my father, the woman had her hands full. She'd had a child every two years since the age of twenty-two, then as soon as she thought she was done she gave birth to my twin brothers, Andrew and Michael, when she was thirty-four years old. Then eight years later, and nine days before my father's scheduled vasectomy, she found out she was pregnant with me. Clearly a condemnation for agreeing to the vasectomy."

He smirked.

"Rumor has it she literally handed me over to Caroline the day I was born and said, 'This one's yours.' My relationship with her was like a relationship with a distant grandparent. I tried as hard as I could to get her attention, but I hated going to church."

"Why did you hate it?"

I shrugged and considered his question. I never understood what Mom saw in God anyway. He didn't save my Uncle Berty when he got lung cancer. He didn't save my favorite cat from the one car an hour that drove down our country road, and he never allowed my sister Caroline to get pregnant with the baby she so badly wanted.

"Probably because my mother was always there and put the church before her family. She always said God's work was never done. But as it turned out, too much of God's work gave her a heart attack."

He smiled at me without an ounce of pity on his face, and I was so grateful for that.

"Well," I said, throwing my arms up, "enough of this rookie therapy session."

He arched an eyebrow, causing me to pull at the hem of my shirt.

"Last time I'll mention it . . . but I'm truly sorry for jeopardizing your trust in me. I really like being with you, and I don't want there to be any bad feelings between us," I said as honestly as I could.

"I like being with you too." He kept his eyes on mine for a beat longer and then glanced at the radar.

"Can I ask you something?"

"Yes," he said.

"Have you kissed anyone else since Jane died?"

"Yes," he answered without hesitation.

I nodded.

"Is there more you want to know?"

I shook my head.

He leaned toward me and brought his face close to mine. "Does that bother you?" His eyes narrowed. "Did you think you were the first person I'd wanted to kiss in four years?"

My body stilled. It seemed as though our minds were on the same page, but I was not about to make the first move.

"No," I whispered. "But if that's the case, can I ask why you reacted the way you did in Bangkok?"

He averted his eyes for a second. "I guess my feelings caught me off guard. It felt different between us, and you're one of the first women I've wanted to spend any length of time with."

I could feel his breath on my skin as he spoke.

"Why?"

He thought for a second. "I can appreciate what you've done with your life and your desire to see the world. Relocating to a foreign city with limited modern amenities is not an easy task for every small-town girl. And I admire what you've done with your students and how much your face lights up when you talk about your work with them. I can tell how grateful you are to be living your life."

His words moved me.

I swallowed. "Well, lucky for you then that I'm stuck on this boat for the next few weeks."

"Yes, it is lucky for me," he said, and then leaned back against the seat behind him. "What about you? What's your story with men?"

I let out a laugh. "This should cure your insomnia. You don't want to know."

"Apparently I do, as indicated by my question just now."

I took a sip from my bottle before answering. "There's not much to tell really. My only serious relationship was in college. I dated a guy for about a year and a half. Besides that, not much to write home about." I shrugged. "I've been busy."

"Who pulled the plug? You or college boy?"

"I did."

"Why?" he asked.

"It was never meant to be. Neither of us ever talked seriously about getting married, and we couldn't have been more different. At least as far as our future goals were concerned. He wasn't a bad guy, just not for me. The only places he'd consider traveling to were football stadiums."

"Stadiums?" He stretched his legs and smiled again, this time more curious, as he sipped his beer.

"We were never right for each other. His dream girl will produce three children, make a killer macaroni casserole, and have a degree in scrapbooking. I couldn't have been more wrong for him."

"Is that why you moved? To get out of Dodge and away from the boys next door?"

"I moved because I never wanted to stay in Indiana. My mother's passing and me losing my job were just the catalysts. There was never anything holding me back except for myself and maybe Caroline. We're very close."

"The sister you just mentioned?"

"Yes. She's like a mother to me, and it was hard to leave her, but she was really the only reason I stayed as long as I did. In the end all she's ever wanted was for me to be happy, but I wasn't happy there."

"Why not?"

"I can hardly tell you." I shrugged and considered his question. There was simply nothing in LaGrange County that appealed to me. On paper my life was good there. I wasn't miserable, and I loved my job and my students, but I always felt out of place. Like I was just biding my time, waiting to be transported somewhere else where people wouldn't roll their eyes at my curiosities and desires to see new things and meet new people. But I was a practical girl with student loans and little savings to fund said curiosities. So I learned to curb my enthusiasm, fly under life's radar, and wait until the time was right to follow my dreams instead of everyone else's.

"Maybe 'happy' is the wrong word," I said. "I was never comfortable. And what I've learned from moving away and living in Thailand is that in the end I think I was running to something, rather than running away from it. Does that make sense?"

He nodded.

"Indiana is not a bad place. In fact, I couldn't have grown up in a nicer community of people. Things like family values and hard work and common courtesy are still revered. It's a place where kids play outside and people leave their doors unlocked, but I never fit in." I scratched the back of my neck. "My mother never let me do anything except come straight home every day after school when I was young. Any interest I had in leaving home or participating in activities that were outside the norm always angered her. I had only a tiny handful of neighborhood friends, and my closest siblings in age are eight years older than me, so I spent a lot of time alone, masterminding a future for myself. I never had any desire to work on our farm, and the only things that interested me were the things I knew nothing about or had never experienced."

"Are you happy in Thailand?" he asked. "It seems like you had high expectations for yourself."

I thought about his question for a moment, then nodded. "I am. I'm not exactly sure how long I'll stay and what lies ahead for me, but I'm extremely pleased with my decision to move there."

We both studied each other for a moment. He had one elbow rested up on the seat cushion behind him and his beer in his other hand. There was a palpable energy floating between us. Sexual, kinetic fireworks bursting around us and staking claim aboard *Imagine*. He had promised me on New Year's Eve that he would kiss me again. If it didn't happen soon, I might not survive the wait.

I went down to my cabin that night, opened one of the drawers beneath the bottom bunk, and pulled out the photo album of my parents' honeymoon that Caroline had sent to me. Maybe she was right. Maybe I was more like our mother than I ever knew.

Maybe my mom was just never able to find the courage to follow her dreams like I did. I stared at a picture of her, so young and beautiful and unrecognizable to me, and began to cry. I longed to know that girl, and I was determined to make her proud and fulfill her dreams for her.

Chapter 22

February 16, 2011

Dear Caroline,

Just a quick note to let you know that we are all still doing well. Grant says we should arrive in Sallalah, Oman, midday tomorrow for a quick 24- to 48-hour stop for fuel and hopefully food. If we can't reprovision there, we'll be eating a lot of pasta and peanut butter on the next passage. With a Pringles appetizer, naturally.

Although this has not been a great sail—and we have run the engine every minute to keep a good pace—it has not been as bad as Quinn or Grant had expected so far. Fishermen present the biggest problem. They are everywhere and make our watch very, very busy, since we never know if they're going to turn out to be a threat or not. We did have one get a little too close for comfort the other night, but thankfully, with the help of our convoy (and the US Navy), we were able to thwart the threat, and it turned out to be nothing.

I don't want to say too much about Grant, but he's been a wonderful support, and I can't wait to tell you more about him. Let me just say that I'm doing my best to keep my heart from going adrift.

Jess

Quinn turned in early the next night while I cleaned up the galley. It was raining pretty hard, and Grant was drenched from checking the rigging when he came back down to the salon.

"You're soaked. Can I get you a towel?"

"I'll grab one from my bunk," he said, and removed his wet shirt as he turned and walked away.

Seeing those two guys shirtless was a regular occurrence, but that night, watching Grant slowly peel his damp clothing off his toned, suntanned arms stopped me in my tracks. My body stilled as my eyes followed him down the tiny hallway to his room, where he towel-dried his hair and slid a white cotton T-shirt over his torso. He turned to return to the salon and caught me staring at him. He stopped walking as we locked eyes and held that moment in time for what seemed like an eternity. No words were necessary. My expression must have conveyed everything that had been on my mind, because he extended his right hand to me and gave me a subtle yet commanding nod. I swallowed and left the dishrag on the counter, never once taking my eyes off of his. My desire for him increased with every step until I reached his grasp.

He guided me into the master cabin and shut the door. There was very little space between us and the bed—a foot maybe—and the only light was from the moon filtering in through the small windows above the bed. As soon as we stopped, I placed my free hand on his cheek. He closed his eyes for a second and then turned to kiss the tips of my fingers. Grant released me, then placed his hands on either side of my neck. I tilted my head upward to look into his eyes again and found them scanning my body.

"I think it's time for that kiss," he said in a low whisper, then slowly removed the dry shirt he'd just put on.

There was nothing for me to say. I'd lost my urge to speak when he extended his hand, and my mind delighted in the thought that my physical hunger for him might finally be satisfied.

He reached for my hand and placed my palm over his heart. His skin was damp, and he smelled like the sea. My eyes went from the back of my hand to his face, and without hesitation he bent forward and kissed me. His lips were soft, in contrast with the stubble that surrounded them, and his hands tightened their grip on my neck as he parted my mouth with his tongue.

"You take my breath away," he said.

I dropped my arms to my side, numb with desire. He pressed my back against a wooden post at the base of the bed, and we kissed with unadulterated abandon. A moment later he lifted me up onto the mattress and continued to explore my neck and ears with his mouth. My breathing intensified when he laid his weight on top of me and spread my legs to make room for him.

"Your skin is exquisite. Has anyone ever told you that?" he paused to ask as he slowly dragged his fingers over my thigh.

I shook my head and pulled him to me, guiding his lips back to mine.

Grant straightened his arms beside my head while keeping our mouths glued to each other and began to press his hips into mine. I could feel him getting hard as I closed my eyes and arched my back to meet his body. He wrapped his hand around my waist and pulled at my shorts while I wiggled out of them. Then he removed his own as I watched him stand for a second, naked, in front of the bed, looking too big for the tiny space. It was dark, but I could see his eyes light up as I removed my underwear and tossed it on the floor. He expertly lowered his warm body back on top of me and parted my knees again. Then he placed his hand on my chest and paused to look at me.

"I've never felt this way about anyone," I said as if to explain my rapid heartbeat.

I lifted my chin and pulled on his hair as he bent forward and kissed between my breasts. He pulled gently at my bikini top with his teeth and placed my right breast in his mouth. I turned my face away from his and moaned, causing him to press himself harder between my legs, which were begging mercilessly for him to come inside me.

"It's time," I choked out—the same words he'd said to me moments before.

He smiled with one corner of his mouth, then took both my wrists in his right hand and placed them above my head before slowly guiding himself inside of me. My body shook, then tightened, then released itself to him completely. He moved with skilled precision, keeping one hand on my wrists and one pressing into the bed beside me as he managed his pace—slow at first, then more rapid and controlled. His head was down, allowing his gaze to be focused on where our bodies were connected.

Finally, he released my arms and put his lips on mine.

"Keep them there," he said, and I was quick to obey.

Both his hands pressed hard into the mattress beside my body as he kissed me, starting at my chin, then moving on to my neck and my breasts before increasing his thrusts until he released himself and drew me closer to him.

He laid his head on my chest, which was pounding like the waves, and then lifted his mouth to mine. Our bodies were sweaty and beat. He rolled over, pulled me on top of him, and wrapped his arms tightly around me.

"You are magnificent. Thank you," he whispered.

I let out a small laugh. "Thank *you*."

Grant rolled to the left and propped his body up on one elbow as I fell to his side. He put his other hand under my chin. "Come here."

I leaned forward. "That was a great kiss, but don't ever make me wait that long again."

He ran his fingers through my hair as we gazed at each other. "Thank you for what you've done for me."

"What have I done for you? You're the one who's done so much for me."

He pulled me close and then released me. He was gazing at me intently and smiling. I loved when he smiled.

"You've . . . how can I explain it? You've brought some *excitement* back into my life."

He kissed me again, nipping my lower lip with his teeth.

Grant leaned back against the wall behind us, and I stretched my legs beside him, my limbs loose and relaxed.

"How about another round of excitement then?" I whispered in his ear.

He slowly trailed his fingers from my shoulder to my knee and then flipped me on my stomach. He sat up and straddled me from behind, kneading my legs with his strong hands and making my head spin.

He leaned over and whispered into my ear, "Try to relax."

"You're not making it very easy," I mumbled.

"Shh," he said, and massaged my inner thighs and buttocks with his fingers until I begged him to stop. I couldn't take it any longer. My need for him was explosive. The weight of his chest on my back released the air in my lungs, and I nearly gasped as he entered me a second time.

My heart was doomed, but it was the best sleepless night I'd ever had.

—◆◆—

At five in the morning, I awoke to a slurping sound and nearly screamed when I opened my eyes. Quinn was standing at the end of the bed, holding a bowl of cereal and wearing a colossal grin.

"Hey, kids," he said.

Grant rolled over and grumbled.

I sat up straight and pulled the thin sheet over my chest, mortified, and shrugged. We were caught, and Grant didn't seem to care, so why should I?

After Quinn left, snickering and shaking his head, I pulled the sheet over Grant's shoulder, got dressed, and crawled out of there. I took a quick shower, grabbed a new pair of shorts and a tank top, and joined Quinn on deck as the sun was coming up.

"Busted," I said as I plopped down next to him.

"It's all good, Jess. Don't sweat it."

He finished his cereal, and I let the wind blow on my face, waking me up a little before saying anything else.

"I like him, Quinn. A lot."

He looked at me. "I can see that, but you don't have to explain. It's all good. I mean it."

"I'm not really trying to explain, although maybe I should be, but you're the only one I have to talk to about it." I leaned forward and patted him on the knee.

Quinn chuckled. "Okay, I gotcha. We can be girlfriends." He placed the empty cereal bowl next to him, sat cross-legged, and folded his hands in his lap. "Let's chat it out."

A smile spread across my face. "I know your loyalty is to Grant, and I one-hundred-percent get that. But, if I asked you to be completely honest with me and tell me if he's had countless other women in that bed, would you tell me?"

"No."

I lowered my chin and raised my brows. "No to what?"

"No, he hasn't had countless other cabin dwellers."

My shoulders relaxed. "Has he had any?"

"I can't diss my boy like that," he said. "But countless is a pretty big number."

"You're right, and it's totally not my place to ask." I glanced out at the water, so smooth and calm that morning. Exactly as we'd hoped. "I'm for sure going to get my heart broken," I mumbled.

"I don't know about that."

I turned my attention back to Quinn. "I can't help it. I'm in too deep already, and I've somehow convinced myself that having any part of him, no matter how small, is better than having none of him. I mean, what was I thinking? I'm going back to Thailand, and he's sailing through the Med and picking up a new crew and has about a year left of his journey, and then God only knows what he has planned after that."

"Fuck, this hurts." Quinn unfolded his legs.

I threw my hands up. "I should've known better than to get involved like this."

"Can I ask a question?"

"Sure," I said.

"Do your girlfriends ever get a word in edgewise, or should I just sit here and nod and snap or whatever?"

"Sorry. I guess we girls usually just talk over one another and interrupt with our infinite wisdom. Got any?"

Quinn straightened his legs out in front of him and leaned back on his hands. "Look, if it's any consolation, which I know it is, I think he likes you too."

"Did he tell you that?"

"Not in so many words."

"Then in how many?"

"Guys can tell. We don't need a neurotic gabfest like this to know when one of our own is interested in a girl, and I can tell he's into you." He paused to raise a brow and lean in. "He was *into* you, right?" he sneered, and I smacked him.

Grant awoke and joined us on the bow. I felt my cheeks turn beet red as he and I exchanged looks and smiled.

"Sleep good?" Quinn said. "Or was the bed a little rocky last night?" he cracked.

"Wow. Seriously?" I shot him a look, and then Quinn stood and patted Grant on the back as he walked away.

Grant sat next to me, his tousled hair and morning stubble in perfect harmony.

"Looks like it's going to be a beautiful day," I said.

"It does," he answered without looking away from me.

I smiled at him, but all I could think about was our limited time together and how I may never see the man again once we reached Egypt.

"I can tell you have something on your mind," he said. "Care to discuss what went on last night?"

I lowered my eyes and fumbled with my hands. "Yes and no. Yes, because I'm desperate to know how you're feeling, but I don't want to put any unnecessary pressure on the situation." I looked up at him. "I mean it. I'm really not that girl."

"What girl?"

I waved a hand in front of me. "You know, that 'what are you thinking?' kind of girl you need to coddle after sex."

He sniffed out a laugh. "Okay, no coddling then."

"And not because I'm scared to talk about the future . . . or lack thereof."

He sighed and looked over the rails at the sea. "Yeah, I've been thinking about that myself."

"You have?" I piped up.

"Yes, I have."

I tucked my hair behind my ears. "What have you been thinking about exactly?"

"Whoa. Didn't you just tell me you're not the 'what are you thinking?' . . ."

I shook my head. "Okay, fine. How about I tell you what *I'm* thinking?" I said, and sat straight.

I learned at an early age the rewards and perils of speaking my mind. Sometimes being forthright would get me into trouble, but more recently it'd gotten me to where I was in life. On my own, halfway across the world, and on a boat in the middle of the Indian Ocean with a man unlike any I'd ever met. How could I ever regret telling him how I felt?

I took a deep breath.

"You're not on trial," he said.

"I'm thinking that I really like you, and that you're the most incredible person I've ever known, and that I don't have anything to lose for telling you."

He narrowed one eye. "What do you mean you have nothing to lose?"

"I mean, I'm not afraid of opening up to you, or of having my heart broken." I looked away. "Only of never seeing you again."

He nodded in a way that didn't quite ease my concerns.

"Oh my God, I *am* that girl," I whispered.

He sighed again but didn't look bothered in the least. "I wish I had all the answers, Jess, I really do. But the truth is that I don't know exactly where I'll be in six months, let alone six weeks. I have a very loose travel schedule, and I've allowed for many changes and diversions in between." He paused. "I definitely don't think this trip will be the last time we'll ever see each other, though."

"I hope not."

He leaned forward and kissed me. He tasted like toothpaste and held the back of my head while he explored my mouth with his tongue before resting his forehead against mine.

"How about we enjoy the time we do have and then worry about the continuation to this story another time?"

"Deal," I said. "But just so you know, I like happy endings."

Chapter 23

I was dreaming about Grant and me. We were in a home. It must have been my subconscious's version of what Grant's house would look like, because I'd never been there. It was in the mountains somewhere at the bottom of a hill. The décor was rustic yet modern. Sleek lines, lots of wood built-ins and flooring, and a singular glass staircase leading up to a lofted master bedroom. The kitchen was clean and sparse with no cabinetry on the walls, only floating shelves to hold the white plates and bowls. There were a few small appliances hidden below the countertops, and I was making microwave popcorn. We were about to watch a movie, and Grant was waiting for me on a large sectional couch near the TV and the fireplace.

We smiled at each other as I tended to our snack in the kitchen. I pressed the preset popcorn button, and after about a minute I heard the signature pop-pop-pop noise and went to give Grant the thumbs-up—but when I looked up, he was gone. Pop, pop, pop.

The sound was real, but everything else was not. When I awoke from my dream, I could still hear the noise. Pop, pop, pop. Only this time it was gunfire, and it was getting louder.

And it wasn't a dream.

By the time I opened my eyes, there were seventeen Somali pirates on board *Imagine*.

DAY ONE

It's very difficult to describe my emotions in that moment. Fear, shock, disbelief hardly scratch the surface of what I was going through. My breathing was heavy and labored due to the sheer terror of it all, and my body temperature rose instantly—to such a dizzying, intense heat that I nearly fainted. Physically, I didn't know how to react. My eyes rolled back for a brief moment, and my mouth went dry as I dared to look at them. Every single one of their faces looked like Death. Dark, hallowed eyes devoid of emotion.

Many of them were chewing on khat, a drug I'd heard of many times and knew that nearly every Somalian gang member was addicted to it. It's a leaf from an African plant containing mind-altering chemicals similar to amphetamines and is used like chewing tobacco, often held in the user's mouth between their cheek and gums.

The devil had boarded *Imagine*.

The raw fear caused my ears to clog, like I was on an airplane, so it sounded like the men—some young teenagers—were trying to communicate with me through a tin can. Three of them were waving guns in my face, trying to get me to move, but there was nowhere to go. The space was crowded with our captors, and my legs were curled tightly beneath me, my face nearly pressed against a wall. It seemed impossible for me to stand because my limbs were petrified. When I didn't move, one of them smacked the left side of my head with a gun. I passed out and had a moment of peace.

I awoke to find two of the men pissing on my bare feet. I tried to scream, but there was something soft and damp in my mouth preventing me from doing so. I swung my feet away from them, and they just continued to let it trickle onto the floor.

I was hunched over, sitting on the floor of the salon, desperate to know where Grant and Quinn were. Blood drenched my shoulder, thick and dark, no doubt from the hit to the face. I began to cry and was hit again in the same spot. The second blow temporarily blinded me. I saw only black and kept trying to blink the darkness away. Eventually, a blurred vision came back to me, and I saw them. Grant and Quinn had been right in front of me the whole time, only I couldn't see them until now because there were so many people standing in the way. The three of us were tied up and seated on the floor of the salon. I squinted, trying to make out their faces. Quinn's head was down and he was slumped over, gently convulsing. The sight of him made me nauseous. Then I looked up at Grant. He was staring straight at me, eyes wide, with a dirty rag in his mouth and his arms behind his back. I tried to read his expression, but the sight of him bound and gagged destroyed me.

I began to shake. I didn't want to get hit again, but I couldn't control myself. My brain and body were in such a state of shock they didn't know what else to do. Grant shook his head slowly; his gaze was intent and heartbreaking. He wanted to die for putting me in this position. I knew it.

"Where is the money?" one of them shouted. "Get it now!"

Grant looked up at him. "We have very little money on board."

"Where is this money?" He slammed the butt of his gun to the floor. "Find this 'little' money," he said to some of the others, and then turned back to Grant. "Where is it? You have American dollars and jewelry?"

Grant gestured toward his cabin. "All I have is in there, top drawer."

The man disappeared and came back with three thousand dollars. All the cash that Grant had on board. "Where is more?" He shook the envelope in Grant's face. "Cash!"

"We carry plastic. Charge cards. That is all the cash."

He spat. "You lie!"

The conversation went back and forth until the man was screaming at Grant and shouting for the others to ransack the boat—which they did. They threw our life jackets overboard; they destroyed our emergency equipment and flares; they emptied drawers and shelves and changed into Grant's and Quinn's clothes.

I turned my head to the wall and did my best to hide my tears. Ten of the pirates were still crammed in the salon with us, menacingly cocking their guns and devoid of compassion. The body odor was debilitating.

Quinn eventually stopped moving and spitting, and either fell asleep or lost consciousness. When the human body endures such trauma, it's literally exhausting to its system. I myself could barely keep my eyes open, but I was scared to close them. Grant attempted to stretch his legs, but there was little room. Just then two of the men started to hit our feet and legs with the tips of their guns, carelessly swinging AK-47 rifles around in that small space and slamming us with them in an effort to get us to move.

Grant nodded at me to get up, then he nudged Quinn with his shoulder. Quinn lifted his eyes as best he could, but it looked as though his neck was incapable of supporting his head. One of the men smacked him in the knees with his rifle, and Quinn winced. Then the man did it again and kept repeatedly hitting Quinn in the knees even after he'd stood.

"Get up now! Move!" they were screaming in heavily accented English.

I stumbled to my feet along with the guys, and the pirates ushered us with their guns into my cabin of all places. The smallest room on the boat. They forced us all into the bottom bunk, and the three of us were soon crammed into a space that a day before was barely large enough to hold me alone. I was in the middle, and when I tried to make space for Quinn, he retracted. I looked at his face. There were tears in his eyes and a look of despair. I pleaded with my own eyes for him not to lose hope.

I need you. Please stay with me, I tried to convey.

He nodded, then looked at my left eye and the side of my face and shook his head.

What had they done to him? Quinn's spark had gone out. I could see it with one look. I tried to touch him, but my hands wouldn't reach.

My left eye was in bad shape. My hands were tied, but I could feel my lid swelling with a prickly burn, and it stung like hell. The pain was more bearable when my eyes were closed, so I shut them and put my head back. Grant pressed his leg into mine, so I turned my face to his. His lips parted when he saw my eye, and he threw his head back against the wall, shaking it back and forth. I silently begged him to stop. I was so worried one of us would be punished for doing anything but lying still. I opened my mouth to say something. He shook his head and silenced me.

Our situation was truly unthinkable. The worst possible scenario—the thing we'd all assured ourselves could happen but never would—had happened. The speed at which our fate had changed was inconceivable. One night I'd gone to sleep dreaming of happy endings, and the next I was being held captive, my air supply limited, my throat dry and raw, my body poked and prodded with machine guns. Machine guns! I'd never even been in the same room with a gun of any kind, and now there were military-grade assault rifles in my face.

My head was filled with a combination of conflicting images. On one hand, I pictured every possible horrific scenario that could happen, and on the other, I was picturing things that had nothing to do with what was happening to me. Things like the tomato plants in the Knights' backyard and the broken chalk I'd meant to replace at school and the air in my bicycle tires. It was low. I'd promised to fill the tires before I left, in case Mrs. Knight wanted to use the bike while I was away, but I'd forgotten.

I closed my eyes again, rested my head on Grant's shoulder, then quickly felt his head press against the top of mine. I must have fallen asleep, because there was a young boy, maybe in his late teens, sitting in the doorway when I opened my eyes. He was heavily armed. Quinn and Grant were both still next to me with their eyes shut. I stared at the boy. His face was not like the others' and despite his weapons, he didn't pose a serious threat. After a second or two, he looked at me. He didn't smile—none of them ever smiled—but he stood and walked toward me with some ice, which he then held against the side of my head. Grant slowly opened his eyes and stared at me wildly as the boy stood in front of me, as if I had any choice in the matter.

A few minutes later a man came in and pointed at me. "Come."

Grant immediately stood and shook his head. "No. She stays here with me."

His defiance was met with a wicked slap to the face that sent him back onto the bunk. I winced and began to shake but could not will myself to stand.

"Come!" he yelled.

I slowly got up and walked toward him. He clamped onto my forearm and ushered me into the galley, where he freed my hands.

"Cook rice," he ordered, and walked away, leaving three men seated on the couch behind me in the salon with their weapons drawn at my back.

I stood, frozen, staring at the tiny stove top, afraid to move a muscle. I blinked, trying to organize my thoughts. I didn't want to do anything that would cause alarm. I slowly glanced over my shoulder and lifted my arm, pointing to a cupboard above me.

"Pot," I said with no idea of whether they understood me or not, then reached for the largest pot we had. It was just big enough to cook rice or pasta for four people. I kept my feet in the same location and just leaned over to the rice canister. It was barely half full. Once I was done, I placed the small amount on the stove and waited.

And waited.

I think I stood there while the rice cooled for at least twenty minutes before anyone bothered with me. Eventually, the man who'd told me to make rice came back and ordered me to make sandwiches. This time he stood and watched me as I made nine cheese sandwiches, hands trembling. Once I was through, he tied my arms behind me, shoved a cloth rag in my mouth, and put me back in the cabin.

DAY TWO

My own vomiting awakened me. The rag must have come from the engine room because it tasted like diesel fuel. I used my right shoulder to try and release it from under the tourniquet covering my mouth and spat onto the floor under the bunk. I bent forward as best I could and felt Grant try to place his hand on my back. I was able to dislodge the rag enough to clear my mouth and leave it hanging on my chin. I wanted to talk to Grant, but I was too scared, so I kept my body forward and tried to piece together how the hell we ended up there.

I could hear my mother's voice telling me everything I'd done wrong, just like when I was young. Back then too much chatter would land me in the "prayer chair," facing the corner, with two rosaries around my neck. Jesus loved peace and quiet, and so did mother. I'd sit there as long or as short as I wanted, scraping paint chips off the wall, because she'd never check on me. Ever.

In high school I had a curfew of 10 p.m. At exactly thirty seconds past ten, Caroline would begin calling around looking for me, trying not to let Mom get wind of my defiance. Then one night around midnight my friend Sarah and I were at Hardee's, splitting an order of fries and watching the door, hoping some boys our age would walk through. When a few boys did walk in, Sarah and I followed them outside to the back of the restaurant and watched them light a joint.

"No, thanks." I shook my head.

One of the boys, Matt Anderson, narrowed his eyes and inhaled. "Take it," he said, thrusting it to me again.

"My mother would kill me if I got caught." The words just came out, and Sarah rolled her eyes, expressing my embarrassment.

He looked around and laughed. "Is she here?"

Sarah reached over and took the joint from him. She held it gently to the edge of her lips and smoked. "Go ahead, Jess," she said. "You know you want to. Your mom would kill you for much less, so you may as well have some fun with us."

Matt got it back from her and then offered it to me again, so I took it.

"If you can't do anything right, then why not do everything wrong?" he said with a wink.

A moment later the cops pulled up.

Everyone ran except for the marijuana and me, and all I could think was that there wasn't a "prayer chair" big enough to hold this mess.

Caroline accompanied my mother—in her Velcro rollers—to the police station. At least she'd shown up. Caroline stood silently as Mom cursed me up, down, and sideways on behalf of the entire family, community, and God in heaven. She was so brutal in her admonition of me that the arresting officer literally jumped to my defense, saying he didn't actually see me smoking and that it looked like my friends ran and deserted me. He even applauded me for doing the right thing by not fleeing.

The worst part was seeing the disappointment on my sister's face. Letting her down was worse than whatever corner of hell my mother had just assured me I was going to.

I looked down at the dried blood on my hands and thought, *Maybe this is my corner of hell.*

I sat back between the guys, whose necks were crammed due to the bunk above us. Quinn was facing the wall on his right, and away from me.

"Are you okay?" I whispered to Grant.

He stared straight through me for a moment, then nodded.

"Is there anything we should do?" I asked.

He shook his head. The room smelled like urine. Likely any one of us had peed our pants over the course of those two days. I closed my eyes again, and we waited in silence.

Some time later the young boy came in with an AK-47 hanging across his chest and a bottle of water. His eyes were kind and not as dark as the others'. He approached Grant first and removed the rope that was holding the sock in his mouth. Grant spat it to the floor and began to cough and spew out what little saliva he had. The boy lifted the water bottle to Grant's lips and let him drink. I swallowed the dry air in my throat as my brain begged for a sip like a junkie begs for heroin. My throat tightened at the mere sight of someone else drinking water. Next it was my turn. I made eye contact with the boy before guzzling down as much as he would allow. After I'd finished, the boy gently tapped Quinn on the shoulder, causing him to flinch.

"Humnmnh?" Quinn mumbled an unintelligible word, then saw the boy. Neither of them moved at first, and then the boy relieved Quinn of his gag.

"Take it," Grant said, his voice hoarse.

Quinn looked like he wanted to kill the boy standing there with a peace offering but instead drank the water. What other choice did he have? He emptied the bottle and laid his head back against the wall.

I began to cry again. I didn't want to cry. In fact, I tried really, really hard not to, but my emotions were out of my control. The boy left, then came back with a tissue for me and wiped my eyes.

"Thank you," I said as he stood there staring at me.

"You welcome," he said after a beat or so.

"Is there more water?" Grant asked quietly, and gestured with his head toward the empty bottle. "Do you think we could have some more water?"

"I check for you."

He left and never came back. Instead, two of the other armed men appeared in the doorway. My head was dizzy and my mind and body were suffering from exhaustion and dehydration. I could barely keep my eyes open.

"Whose boat?" one of them said aloud. He wore a bright orange shirt and appeared to be in charge. He wasn't very tall or physically threatening, but everyone on board feared him. His head was shaved, he had a scar on his left cheek, and he looked at us with his dark eyes with complete and utter distaste.

"Mine," Grant said.

"Where is more money?"

I couldn't believe he was starting that interrogation again.

"There is no more money on the boat."

The man studied each of us. He wasn't pleased with Grant's response. "You give fifty thousand dollar, and we leave." He shrugged his shoulders like he was our pal.

Grant, Quinn, and I just stared at him. No cruisers carried that sort of money, and if they did, I'm sure the hijackers would assume there was much more where that came from if someone could easily produce fifty thousand dollars.

Grant stood. "Let them go, and I will get you the money."

The man looked at Grant as though he'd said something amusing. "Now you have it?"

"I don't have it on board, but I can get it for you. If you let them go." He looked at me.

"If you don't have money on boat, price goes up." His eyes settled on Quinn and me. "And they are not going anywhere." He waved his rifle at Grant. "Come."

Grant hesitated.

"Now!" the man shouted.

After nearly two days with his lanky body folded up in that tiny space, Grant struggled to stand, and collapsed as soon as he tried.

He looked at Grant with his dead eyes. "I say move, you move. I say come, you come!"

Grant didn't move. "I need to know they will be safe."

The man looked at us again before speaking. "You a business-man?"

Grant said nothing.

"I'm businessman too." He turned and shouted something in Somali to the guy next to him, then turned back to Grant. "We do business. Now come!"

He smacked Grant on the head with his rifle as another one of the men grabbed him by the forearm and led him away.

My despair grew.

The boy came back without any water but brought more ice for my eye. "I will untie you so you can hold it."

He released my hands and handed me the ice, which was wrapped in toilet paper.

"Thank you," I whispered, and immediately placed one of the cubes in my mouth and shoved one in Quinn's as the boy turned away to seat himself in the doorway. Quinn hadn't moved.

I held the ice to my head and stared at the boy. "What is your name?" I asked, and waited about a minute for him to answer.

"Baashi."

"I'm Jessica."

"Okay."

"Do you know how long we'll be here?"

He shook his head.

"Do you know where we're going?"

He shook his head again.

"Thank you for the ice," I said as Grant was ushered back in. His eyes went wide when he heard me talking to the boy.

Baashi left the room soon after.

"Do not speak to him," Grant said to me.

"I was just thanking him for the ice."

"Look at me." He was breathing rapidly.

I did.

"They have no intention of being your friend or helping you or showing you an ounce of kindness. They want a ransom. End of story. Please, Jess, do not speak to any of them unless they ask you a question."

"Okay." I said, nodding. "Where did they take you?"

He looked at the door. "The boat is too sophisticated for them. They have no idea how to work the controls, so they had me do it. I tried to trick the navigation system and put some added strain on the engines so we'll burn a motor and buy some time." He shook his head in disgust. "They invade our boat with little or no knowledge of how to use it and expect me to comply and be helpful. There's clearly one guy in charge, but he's answering to a higher power. He keeps dialing the sat phone and saying God knows what to God knows who on the other end." He paused. "There's a kill switch in the master cabin underneath the mattress near the top-right corner. It's a red dial covered by a small panel. I'm going to try and get in there and kill the motors. They won't know what's hit them, and there's no way to restart the engines without first reengaging the switch. That will at least stall us so the navy can get closer."

"Please be careful. They always have someone following you."

He shrugged and shook his head. "I don't even know how I'll get in there, but I will be careful."

"Where are they taking us?"

"They had me set a course to Somalia. They're trying to reach their mother ship, which is a few miles off the coast." He sighed. "And if we reach it before help arrives . . . it's not good news for us."

DAY THREE

I awoke slowly that morning with not much of a start. It was still only Quinn and me in the room; Grant was gone again.

The thought of what they might've done to him sent a chill down my spine. Was he even still on the boat? Had they tossed him overboard and sped away? Was he beaten and lying in pain somewhere?

Quinn woke up when I began to stir, and Baashi came in about a minute later. I had no idea what time of day it was, but it was light outside.

"Where is the man?" I asked eagerly, and looked at the spot where Grant had been. "Where is the other man who was here?"

The boy pointed up. Quinn and I exchanged glances.

Baashi produced another water bottle. "I have more water," he said.

He pressed the bottle to my lips, and I drank furiously and then nudged Quinn to have some more. Once we were through, he turned and was about to leave.

"Baashi?"

He looked at me.

"Do you think we could have something to eat? Anything."

"I will check for you."

"Thank you," I said, and he left.

I wanted to hate him, but I didn't. I felt sorry for him. It was obvious that he was being forced to act against his will just as we were.

Quinn adjusted his body next to mine. "Are you all right? Are you hurt? I saw those bastards hit you."

"I'm okay. I'm just worried about Grant. How did this happen?" None of us had had a moment to discuss the chain of events that led us to our fate.

Quinn attempted to arch his back where his hands were secured behind him and rolled his neck. His eyes were red and bloodshot. "I was on duty. The whole thing happened so fast. I saw two skiffs, and they were coming at us fast like these fuckers weren't even going to think twice about it. I woke Grant, and he put a distress call in to MARLO and a mayday call on the VHF, but before I knew it they slammed their boat alongside ours, and seconds later there was an RPG pointed at my face." His voice cracked. "A fucking grenade launcher in my face!"

"Shh." I shook my head and glanced at the door.

He continued to rattle on. "They struggled to climb aboard at first, but the whole time the other guys in their boat were pointing their guns at us. Once the first two guys had boarded us, it was a matter of seconds before they were all on. Then a second skiff slammed into the stern and more of them clamored to get aboard. One of them began shouting at the first group—the asshole in the orange shirt, I think. I couldn't understand a fucking word. It was mayhem. They were shouting and firing off rounds and pointing flashlights in our eyes and throwing weapons around. Some of them looked as clueless and uncertain of what to do as we did. They kept asking how many people we had on board. We put our hands up, didn't try to be fucking heroes or anything.

"Grant was so worried about you, Jess. If either of us could've warned you or done anything, we would have. You know we would have! Grant too. He was sick about it."

"I know, I know. Please, there was nothing you could've done," I said.

"I'm so sorry. I just want to get off this boat and back to my girl," he said, slamming the back of his head against the wall.

"How much time was there between when you first saw the skiffs and when they boarded the boat?"

"Ten minutes maybe," he mumbled. "It was really quick."

"Quinn, are you sure Grant got the distress call out?"

He nodded.

"What did they say?"

He sighed. His mind was elsewhere.

"Quinn, please. Did they respond? Are you sure Grant made contact?"

"I'm sure," he said, fidgeting beside me, trying to manage an ounce of comfort with his wide shoulders. "Just like the other night, he put a call into MARLO, and they said they'd get a US warship on it as soon as possible. He told them we didn't have much time, and the guy at MARLO said he understood. There could be a ship out there as we speak—I have no idea. It hadn't come by the time these fuckers came aboard, but I know MARLO understood the severity of the call. I know he made contact."

I rested my head on the wall behind me and did my best to arrange my tied hands in a position befitting my posture. My stomach was empty and tight. At least Grant got a distress call in. I had no knowledge of piracy protocol but was grateful the navy had been alerted.

In that moment of silence and brief hiccup of hope, I thought of my sister. I had promised to e-mail every day, even if it was short and sweet, and since I'd forgotten to send one the day before all this happened, she would be worried sick. I hated to think of her upset.

I have no idea how much time passed before Grant returned, but Quinn and I sat up like lonely puppies in that dark room once he did. His hands were untied, and he was holding a loaf of bread. Behind him were three men. One squeezed past Grant and released the ropes around our wrists. As soon as mine were free, a searing pain ran through my arms as the blood flow went back to normal. Grant quickly handed us the bread, which we devoured, then he turned to the men behind him.

"Can she go to the top bunk?" He spoke to them in English but mostly used his finger to get his point across.

All three of them stared at me long and hard before one of them nodded.

"Get up there," Grant said to me, and I did.

Two of the pirates walked away, leaving one to guard us with his rifle. He leaned on the doorframe, chewing khat. Some time later, he was seated on the floor, passed out.

"The navy is on their way," Grant whispered.

"How do you know?" Quinn asked.

"They brought me up there because they were having trouble with the autopilot, so I ran around from the cockpit back down to the computer below like I was in a frenzy and got an e-mail out to MARLO. About two hours later, I got a look at the radar. I could see a ship on our approach, and when I glanced out at the water I could see them. There's two ships, and they should catch up to us in a couple hours."

"Fuck," Quinn said, shaking his head. "What then? They're not going to pay a ransom for us."

Grant looked up at me. "I don't know, but I'll figure it out. I've offered to wire them money, but they want millions," he said, and then took a step toward the top bunk, and I leaned forward and threw myself into his chest, trembling with fear as he stroked my back and kissed my head. He pulled away and grabbed the sides of my face, rubbing my now only slightly swollen eye with his thumb. "I'm so sorry," he mouthed. His lids were heavy.

I nodded. "I know," I mouthed back. "Have they hurt you?"

He glanced at the floor and shook his head. "I'm doing what they ask."

"What have they asked?"

"Just to increase the speed, work the sat phone. The guy with the scar is definitely in charge and has a short fuse. We have to make sure we don't set him off for any reason. I've seen him pistol-whip his own guys."

My stomach sank. Grant gave me a quick squeeze and then stepped back and sat down on the bottom bunk.

Over the next couple hours, Grant negotiated with them to show us an ounce of respect. He'd demonstrated to them how to activate the secondary water supply, and they agreed to allow us to wash ourselves—our faces, our mouths, our hands. Deep down I knew they had to keep us alive in order to accomplish their goal, that if we died of starvation, they'd wasted their time. Once we finished, we were sent back to my cabin.

Just after sunset we heard shouting and confusion above us. Company had arrived.

DAY FOUR

From what little we could understand, the navy had arrived, and negotiations for our release had begun. Our lead captor had increased the engine speed, and Baashi had not come with water that morning. Sometime after dawn, we were dragged into the salon and tied up again.

One by one, we were then taken up top. They likely had to traipse us out on deck to prove we were alive. Grant went first.

"You!" The leader pointed to Grant and gestured for him to get up.

Grant managed to stand as quickly as possible but was shoved by another pirate and fell to his knees. Two men forced him to stay down, and another blindfolded him.

"Now!" the man shouted.

Grant recovered and was pushed clumsily up the stairs. Once he returned, his blindfold was removed.

"Come!" He pointed at Quinn.

My heart skipped a beat at the sound of his voice. His abrupt commands were filled with hatred. Perhaps he liked being there as little as we did.

Quinn's eyes were covered, and he was jabbed in the back with a rifle as he made his way up from the salon.

I counted twelve men standing below with us. The place had been destroyed. The smell, the trash, the odor. My heart broke for what they'd done to the beautiful *Imagine* in only a few days. Unknown liquids were doused on every surface, and small splatters of spit and saliva were everywhere from the khat. Food and garbage were smashed into the carpet and couches. And the urine. Again, the smell of urine was overwhelming, making my eyes water. When they led us past the once-pristine bathroom, I got a glimpse of the clogged toilet and fluids all over the floor. The sight and smell of both nearly made me vomit again, but I had nothing inside of me to give up, save for a few sips of water and a slice of bread.

I bent my head close to my chest because the stench in the salon was too much to bear. I buried my nose in my shoulder as best as I could and tried to take in as little air as necessary through my mouth. There was no way I could remain there much longer without becoming queasy again. My body began to shake and dry heave when Quinn reappeared.

They came for me third.

Once I reached the top of the stairs, my lungs gasped for fresh air. My blindfold had been tied high up near my eyebrows with little care, so I was able to lift my chin and see underneath it. I saw the vast open water out of the corner of my eye and wanted to jump. The ocean breeze filtered through me and represented my only chance at freedom.

I tilted my head back a little farther and could see a massive navy warship, but its presence gave me a false sense of hope. I lowered my chin and tried to sit on one of the benches. I could not go back down into that salon. The men pulled me back up, but I still fought against them with what little weight I had and wriggled free. Miraculously, they'd lost their hold on me.

"Do not move!" I heard the leader shout, but I ignored him. "Get her!"

I jerked my head up and down, trying to get a glimpse of the water again, and ran lopsided toward the bow with my hands behind my back.

If I could just get into the water, everything would be okay. The shouting behind me was nonthreatening in that moment, like the white noise of a television playing in the next room. All I needed to do was get off the boat.

The glorious scent of saltwater replaced the rancid stench that lingered in my nose for only a second before I felt a hard tug on my hair.

I almost made it.

My whole body jerked backward in one motion, and I fell hard, slamming my tailbone against the surface of the deck. The man still had my hair in his hands and was pulling me back to the cockpit. The pain was intense as I struggled to my feet and tried to keep up with him. As soon as we got back to where the leader was standing, I was thrown to the floor.

"Stupid fucking bitch."

He kicked me in the ribs, and my whole body shook as I clambered to my knees.

He bent down close to my face and screamed, "Idiot! Get up!"

"Please! Can I please stay up here?" I said in a voice I hardly recognized.

I repeated myself as he shoved me to the floor again, where I couldn't be seen, and kicked me three more times. I curled up into a ball, my body convulsing as I tried to speak, even though no one was listening.

"Enough! Leave her alone." I heard Grant's voice but didn't see him. "She's down. Let me take her. She's not going anywhere."

"I can't go back down there." My voice trailed off in a weak murmur, until I was pulled to my feet and tossed down the stairs. With my hands behind my back, I landed on my head and blacked out.

—◆◆—

Grant's face was the first thing I saw, and for a moment I was happy again. He sighed, relieved to see me open my eyes, and then his face went hard.

"What did I tell you? You do not speak to them, and you definitely do not argue with them!" he said sternly in a low growl as I lay on his master bed while he stood over me, gripping my elbow. "Have you lost your mind?"

Yes, I had.

"They will kill you, Jess. Do you understand?" He shook his head in amazement and then held me tight. "I can't believe he didn't shoot you. Thank God, you're all right."

I closed my eyes and nodded as he brought his face closer to mine and whispered loudly, "They will show you no mercy because they have *nothing* to lose. Do you understand? Nothing! They have no money, no hope, no promise of any life other than this drugged-out, miserable existence." He paused and scanned my distant eyes. "Can't you see that they're as in control of their own lives as we are of ours right now? They're being forced to produce. They've increased the speed, and they need to get us to their mother ship before the navy reaches us. If they return without the means to acquire some huge ransom, then their lives and the lives of their families are in just as much danger as ours." He sighed. "Don't ignore what I'm saying to you. You need to be as invisible as possible. Make them forget you're here. You will not escape. You will not bargain with them. You will not befriend any of them. Not even the boy, so don't try. Just do *exactly* what they say. Do you understand?" His eyes were wide as he studied my face with desperation, then loosened his grip and lowered his voice. "Please, Jessica, please tell me you understand?" he pleaded.

I nodded again, and he pressed his mouth hard against mine and devoured my lips like it was the last chance he'd ever have to kiss me. I didn't doubt that it might be.

He stood up and glanced at the door, then grabbed a paper towel with some ice folded in it that was lying next to my head.

I struggled to speak. "I'm so sorry. I don't know what I was thinking. I wasn't thinking. I was trying to jump." My voice was weak, and I burst into tears. "I didn't want to come back down here." I paused to catch my breath, and Grant dried my eyes. "I will do exactly what you said. I promise." My voice broke as I tried to get the words out without sobbing. "I just want us to get out of here alive." I wiped my face. "I'm so scared. Scared of what they might do to me . . . to all of us. I keep thinking they're going to rape me or kill you guys and then rape me to death . . ."

Grant jerked his head to the side, while his eyes and mouth were tightly closed as I spoke. He'd been thinking the same awful things I had—I just knew it. My brain wouldn't allow it.

"I'm losing hope. I'm sorry." My throat was so dry I could barely speak, and my stomach was cramping from deprivation.

He opened his eyes, scooped my upper body into his arms, and held me tight. "I'm not going to let anything happen to you," he said, but we both knew it was likely a promise he couldn't keep. He couldn't save his wife, and there was no guarantee he could save me either, but I wasn't about to challenge his optimism.

"I'm so happy they untied you," I said.

"Just to get you off the floor and out of the way."

"What is going to happen to us?" I dared to ask.

He stroked my hair. "I don't know," he whispered into my ear. "I know it's hard, trust me, but you need to think positive. The navy knows we're here now, and I have to believe they're going to do everything in their power to put an end to this thing."

I shook my head. "Why haven't they rescued us yet? It's been days. What are they waiting for?"

"They can't." He raised his voice slightly and quickly looked over his shoulder. "They can't intervene unless they are attacked, or they visibly see us being harmed."

"Why?"

"They just can't yet!" He inhaled slowly and closed his eyes for a moment. "It's like any hostage situation. They can't just storm in here, or we'll all be killed for sure. There are certain regulations that have to be followed. They have to tread lightly, and so do we for our own safety, so please . . . just concentrate on their presence and try to find some peace inside your head. Don't get desperate. If these thoughts you're having lead to desperation, then you're bound to do something that will get you killed. Please just relax in any fucking way possible."

With my body bordering on dehydration and having no use of my hands and no food, I was the pure definition of desperate. How could I not be? My brain was beginning to play tricks on me, and short hallucinations became commonplace. Many of the images that flooded my mind were of my youth. Riding my bike across the road to the Yoders' farm for fresh eggs, brushing my horse and braiding her mane, feeding the cats in the barn. A wave of contentment came over me as I relived those moments—happy, beautiful, peaceful, safe moments that went unappreciated until then.

And then there was Mom. I hardly remember her ever being cheerful, but there she was right beside me on the boat, nodding and smiling and praying with her rosary beads. Was she praying for me? After all this time, did I finally have her undivided attention? I closed my eyes and held her hand, and we prayed together. My heart rate slowed to a healthy pace, allowing a lightness to emerge inside of me. My concept of wisdom and patience and understanding became clear again, and for the first time in my life I realized that my mother was always—and would always be—there for me.

I thought about the cats we used to have on the farm, and how much I loved the time when one of them got pregnant and had kittens. My dad built a little pen for the mother to rest in and feed her babies. I used to sit there for hours and watch them sleep and eat and explore. But there was one in particular that I connected with the most. It was a little boy kitten, who was the last one in the litter of six to open his eyes, and he always had the hardest time finding his mom when he was hungry. He would just sit and cry with the tiniest meows while she lay there feeding the other kittens. I never understood why she didn't come to him and help him, how she could bear to listen to his sweet, panicked cries and not do anything about it. But she was always there for him, and he'd always eventually find his way to her.

That's just it. She was always there for him—she knew it, and so did he. I looked over at my mother and apologized for losing faith in God and in her. She just smiled.

Grant laid me down on my side and gently rubbed my forehead. "Try and relax, okay? You need to heal, and right now rest is all you have."

"I'll try."

He looked at the door and then back at me. "I have an idea," he whispered in my ear. "How about I tell you a story about my trip? You love that."

My eyes teared up. "Thank you."

He leaned over me and began to speak, his voice low and comforting. "By the time Quinn and I arrived in Phuket, we were exhausted. We'd just endured a long, rainy four-day sail from Malaysia and couldn't wait to pull into Thailand. We'd heard such wonderful things about the people and the beaches and were eager to set foot on solid ground. When we docked at the marina, we were thrilled with the clean and modern accommodations, and the people were some of the kindest we'd encountered thus far." He stroked my hair. "Quinn and I decided early on that we'd try and stay there as long as possible, since we knew the next leg of our trip was going to be a difficult one. After about a week, we discovered this wonderful little bar and grill called The Islander."

I looked up at his face, and he was smiling.

"The very first night we went to eat there I noticed a beautiful young blond woman. She obviously wasn't a native, and she piqued my interest from the moment I laid eyes on her. The way she carried herself and the way she moved without a care in the world. She held her head high, she smiled at everyone, and she ran around that place working her little tail off. The next night I introduced myself to the owner and asked him who she was."

My eyes went wide.

"He told me she was an American girl working at the bar part-time and teaching English at one of the local schools." He paused to wipe the tears that were now streaming down my face. "So I went to find her and to learn more about her, and to see if she liked storytellers. Sure enough, my initial instincts were correct." He kissed my cheek. "She was even more beautiful close up. And kind. And generous. And above all, brave."

I gave Grant a nod, indicating that I would do everything in my power to survive. For him, for Caroline, for my mom, and for myself. Our eyes met, and he kissed me one last time.

"That is enough," I heard the voice of evil say from behind Grant.

We turned to find the leader standing in the room with two men.

"Get out," he said to Grant, who was quickly dragged away by the others, leaving me alone with the man in the orange shirt. I blinked my eyes and scooted my body away from him toward the wall behind me.

"There is nowhere to run, idiot."

My heart was pounding in my ears. I said nothing.

"Are you in charge here?"

I shook my head.

He leaned in close and shouted, "Are you a *fucking idiot*?" His spit sprayed my forehead. "Are you?"

I nodded, certain I was going to die.

"That is right. I am in charge, and I am no idiot."

He slapped his chest and yelled something in his native tongue. A man appeared with a banana and a bottle of water and handed them to him. The other man left, while the leader stood in front of me and slowly ate the banana, then drank every last drop of the water. Once he was through, he tossed the empty bottle at my head and walked out.

Something that Grant had said earlier occurred to me as soon as the man was gone. I gritted my teeth and sat up, with debilitating pain searing through my head and blurring my vision. I glanced at the door and slid off the bed, positioning myself near the top right corner of the mattress. My knees cracked as I bent down with my back to the bed and shifted the mattress to the side. Sweat was pouring down my face. Once the mattress was moved, I turned around and could see the panel. Next, I stretched my arms as far as I could and positioned my hands so that I could remove the cover. My left shoulder was shaking as I placed my fingers on the red switch and killed the engines.

DAY FIVE

There was mayhem when the engines went down, but I was alone in the master cabin with my hands tied behind my back, so no one bothered to check on me for quite some time. I only hoped Grant and Quinn had not suffered for it.

I awoke that morning to the sound of a speedboat. The room was so hot and devoid of fresh air, and the pillows were drenched with perspiration. There was a lot of activity going on up on the deck above me, and I could hear the men talking and shouting, and it sounded like some of them were stepping off *Imagine* into a skiff beside us. I shimmied my body to an upright position and tried to look out one of the portholes. Sure enough, I saw four pairs of legs get off the boat. All pirates. My head felt like it'd been repeatedly hit with a cast-iron pan. There was pressure in my left ear, and my headache was so intense that even the slightest bit of light was painful on my eyes.

Beyond the skiff, I could see a small naval speedboat waiting for them. The good news was that they were obviously starting negotiations with the navy, but to what end? We all knew they wanted much more than fifty thousand dollars. Quinn had overheard them talking more in the realm of four to five million. There was no way the United States was going to write that check. It doesn't negotiate with terrorists. So I was forced to *imagine* that somehow, some way the navy was going to bargain for our release—and after spending a few days with these people, I couldn't fathom it.

Once the skiff was untied, I got a better view of the men on board and was surprised to see that the leader was not among them.

I turned toward the door, desperate to know if Grant and Quinn were all right, and thought about calling out to them but instead gently leaned my body back against the wall, kept my eyes closed, and just tried to breathe. Sometime later, a man came in and jammed the tip of his rifle into my chest and knocked the wind out of me. He laughed as I gasped for air.

"Come!" he shouted above my hacking coughs, then hit me again in the same spot.

I saw stars but heeded his command. Grant's warning was at the forefront of my brain.

Do not argue with them. Be invisible. Do exactly what they say!

I staggered to my feet. My hands were numb, and my shoulders were badly cramped from being inverted for so long that I had to literally bite my tongue to keep from screaming. The men grabbed me by my hair and dragged me into the salon. When I arrived, a muffled sound came from my throat that was so guttural and foreign it sounded like the cry of a wounded animal.

Until Mom's funeral, I'd never seen a dead body before, but even without obvious wounds there was no mistaking one. Three of the pirates were dead. Lying on the galley floor, one on top of the other. Baashi was among them, and had the stench in the salon been nauseating before, this was otherworldly. Only one of them had any visible injuries—a slash to the throat. The other two, including Baashi, were just lifeless and left to rot.

I was tossed to the floor inches from the bodies, where I sat with my eyes tightly shut until my body went into shock. Rapid breathing. Blurred vision. Cold sweat. My brain rendered powerless when I finally opened my eyes and just stared at Baashi. All I could do was scream. Loud, rasping screams. Why? How? Why had they done this to him? I could hear my voice belting out those questions, but I was not in control of what I was saying. Nor did I care. None of the other pirates even bothered to look at me. I sobbed and rocked my body. The boy's bare feet were small and calloused, but the rest of his skin still young and soft. His eyes were closed and his mouth open, but he still had a baby face, unlike the others. I shook my head and thought of his mother. It was easier to *imagine* someone loving this young boy at one time than it was to fathom how anyone could love the soulless men remaining on board. I thought to myself that if they would allow this to happen to him, I was going to die for sure. All three of us were.

Grant and Quinn were brought out a moment later. Both of their faces were covered in stubble, and Quinn had a black eye.

"Shh!" Grant said to me.

I hadn't even realized I was still shouting.

We all looked at each other and then at the floor. I took a deep breath when I saw the two of them were alive and continued to weep quietly to myself. I'd wept so much in those few days that it was the only thing that gave me comfort. I wasn't eating. I wasn't drinking.

I wasn't working or talking or thinking clearly. I wasn't safe and I wasn't happy. In fact, crying was the only thing that reminded me that I was still alive.

"Do you know what happened to them?" I asked Grant as the two of them were told to sit. I didn't care who heard me anymore.

He shook his head. "Try and relax, Jess. I know it's a lot to ask. Please just try."

I closed my eyes and willed myself to calm down.

I looked at Quinn, who was unrecognizable to me. "They're going to kill us," I said to Grant. My voice was composed as I contemplated my own words.

But my life had just begun, and I wasn't ready to die. Was I being punished for being selfish? For wanting more out of life than I deserved? No one ever died from following their dreams . . . or did they? Caroline would be so disappointed in me. She could've gotten me another job back home, and I'd be safe and sound, returning DVDs to the library and calling numbers on bingo night at the church. No one in Wolcottville owns an AK-47.

Grant looked away and didn't answer.

"She's right," Quinn said, and began to cough. "If this can happen to their guys . . ."

Three men walked in behind Quinn and dragged the bodies into the master cabin and closed the door as we all watched.

"They don't care about their guys," Grant said in a loud whisper. "They care about one thing and one thing only. Money! And if we die, then they don't get shit, and they have no chance at getting out of here. They are going to try and use us to secure a ransom and safe passage back to Somalia or to their mother ship. If we're dead, so are they."

Quinn pondered what Grant was saying and then looked over at me and winked with his bruised eye. And with that one gesture—that one glimmer of hope—all was right in the world.

The boat was silent, and Mom was back. Sitting next to me. I'd stared at the pictures from her honeymoon so many times, I recognized her immediately in her bell-bottom jeans and long blond hair.

"Is it really you?" I whispered, and she just smiled. "It is you. *This* is the real you, isn't it? Who you always wanted to be."

She said nothing.

"What happened?" I asked.

She looked away.

"I'm so sorry you never got what you wanted out of life. I thought you hated me."

She shook her head.

I lowered my head. "If I make it out of here, I will forever follow my heart and my dreams . . . for you. I will never think twice about it again." I choked back a sob. "I love you."

She smiled at me, and I couldn't wait to tell Caroline that I'd seen Mom again.

Almost as soon as we were told to sit down, we were ushered upstairs into the cockpit, where we sat on one of the benches. The same one where Grant and I shared our first kiss. It was an ugly night. The sky was dark, and ominous gray clouds prevented the moonlight from shining through.

Again, the fresh air smelled of freedom and fear at the same time yet gave me one more reminder that I was still human. Our fate was in the hands of others, and that left me with little comfort. I was somewhat relieved to see the lights of the naval ships that were still in close proximity.

This time the men kept us in the covered cockpit instead of traipsing us out onto the bow like last time. Showboating was over, I guessed—maybe on account of my failed attempt to escape—but I couldn't figure out why they'd brought us out there. I didn't dare think they were being kind to us for a moment. The men were speaking in their native tongue, four of them in a heated conversation over something with the leader.

Quinn and I made eye contact. I'd barely seen him in the past couple of days. I managed to force a hint of a smile when he looked at me. His expression back was one of utter sadness and regret. If I could have hugged him, I would have.

Just then two of the men started frantically looking for something. They began tearing through everything in the cockpit, as if there was anything left that they hadn't discovered or destroyed, looking under the wheel and taking things out of lockers and throwing thcm overboard. They tore through a stack of remaining papers and travel logs that were tucked next to the console and, without a second thought, tossed *Emma* and the letter she'd so dutifully guarded into the Arabian Sea.

Quinn and I spun our heads in Grant's direction. We all saw the same thing. My body slumped forward, and my lungs emptied as I did my best to convey an apology with my eyes. He looked from me to Quinn and then in the tiniest motion shook his head, not wanting us to bring attention to anything. *Emma* was gone. Miss Woodhouse was floating in the water with a smattering of other papers and maps and journals. I closed my eyes and prayed for her to sink gracefully to the bottom, letter in tow.

What happened next changed me forever.

Aboard a boat named for such hope and promise came . . . the unimaginable.

Chapter 24

The skiff I'd seen earlier was coming back toward us, but only two of the four men that had initially boarded it had made the return trip. The conversation between the men in the cockpit turned heated as our six remaining captors came up from below and walked out onto the uncovered stern of the boat. I kept my head down, just grateful to be away from the salon, and prayed. One of the captors who'd come from below was holding a rocket-propelled grenade and was none too happy that only two of the four pirates who had taken the skiff earlier had returned from the navy aircraft carrier. In fact, he began pointing at them and shouting at the man in the orange shirt as the skiff slammed into the side of *Imagine*. Obviously, the navy had managed to secure some bargaining chips of its own.

Grant stood. "Let me talk with the navy."

They looked at him.

"The engines are dead. They have two of your guys. We all want to get home safe, right? Let me talk with the navy." He repeated. "I can get your men back if you let me speak to them."

The leader held the sat phone to Grant's ear as the man with the RPG glared at both of them.

"This is Grant Flynn. Yes, three of us." He paused and looked at Quinn and me. "Not good." He paused again to listen. "I want my friends taken off the boat, and I will wire them the money. Yes, I do."

The leader began screaming at Grant in his native language.

"They want their men back," he said into the receiver. "I will trade my crew for their men. This needs to happen fast," Grant yelled as the phone was ripped away from him.

"No trade! Send our men back with a boat. Alone! No one else going anywhere!" the leader screamed into the sat phone before tossing it into the water.

The other man—the one with the grenade—began yelling at the leader and waving his weapon around, repeatedly pointing at the skiff. I began slowly rocking back and forth as they continued shouting at one another. I closed my eyes tightly and prayed for them to come to a resolution. They did not.

Four other pirates ran below while the man with the rocket launcher stepped onto the narrow deck beside the cockpit, raised his weapon, pointed it at one of the two naval ships, and fired.

"Holy shit," I heard Grant say as he knelt beside us. "They're firing at the navy. Stay down!"

What ensued was complete and utter chaos.

Immediately after the grenade was fired, gunfire erupted in the cabin below, and the leader drew his automatic weapon and shot the rogue pirate with the grenade launcher, then fired off a round of wayward shots—some below, some on deck, some into the air. The man he'd shot fell overboard and splashed into the water. There were now two pirates in the skiff, unarmed and unsure what to do, and twelve others still aboard *Imagine*, with only nine of those alive. Grant, Quinn, and I hit the floor of the cockpit, and Grant covered my body with his.

"Stay as low as you can," Grant said to Quinn and me, and we both nodded. "Do not fucking move! The navy is here. I can see them, and some of the shots are theirs. Stay down!" Grant yelled to us.

Within seconds a speedboat with Navy SEALs appeared next to *Imagine.* I could hear the roar of its engines. They were shouting orders through a megaphone, and our captors were running everywhere as the gunfire continued. Several of them—five at least—dropped their weapons and moved to the tip of the bow and sank to their knees with their hands raised in surrender. One Somali who would not relinquish his weapon was shot in the head by a navy sharpshooter and fell into the ocean. The rest of our captors then began an exchange of gunfire with the US Navy.

My body rocked faster. I was crouched over my knees with my eyes closed and Grant covering me, praying. "Oh my God, oh my God, oh my God," I repeated over and over. My limbs were beginning to go numb, and I could feel my circulation coming to a halt, but I knew I couldn't dare sit up. I went to move my leg to better support myself when my knee slipped on a puddle of liquid beneath it. When I opened my eyes, I looked down to find dark red blood pooling beside me. I lifted my head and saw it coming from right next to me, where Quinn's body was slumped over.

"Quinn!" I screamed. "Quiiiiiiin! No!"

Grant sat upright in an instant; his face went pale. He leapt to Quinn's side, forgetting his hands were tied, and then spun around and positioned himself in front of me, with his back to me, and shouted, "Can you see the knot, Jess? Can you turn around and untie me with your hands? Now!"

I couldn't see anything. Tears were blurring my vision.

Grant craned his neck over his shoulder. "You have to try and free my hands! It doesn't feel very tight. Do it, Jessica!" He was shaking uncontrollably.

I turned around, and with our backs to each other I managed to free Grant. He rushed to Quinn's side, released his hands, and sat him up. Blood was everywhere. His shirt was covered in it, and it looked like gallons of red paint had been tipped over on the cockpit floor, spilling everywhere.

"Quinn! Hang in there, buddy. Don't fucking leave me, okay? I need you, man." Grant's voice was high pitched and upbeat as Quinn's head rolled from side to side. Grant tore off his shirt, rolled it into a ball, and pressed it hard to Quinn's chest. "The navy is here, Quinn. They're here. We're being rescued right now, so don't you dare even think about doing anything else but staying with me. Bridget is waiting to hear from you, and you can call her today, Quinn. Today! The navy will have a phone for you to call Bridget and tell her you'll be coming home soon. Can you hear me, buddy? Hang in there for her, Quinn. Please!"

My hands were still tied, both literally and figuratively. Time seemed to be moving at a snail's pace for the three of us, while all around us was complete pandemonium. Two of the pirates had jumped overboard in an attempt to reach the skiff and escape, but the navy had dispatched a second boat from its ship with what looked like ten armed men aboard. I watched as they fired artillery into the skiff and sank it before the two men were able to reach it. After that the gunfire stopped. Most of the other pirates were still standing on the bow with their hands behind their heads.

I looked back at Grant, who was anxiously trying to get Quinn to say something. I swallowed the lump in my throat, knelt amidst the blood, placed my forehead on the bench cushion, and said a prayer for Quinn.

Dear Lord,

Please save us. Please just get the three of us off this boat alive . . .

My thoughts were interrupted by the sound of Grant's voice. "Up here! Up here! He's been shot. We need a medic now!"

Two naval officers and a medic rushed to Quinn's side as Grant stood and stepped away from his mate. Grant's hand was over his mouth, and he was pacing the small bit of space at the top of the stairs. He was covered in Quinn's blood. The medic quickly went to work, laying Quinn down and performing CPR. It looked as though he was still alive, but I couldn't be certain. I could see the smallest movement under his eyelids, and his head was moving without being forced to do so. A third naval officer came up with a large first- aid kit and assisted in trying to stop the bleeding.

Grant and I finally made eye contact. His hands were now behind his neck, and his expression was distraught. A second later, when he realized my hands were still tied behind me, he rushed to my side, freed my arms, and wrapped me in his.

"Not Quinn, Jess. Not Quinn."

Grant squeezed me hard and broke down. His body convulsed with mine, and we wept and prayed and pleaded for Quinn's survival.

As our captors were being led off the boat onto the US warship, their hands secured behind them with cable ties, Grant and I went from one personal hell to another. The three naval personnel who did everything in their power to save Quinn slowly sat back and exchanged glances. Then the officer in charge turned to us. One shake of the head was all it took to convey the message. Quinn was gone.

Chapter 25

I sat motionless with my arms at my sides until someone spoke. "We need to get you both off this boat and get you immediate medical attention. Sir," one of the men said to Grant, "it looks like your leg is in pretty bad shape."

I wiped my eyes and looked at Grant's leg. It was a miracle he was standing. His calf was torn open, exposing muscle tissue and oozing blood. He leaned into the captain's chair and allowed the men to put a temporary dressing on it. He didn't care. He was void of expression, lost in his despair over Quinn, and the pain in his leg was likely nothing in comparison to the pain in his chest.

An officer knelt beside me. "Ma'am, I need you to come with me. Can you tell me your name?"

I turned away from Grant and looked into the eyes of our savior. My prayers were answered. Everything I'd hoped and prayed for over the last few days was now right there in front of me, gently talking to me and asking my name. I mumbled something to him.

"Jessica?" He paused. "Jessica?" he repeated. "I'm Noah, and I'm here to take care of you, so there's nothing to worry about. Can you stand up on your own?"

I focused on his strong, confident face. *Is there really nothing left to worry about?* I thought.

"What about Quinn?" I whispered, fighting back more tears, and pointed toward his body without looking at it.

Noah held my gaze. "We will come back for him and take good care of him, but right now we need to get you off this boat and make sure you're okay."

In that moment Bridget came to mind. She was back in Miami, counting down the days to a homecoming that would never happen. Thirty-six hours had been the longest he'd ever gone without talking to her or e-mailing her. She must've been worried sick. Her worst fears had been realized and her prayers had gone unanswered.

"I need to get something," I told him.

He shook his head. "I can't let you down there. Please let me get it for you. We really need to get you out of here. What is it?"

"It's downstairs in the forward cabin. It's a quilt. I need to give it to Quinn. It belongs to him, and I know he would want it."

He studied my face for a moment, then radioed my request to someone else. Moments later one of the SEALs came up from the salon carrying the quilt Bridget had made for Quinn.

Noah spoke again. "How about we hold onto it so it stays clean, all right?"

I nodded and stood as he pulled my body up in one fluid motion. I looked over at Grant, who was wincing in pain. His head was hanging over the back of the chair, and his leg was being splinted.

"Can I say good-bye to Grant?" I asked.

"He'll be right behind you."

"Okay," I said, and followed him to where the speedboat was tied on our stern. Two men quickly came to my side and lifted me off *Imagine*. They covered me in warming blankets and handed me a bottle of water, which I guzzled. About five minutes later, Grant was put on a stretcher and carried onto the boat.

◆◆◆

A team of naval officers and medics tended to each of us once we reached the aircraft carrier, the USS *Enterprise*. I was separated from Grant and given a shower and food and as much water as I could drink. Next I was brought to a cabin with two twin beds and an attached bathroom. I was told that *Imagine* was in pretty bad shape but that the navy would send some people on board for us and do its best to try and recover any personal belongings that were not destroyed or desecrated. They also told me that they would bring back our computer and any equipment that could be salvaged.

I was sitting on one of the beds, alone for a rare moment, when a female officer named Audrey came in with a handful of fresh towels.

"Where is Quinn?" I asked her.

"I believe he's in surgery. His leg needed stitches."

"No, no, that's Grant. Quinn was with us too. He didn't make it." I paused and covered my mouth for a moment. "Can you tell me if he's off the boat?"

She smiled apologetically. "Let me see what I can find out."

Alone again, I moved over to the small window. *Imagine* was on the other side of the boat, so all I could see was the vast, beautiful ocean that'd held so much promise and excitement for us only days ago. I grabbed one of the small washcloths that Audrey had left and wept silently for Quinn and thought about my mom. How her whole life she'd kept the faith and gone to church and prayed for God to protect the people she loved. How she'd invested so much time and energy in worship, even at the expense of her own family. Where was He this week? How does something like this happen to someone like Quinn? How could God allow that to happen to Quinn? I ached, thinking about Grant's failed attempt to save his friend. His manu-factured enthusiasm in those last few minutes, pulling out all the stops, talking about the navy's presence and about our imminent rescue . . . about Bridget. So eager for Quinn to hear him and climb out of the black hole he was slipping into. Where was God then?

I jumped when there was a knock at the door. "Come in," I said after catching my breath.

The door opened, and it was Noah. "Pardon the interruption, ma'am, but I wanted to check in on you and bring you this."

He held the quilt in his hand. I choked out a small thank you.

"Please call me Jessica." My voice was shaking.

"Yes, ma'am."

He sat down on the bed opposite me and respectfully placed the quilt beside him. He let me cry until I was ready to stop. His presence brought me comfort, and I owed him my life.

"Did you capture any of them?" My stomach turned just picturing their faces, both dead and alive.

"Yes, ma'am, we did."

"Where are they?"

"They'll be taken down to the brig."

I curled my lips inward. "And then what?"

"And then they will stay there until we're told where to transport them to. After that they'll be held and then likely brought to trial for what they've done."

I shook my head. Whatever would happen to them would never bring justice to Quinn and his family, would never bring comfort to anyone.

Noah sat with me in silence, making no attempt to spur conversation.

"Thank you," I whispered.

"You're very welcome," he said. "When you're ready, we'd like to get a full account of what happened to you and Mr. Flynn." His voice was gentle and kind. "And to Quinn."

I nodded. "Could I e-mail my sister first?"

"You can call her if you'd like."

I was relieved to hear that. "Thank you," I said, and closed my eyes for a second, and sighed. "What about Quinn's family and his girlfriend? Who is going to call them?"

He scratched his neck. "However you and Mr. Flynn would like to handle it is fine with us. I know it's not an easy call to make."

I *imagine*d he did know that. I also figured that Grant would like to speak to Quinn's family and to Bridget.

"What will happen to his body?"

"He will be paid his respects right here on the aircraft and his body will be placed in a casket. Then, dependent on the family's wishes, we can bury him at sea or fly the body back to his hometown."

I glanced at the floor. Quinn didn't deserve to arrive home in a casket. He was so much more than a body. He was the light of so many lives. I wanted to explain to Noah how much fun it was to be around Quinn. How he made every woman feel beautiful and every man like he was one of the cool crowd. He never passed judgment on people, just wanted everyone to have a good time and be happy. How could someone who loved life be deprived of it so quickly?

He stood. "Would you like to come with me now and call your sister?"

"Noah?" I looked up.

"Yes."

"Could you please get this quilt back to Quinn?" I asked and handed the blanket back to him.

He nodded. "Of course. I will make sure that it is with him at all times."

"Thank you."

Chapter 26

I stood in a windowless room behind an officer wearing a green shirt sitting in front of thousands of buttons and switches and various dials. He looked way too young to have lived enough years to learn how to function each of those controls. Also in front of him were five phones. I gave him my sister's phone number and waited. Moments later he spoke into his headset.

"Good afternoon, ma'am, this is Petty Officer Harris with the United States Navy. We have your sister Jessica here with us, and she would like to speak with you," he said, and I could hear Caroline scream on the other end.

Officer Harris pressed a button, then lifted one of the five handsets off the console and handed it to me. Tears were flowing down my cheeks before I could get one word out.

"Caroline?" I choked.

"Jessica! Oh my God! Where are you? Who was that? Are you all right? I've been worried sick."

I placed my hand over my mouth and sniffed. Hearing her voice was both comforting and difficult. "I'm okay. I'm safe now. We had a terrible thing happen to us."

"What happened? Are you sure you're okay?"

"I'm sure. We're with the navy now, aboard an aircraft carrier somewhere off the coast of Oman I think. Our boat was attacked."

I'd shared very little with her about the threat from Somalian pirates before we left because I didn't want to worry her, but she was no idiot. She'd told me she'd done her own research and had begged me to reconsider.

She gasped on the other end of the phone and then began to cry.

"Please don't get upset," I said. "I'm so sorry I gave you such a scare."

Her breaths were loud. "I don't know what I would have done if something had happened to you. I've been frantically checking my e-mail every five minutes. I can't begin to tell you what a relief it is to hear your voice. I'm just so thankful you're okay. You promise me you're okay?"

"Yes," I promised. "But I can't say the same for Quinn." My throat went tight as I tried to get the words out.

"Oh no," she said. "What happened?"

I couldn't speak. Just shook my head and rubbed my eyes.

"Jessica?"

"They killed him! Minutes before our rescue. Quinn is gone. Just gone. Oh my God, Caroline." My stomach was in knots. Would I ever be able to say those words without falling apart?

"I'm so sorry," she said slowly, and then paused. "That is unbearable. I'm so sorry you had to see that. What about Grant?"

Noah handed me some tissues, and I wiped my face. "He's okay I think. He was shot in the leg, and I haven't seen him in a few hours, but he's alive. He did everything he could to save Quinn. Everyone did." My voice was raised at the end like I was trying to convince her of something.

"Oh my God, Jessica. I can't *imagine* what you've been through. Please come home. I need to see your face. When can you come home?"

I looked over at Noah, who was still with me. "I don't know what the plan is."

"I want you out of there as soon as possible. Enough of these reckless antics. It's time you come home now."

"I will call you as soon as I know anything."

We said our good-byes, and I was glad to have finally brought her some relief. Afterward, I asked to call Sophie.

"Jessica, my God! We heard the name of the boat on the telly," Sophie said. "Are you hurt?"

I began to cry again.

"Oh darling," she said in a softer voice. "Oh my dear, are you all right? I'm just so glad to hear your voice."

I took a deep breath. "Grant and I are all right, but Quinn . . . he's . . ."

"No."

We sat in silence on the phone for a moment. "I can't talk about it now. I'm so sorry; it's been really hard."

"Shh. Oh God, it's okay, love." She was sniffling.

"Sophie, can you please go to the Knights' house for me and tell them I'm okay and tell them I'll call them as soon as I can? Can you go today and do that for me?"

"I'm on my way. Consider it done. When are you coming back here?"

"I don't know yet. We have to bring Quinn home first."

"I miss you, love. Please be safe."

"I miss you too. And Niran!" I was smiling now through the tears, laughing almost. "Please give him a kiss and a squeeze for me."

"You can bet I will."

As soon as I handed the phone back to Officer Harris, I asked to see Grant.

Noah led me up an interior stairwell, up two flights of stairs, to the infirmary. He rapped twice on a gray metal door and was greeted by a medic. They exchanged a few words and then moved aside, allowing me to enter.

Grant's attention was already on the door when I walked through it. I paused for a moment and then ran to him. He was lying on a hospital bed with his leg elevated but all else intact. I buried my head in his chest, and he stroked my hair. As soon as I caught my breath, I lifted myself up and bent over to kiss him. I placed one hand on the side of his face and savored the warmth of his lips.

"Are you okay?" I asked.

He nodded.

"I'm so glad."

Grant reached out to hold my hand, and Noah brought me a chair and then left.

"How about you?" Grant said.

"I'm fine. I spoke to my sister. They let me call her. She was worried sick, obviously, and very, very glad to hear from me."

"That's great."

I rubbed Grant's hand with my thumb and stared at our intertwined fingers. We sat silent for a moment before I spoke. "We need to call Bridget."

Grant furrowed his brow. "Yes," he said, managing to sound in control.

"It's so awful, Grant." My voice cracked.

"I know it is."

"He didn't deserve to die."

"No, he didn't. None of us deserved what happened. I wish I could fix it all—rewind and start over and take it all back—but I can't. I've done nothing in the past twenty-four hours besides think of you and Quinn. I have no words to express how terrible I feel for putting both of you in this position."

Our eyes met, and I squeezed his hand.

"But we need to move on," he continued. "We need to get you home, and take care of Quinn and his funeral and his family."

"I don't want to go home. I want to stay with you."

He cocked his head to the side, his eyes downturned. "Your sister and your family deserve to have you back with them. And safe."

"My sister needed to know that I was all right, and now that she does she'll be okay. I'm not leaving you."

Noah walked in with two officers behind him. "Excuse me. I'm sorry to interrupt, but we do want to talk with you both as soon as possible. A report needs to be filed, and Quinn's next of kin should be contacted."

"Yes, of course," Grant said, then turned to me. "Let's discuss this later."

Noah pushed a wheelchair next to the bed and helped Grant into it. We all left the room and went to an elevator, which took us back to the communications room, where I had called Caroline and Sophie. Noah asked Grant for Quinn's last name.

"Asner. Quinn Asner. He's from Miami. He lived with his girlfriend."

"Bridget," I added.

Noah nodded. "We'd like to see if we could reach his parents or family first. Would you agree?"

"I do," Grant said. "But I honestly don't know where they live or how to find them. I think we should start with Bridget. I'd like to be the one to talk with her." He swallowed.

I placed my hand on Grant's shoulders. He knew all too well what it was like to lose someone you love; surely he felt not only a responsibility to tell her about Quinn but a kinship with her. Like being the member of a private club no one ever wanted to join.

As we were discussing, Petty Officer Harris was busy tapping away on a keyboard and came up with Quinn's home phone number in a matter of seconds.

"We have the number, sir," he said to Noah.

Noah turned to Grant. "Do you need more time?"

Grant shook his head, and they dialed the number.

It was just past midnight in Miami. On what must have been the last ring, someone answered.

"Bridget?" Grant confirmed. We could only hear his side of the conversation.

"This is Grant Flynn."

He paused to listen to her.

"Uh, yes, that is why I'm calling."

Pause.

"We had some trouble last week. The, uh, the boat was attacked . . ." He rubbed his forehead, elbow resting on the arm of the wheelchair. "We were being held captive for five days, and Quinn was shot yesterday just as the navy was coming to our rescue. He didn't make it."

I bent next to his chair and could hear her repeating the words "no" and "what?" Grant rested his head in his hands and let her finish. She wanted to know what happened. Wanted every last detail of Quinn's last days, and Grant gave it to her. He spared her the most gruesome parts, leaving out anything that indicated Quinn might have suffered at the hands of the devil, and wept with her for a good thirty minutes. She was initially in shock, but by the end of the call she said that she would like to be the one to break the news to his mother.

"We will bring him home," was the last thing Grant said to her.

Grant handed the receiver back to Petty Officer Harris and took a deep breath.

"Is there anyone else you'd like to contact, Mr. Flynn?"

"No," he said, shaking his head.

Once we were through, Noah took us both upstairs to the main deck, where there was a meal waiting for us.

Grant stared at his food, then pushed the plate away. "This isn't right. Being here. The whole week. The boat. Everything."

"I know." My hands were folded in my lap.

"I just can't stop thinking, what if?" He leaned back in his chair. "I never should have had either of you in that situation."

"Stop. You can't do that to yourself."

"This time it was my fault. It was a situation of life and death that I could have controlled, and I fucked it up."

When Jane was sick, his hands were tied as well, but it was out of his grasp. Before, during, and after. She was sick, and her illness had the power. No amount of money, no personal choice, no experimental drug could make the difference. He knew that, and he could eventually live with that. He had to. But now, I could see it in his eyes: he felt solely responsible for what happened to Quinn and me.

"None of us should have been on that boat on that day. This is all my doing." He gritted his teeth and stretched his neck.

"Do not do this to yourself. Please, Grant. If it's anyone's fault, it's mine. I was the one who signed up for this and begged you for the opportunity."

He pressed his fingertips into his forehead and closed his eyes just as Noah approached our table.

"Pardon me," he said. "I'd like to discuss a couple things with you both, if I may?"

"Of course." Grant looked up at him and nodded.

"The medic has cleared you for leave, and we'd like to get you and Jessica back home to the States as soon as possible. Ideally, we can have you both on a plane first thing in the morning."

"What about Quinn?" Grant asked.

Noah rubbed his chin. "We don't store caskets on board the ship, so we need to wait for the next military supply corps to bring us one. We've gone ahead and put in the request, and it should be here in a couple of days."

Grant looked over at me. "I'm not leaving without him."

I gently nodded.

"But if you want to get back to your sister, I completely—"

"I'm not leaving without you," I said.

Both Grant and I glanced back at Noah, who said, "I understand, and if you're both willing to wait it out, then we will have you all flown out together."

"Thank you," Grant said quietly.

"Is there anything else I can get for you?" Noah asked.

I looked at Grant, so defeated and disheartened. Nothing's worse than a captain who's had the wind knocked out of their sails. I placed my hand on his forearm, then turned to Noah and shook my head.

Chapter 27

"Are you sure you don't want to call your family?"

Grant shook his head.

"Can I ask why?"

He sighed and rubbed the back of his neck. "I don't want to worry them." He looked up at me. "I e-mail my parents about once a month and check in with my friends even less than that. No one is looking for me, and I'd like to keep it that way. They don't deserve the added stress."

I nodded. So was he just going to slip back onto his boat and sail away without missing a beat? My mind was conflicted, trying to understand how he could let this go unnoticed by his family and friends. How such a life-altering—life-ending—event could go unmentioned to the people that care about him. Out of respect, I kept my mouth shut about it, but it didn't sit well with me.

◆◆◆

We spent two long days aboard the USS *Enterprise*. Grant was advised to move his leg as little as possible, so I would sit with him in his room most afternoons and evenings. I called Caroline both of the days once I knew what our schedule was, and she arranged to meet us in Miami, which is where the navy would eventually send us, along with Quinn. Once the casket arrived, they were eager to get us all home to our families.

The morning of our departure, I climbed the stairs to the flight deck with nothing but the clothes I'd been given. A light blue shirt, khaki shorts, a navy baseball cap, and gym shoes borrowed from one of the female officers. Grant followed me. He was out of the wheelchair and supporting himself with one crutch. It was very loud on the flight deck. The wind and the sound of the ocean made it difficult to hear what everyone was saying. When I reached the top and stepped outside, I was overcome with emotion. Everyone on board—hundreds of men and women—was standing on either side of a makeshift aisle that led from one end of the flight deck to another, where a plane was waiting.

Noah turned toward Grant and me. "These are military honors for Quinn. Everybody has come here to pay their respect."

Tears were streaming down my face as we were led to the front of the aisle, where Quinn was waiting. Six members of the color guard held his casket, while a seventh member stood in front. All wore their dress uniforms.

"We're about to begin," Noah said.

A moment later we heard a voice over the loudspeaker: "Attention!"

Each one of the people standing aboard the flight deck stood straight, hands at their sides, fists clenched. My heart ached as we walked behind the color guard. Grant had chosen to leave the crutch behind and was walking with a limp. Halfway down the aisle he grabbed hold of my hand. Once we reached the plane, we heard "Parade rest!" announced, and everyone stood with their feet apart and their hands behind their back. We stood and watched Quinn's body loaded onto the plane. I wiped my eyes, let go of Grant's hand, and embraced him. He lowered his head to my shoulder, and I could feel his body quiver. He kissed my forehead and turned to shake Noah's hand.

"I have no words, my friend," Grant said to him.

"None are necessary. I'm only sorry we couldn't have done enough for Quinn. We all are."

Grant scanned the impressive crowd. "Thank you."

Noah turned to me. "Ma'am, have a safe flight home."

I smiled as best as I could and caught him off guard by leaning forward and wrapping my arms around his shoulders. "Thank you, Noah. For everything."

He tentatively patted my lower back. "You're very welcome."

Grant tapped me on the shoulder and then read my face, making sure I was ready, before we boarded the plane that would deliver us back to the States.

Chapter 28

We were flown to a naval air station in Turkey, where we then switched planes and boarded a three-hour military flight to Germany. Grant and I were inseparable during the journey, but neither of us was very talkative. We held hands and I laid my head on his chest for most of the trip. He slept for about an hour, but I was too anxious to sleep. I thought of Quinn and *Imagine*, and my heart broke for Grant's shattered dreams and Quinn's shattered future. It all came crashing down so quickly that it was hard to wrap my head around everything. One moment I'm falling in love on a sailboat in the middle of the Indian Ocean, and the next I'm on a military flight back to the States. My chest ached for so many different reasons that had I not been glued to Grant's side, I'm not sure I would have survived the mental torture I was inflicting on myself. And then I began to question everything. Would I return to Thailand? Would Grant leave me and move on with his life? Would I be forced to go back to Indiana with Caroline? How could I leave again and upset her like that? But more importantly, how could I leave him?

Grant awoke with a start as we were making our descent and looked over at me. "You okay?"

I nodded, and he pulled me close.

Once we landed in Germany, we were led to the officers' quarters on the base and told we'd be spending the night and then boarding a flight to the States in the morning. We were given separate rooms, but I never went to mine. We were also given dinner, a change of clothes, winter jackets and boots, and then we both retired to Grant's room.

"I'm going to take a shower," I said.

"Can I join you?"

I nodded.

I turned the water on and let it warm up for a moment. We both undressed, and I hesitated, with my arms in front of me, for a moment.

"You are the most beautiful sight," Grant whispered.

He gently cradled my hand as we stepped into the shower together, and for a moment everything in the universe disappeared except for his adoration of me. I stood under the water first, wetting my hair, as he wrapped his hand around my waist, and then I gingerly moved out of the way, being mindful of his leg. I stared at the muscles in his back as he faced the faucet and shook his hands through his hair, letting the water beat down on his head and shoulders. Once he was dripping, he grabbed the shampoo and turned to face me. He poured a few drops into his hands and motioned for me to come closer.

"Can I wash your hair for you?"

I nodded and turned my back to him. He kissed me from my shoulders to my chin on both sides, then massaged my scalp and temples with the tips of his fingers. He whispered my name, and I moaned as his hands slid over my neck and breasts, circling and kneading as he kissed me softly behind the ears. I placed my hand on the wall to steady myself, and then he spun me around and lifted me off my feet and onto the tiled bench at the other end of the shower.

"I've been wanting to kiss you and look at you for too long," he said, his lips close to my ear.

He slid next to me and kissed the tips of my fingers and my forearms and my thighs. Then he paused and placed his hand on my face.

"You were so brave," he said softly, then closed his eyes and placed his forehead on mine. "Are you getting tired of being brave?"

I shook my head. "Never."

The water was beating down on both of us as Grant carefully bent down and lowered himself to his knees, spreading mine with his hands and then gently circling with his fingers between my legs before sliding them inside of me. I clutched his wet hair as he moved his hand in and out of me, rotating his fingers until I cried out. My hands moved to his neck and shoulders, relishing the flex of his muscles as I pushed closer to him and embraced his touch. I closed my eyes and tilted my head back, clinging to him and then unraveling from the inside out.

I never *imagined* I'd fall so deeply in love under such duress. Before I dared to dream about what I truly desired, I'd always envisioned myself with a cookie-cutter courtship. A few good dinner dates peppered with movies and meeting the family. Yet there I was, on the heels of facing death as if it were a schoolyard bully, falling in love and out of control. My adoration for him was immense, and our courtship anything but typical. I wanted to care for him and bring his demons to light, because I knew they lived in the darkness of his mind—I just didn't know what they were.

After a few quick breaths, he pulled my waist to his lips, kissed my stomach, and laid me onto the ceramic tiles of the shower. I brought his mouth to mine, and we inhaled each other through the heavy spray of the water. Grant quickly lowered himself on top of me and entered me slowly with care and concentration on the one thing we'd been deprived of—pleasure. I melted beneath him, and my mind became disconnected from everything else but his body moving inside of me. My shoulders were pressing into the shower floor, as he was unrelenting. His movements were determined but meticulous, and his hand cupping the back of my head, protecting it.

All at once his body shook and he fell forward. I wrapped my arms around his back and held on for dear life. We lay there, panting together, as the water beat down on us and we both slowly caught our breath. He kissed me softly on the lips and sat up, but I could barely open my eyes. Then he leaned forward and turned the shower heads off before reaching for my hands to pull me up. We embraced as though nothing could come between us. Not even water.

"I need you so badly," he whispered.

"I need you too."

We sat, naked bodies entwined, allowing ourselves to cherish one another for one final moment, until he pulled away and stood with his weight on one leg. We dried off and dressed in the pajamas that were given to us before crawling into bed. Exhausted.

There was so much to discuss, but I sensed that neither of us knew where to start. We first had to face Quinn's family and pay him the respect that he deserved. I glanced over at Grant, and he was scrolling through his cell phone, which had been returned to him right before we left the aircraft carrier. I could barely keep my eyes open.

"Grant?" I whispered as I was drifting off.

He looked over at me. "Yeah?"

"I love you," I said, and fell asleep about two seconds later.

The next morning we boarded a nine-hour flight to the naval station in Norfolk, Virginia, and touched down on US soil at about three o'clock in the morning. We were driven to our quarters and given some food and then greeted by a man who reminded me of Kevin Spacey in *The Usual Suspects*.

"I'm Walter Morgan from the State Department," he said. "We want to give you both some time to get your body clocks adjusted, but we'd ideally like to have you on a noon civilian flight to Miami, if that's okay with you." He paused. "We've contacted Mr. Asner's family, and they'll be at the airport to meet the body, along with your sister, Ms. Gregory." He looked at me.

"Thank you," I said.

"That way you should both be able to get to bed on time tomorrow. I know how taxing jet lag can be." He flipped a page on the clipboard he was holding. "Very well then, once you land in Miami, you'll be greeted by someone from the State Department there who will direct you to Mr. Asner's family—per your request—and then you're free to go. Are there any questions?"

"My boat," Grant said. "Do you know anything about its whereabouts?"

Walter scratched his head and checked his papers again before looking up. "Let me see what I can find out."

"Thank you," Grant said.

"In the meantime, I'll check back in a little bit, but please let me know if there is anything I can do for you," he said, and then left the room.

The guest quarters we were waiting in looked like your average cheap hotel room. Two double beds, a kitchenette on one wall, striped carpeting, and a wooden desk with matching chair.

"I guess we should try and get some rest," I said, and Grant nodded.

He sat down on one of the beds and turned the TV on while I washed my face and brushed my teeth. After I finished, I joined him on the bed.

"Anything good?" I asked. It'd been a while since either of us had flipped channels.

"Mostly infomercials and shit. There's this blanket with sleeves I'm thinking you might like."

"Sounds cozy."

Grant leaned over and gave me a kiss. "I'm going to take a quick shower."

"There's a toiletry kit in there for you as well."

After he bathed, we both crawled into bed and tried to get some sleep, but an hour later we were both still awake.

"Grant?"

"Yeah?"

"Would this be an inappropriate time for me to ask what's going to happen once we're in Miami? I mean, after we meet up with Quinn's family and such."

Grant turned on his side and tucked my hair behind my ears, then placed his lips on my forehead for a long moment before pulling away. "I don't know," he whispered.

"I was afraid you'd say something like that."

He furrowed his brow. "It's not that I haven't thought about it. I've been wondering about the boat, and I'm sure I'm going to have to retrieve it at some point. I've also been thinking about the trip—you know, whether I should carry on or accept defeat. I'm obviously not going to sail the Indian Ocean again, but if I get my boat back I could pick up in Egypt . . ."

"With what crew?"

"It's not hard to find a crew, Jess."

"So you would just go on like nothing happened?"

He shook his head. "No, not like nothing happened, but what should I do? What should we do?"

That's what I didn't know. I knew Grant wasn't being insensitive to Quinn, and I didn't want to get defensive because, selfishly, I was more concerned with losing him than anything else. If anything, Quinn would have wanted Grant to finish his journey and his dream of sailing around the world. And then I thought about how he didn't want to contact his family after we were rescued. Maybe he wanted to just go on with his life all along. Maybe he'd suffered enough with the death of his wife for one lifetime, and he was resigned to never look back no matter what. But was he willing to look forward?

He lifted my chin. "Hey, look at me. I'm going to have to make a decision soon, and leaving you is a huge factor. Please know that. I left my life—or what I had of it—to rebuild and to accomplish something I'd always wanted to do . . . just like you did." He ran his hand through his hair. "Now, I can't speak for you or tell you what to do, but I will do everything I can to make sure you don't let them—those dirty Somalian pricks—derail the plans you had for yourself. The dreams you had.

"You and I and Quinn had a very, very bad, terrible thing happen to us. And I will work for the rest of my life to not blame myself for what happened. For Quinn and for you. If there is any solace in this tragedy, it has to be that we don't let it rule our future. If this event changes who you are and catapults you back to a place you clawed your way out of, then I will never forgive myself." He propped himself up on one elbow. "I don't want you to make any promises to me, but please don't let this ruin the life you've always wanted for yourself. I simply couldn't live with that."

I managed a smile. "And I simply can't live without you."

He released a small breath through his nose.

"I know that sounds dramatic and filled with pressure you don't need right now, but before we'd even left Thailand, I was worried about saying good-bye to you at the end of the trip." His face was stoic. "It's no secret how I feel about you, and as much as I want to go back to my life in Phuket, I won't be happy there or anywhere without you."

It wasn't lost on me that he hadn't reciprocated my sentiment when I told him I loved him. I thought about that the instant I woke up the next morning. And while I didn't say it just to hear it, I couldn't help but wonder how he really felt about me.

He kissed me. "Well the last thing I want is for you to be unhappy."

A few hours later, we awoke to a knock on the door. It nearly scared me out of my skin and it took me a few minutes to make sense of where I was and what time it was. The first thing I thought of was Quinn. I craned my neck and looked at the clock that was on the nightstand next to Grant: 9:45 a.m. My brain hurt when someone knocked again. I swung my legs out of bed and walked to the door.

"Yes?" I said, my voice cracking.

"It's Walter Morgan, Ms. Gregory. We're going to need you both outside in thirty minutes."

"Okay, thank you."

Grant was awake and stretching when I turned around.

"They need us in a half hour."

He nodded and then spoke. "Come here."

I sat next to him on the bed. He was naked, with only the sheet covering him from the waist down, and he looked glorious. Tan and strong and beautiful and alive.

I placed my hand on his chest. "Today is going to be so hard, Grant."

"Yes, it is."

"I just can't wrap my head around the fact that I'm back in the States, about to see my sister again. My life in Thailand seems so far away from here."

He pulled me closer, and I laid my head over his heart.

"It's going to be a rough day, for sure. It's all I've been thinking about—having to face Bridget and Quinn's family—and what can I say to them? What can I possibly say that is going to ease an ounce of their pain? That is, if they can even look at me."

I sat up and met his eyes with mine. "You just be yourself. They will know in an instant what a good man you are and how much this pains you. They are not going to blame you. They can't."

"They can," he said quietly.

"Whatever they do and however they act is out of your control. Just express how you feel the best way you can, and that's all you can do. Quinn knows how much you cared about him, and how lucky any of us are to be alive. He would never, ever hold you accountable for what happened, and that's all that matters. He's all that matters."

Grant pursed his lips and nodded.

As soon as we were dressed and bundled up, Walter Morgan, along with a junior navy officer, drove us to Norfolk International Airport, where we boarded Delta Airlines Flight 453 to Miami.

When we landed, we were asked to stay on board the plane until all the other passengers had left, and then a woman dressed in a dark blue pencil skirt, white short-sleeved blouse, and heels met us on the plane.

"Grant Flynn and Jessica Gregory?"

"Yes," Grant answered.

"I'm Dana Williams, with the NTSB. It's lovely to meet you. The ground crew is just removing the Jetway and affixing the ladder so we can exit outside. I'll be taking you to one of our staff rooms on the lower level of the airport, where your families are waiting."

Grant didn't have any family waiting for him, only Quinn's.

Once the ladder was ready, we followed Dana down to the ground level and were shown into a room with two doors, where we finally removed our coats. It was nice to be back in a warm climate.

"Wait here one moment, if you will," Dana said.

About two minutes later, my sister Caroline burst through the door.

Chapter 29

I ran into Caroline's arms and embraced her like I hadn't seen her for years. She smelled like home, and I inhaled her scent like it was a drug. Caroline sobbed and laughed and looked me up and down like we were meeting for the first time.

She embraced me again and then pulled back, with her fingers still gripping my shoulders.

"I just can't believe it's you. I've missed you so much, sweetie. Your hair is so long and blond, Jess. You look beautiful." She clasped a hand over her mouth. "I can't tell you how wonderful it is to have you standing here with me." She glanced at the man standing awkwardly next to her.

"Welcome home," he said. "We're so relieved."

Short, portly, bald, and wearing wire-rimmed glasses, Allen Hamlish looked every bit the banker he was. He was kind and polite but had about as much of a sense of humor as he did hair. Caroline had been dating him since the week after Mom's funeral. I'd only met him twice before, but I was grateful she had someone.

"Thank you," I said to him.

Grant walked up from behind me and introduced himself.

"I'm Grant. Jessica has told me so much about you," he said, and extended his right hand, but Caroline pulled him to her and hugged him instead, still sobbing.

"Thank you for keeping her safe and returning her to us in one piece," she said. "I can't tell you how worried I was."

Grant shook his head and furrowed his brow. "Please don't thank me. If anything, I put her in danger, and I am so sorry for that."

"Um," I interjected, and tapped her on the shoulder so she would release him. "I think Grant and I need to find Quinn's family, and then we can meet up with you later, okay?"

She latched onto my hand tightly. "Do you have to go?" she whispered.

"I do, but I'll be back. I promise."

Just then I saw Grant turn his attention to the two large windows that overlooked the runways, and the five of us watched as Quinn's casket was brought off the plane.

Caroline mustered a tiny smile and looked at Grant, then at me. "Of course." She dabbed her nose with a tissue. "I understand. We'll be waiting for you in here when you're through. Please take as much time as you need."

Grant and I looked over at Dana.

"Follow me," she said, and we did.

Grant and I were led to a larger room down the hall. There were six people waiting for us when we entered, and I burst into tears as soon as I saw them.

"I'm so sorry." I lifted a hand to shield my face as a young woman whom I recognized all too well approached me. I lifted my arms to embrace her, and we hugged.

"I'm so sorry, Bridget. You have no idea."

She wept into my shoulder and then pulled away and tried her best to put on a brave face. She held my hand as we followed Grant to where Quinn's parents and brother were sitting, along with Bridget's mom and a woman who leapt to her feet and ran into Grant's arms as soon as she saw him.

She was petite and blond like me, and about ten years younger than him—also like me. She was impeccably dressed—so much so that I glanced down at my shapeless navy-issue blue polo shirt and khaki pants and recoiled. Her eyebrows were expertly shaped, her hair blown to perfection, her designer sandals with nary an ounce of dirt, and her French-manicured nails were on his back. She gently quivered as they hugged. Grant cradled the back of her head before pulling away and approaching Quinn's mom and dad. He crouched before their chairs. I took a couple steps forward, still holding Bridget's hand, as the blond mystery woman stood closely by Grant's side.

Quinn's parents acknowledged him with a nod. They weren't crying in that moment, but you could tell they had been. They were simple-looking people with nondescript clothing. Quinn's father looked like he had just come in from a day of fishing, and his mom was wearing the same gray, Easy Spirit lace-up shoes that my mom used to wear. What do you wear to pick up your son's casket from the airport? You can't very well justify getting dressed up for that.

Quinn's dad placed a hand on Grant's shoulder. "Thank you for bringing him home."

I closed my eyes and fought back tears.

Grant nodded and then quietly broke down. He placed his elbow on his knee and his head in his hands. Blondie rubbed his back until he gently lifted his hand to stop her.

"This is not how I wanted to bring him home." He choked out his words and then sniffed. "For days I've been trying to think of what I can say to you, but I have no words to express my regret. Quinn was beyond compare. He was always there for me, with a smile and a wisecrack, and I will never, ever forget him for the positive influence he had on my life."

He turned, bleary eyed, and stood to face Bridget. He was about to speak but just threw his arms up in defeat. My heart broke over and over for him and everyone in that room.

Grant sniffed again and wiped his face with the back of his hand. "Bridget, he loved you so much." He paused. "I know you know that, but you should also know that you were all he talked about and thought about and dreamt about. I don't want to make this any harder on you; I just want you to know that you were the light in his life and you were with him until the very end."

She let go of my hand and embraced Grant.

"Thank you," I heard her say softly, then pull away and place her hands on his shoulders. "You're so right. He was a positive force beyond compare, and he would hate to see everyone so sad." She paused to wipe her cheek. "All he ever wanted was to lift people's spirits, not to crush them. You must always try and remember that when you think of him. I know I will."

Grant nodded.

She stepped away, and Grant took my hand, but it felt wrong for some reason, so I casually pulled it back.

"Jessica," Grant said, "this is my sister-in-law, Marie." The blond woman stepped forward. "Marie, this is Jessica. She was also with us on the boat when we were attacked."

Jane's sister smiled at me and nodded. "I'm so glad you're safe now," she said quietly, and then looked at Grant. "That you both are."

Grant spoke to me. "Marie and Quinn were friends. They used to work together a few years back when Quinn was interning at the station. Marie is a news anchor in Fort Lauderdale."

"I see," I said, and cocked my head to the side. "I'm so sorry for your loss." The words were stale and void of compassion, so much so that I almost didn't recognize my own voice. I shook my head. "I'm . . . this has been so hard. I don't know what to say. It's just awful, and Quinn was so amazing . . ." I began to cry, and Grant wrapped me in his arms.

"Shh. It's okay."

I let go of him, and Marie rubbed my arm with her hand. "You've been through a terrible ordeal. We're all so sorry for what you went through. I can't fathom it." She made a tsk sound and shook her head. "It's inconceivable, evil like that."

"Yes," I agreed.

Dana entered the room with two other people. "We're ready when you are. No hurry," she said.

Quinn's brother hooked his arm around his mother's arm, and they followed Dana out, with Bridget and her mother in tow. I grabbed Bridget's elbow just as she was about to walk past me, and we made eye contact.

"I just wanted to tell you that your quilt is with him."

She placed her hand over her heart. "Thank you," she whispered, and walked out.

Grant reached for my hand again, and I saw Marie's eyes glance at our entwined fingers. I didn't want to hurt his feelings by letting go a second time, but I wasn't comfortable.

"Can we sit for a minute?" she asked us.

"Of course," Grant said, and we all took a seat at the table where Quinn's family had been sitting.

Marie sighed and looked at him like he was a child. "Why didn't you call anyone?" she asked.

Grant looked down at his hands, now folded in his lap, and shrugged. "I don't know."

She gave me a quick look and then turned her attention back to Grant. I thought about excusing myself and running back to Caroline, but I sensed he needed me there with him.

"Who told you?" he asked.

"Things like this make the news, Grant," Marie started. "But actually a close friend of Bridget's had posted something on Facebook, and a mutual friend of ours asked me about Quinn, not even realizing that I knew you."

Grant rubbed his forehead, then rested his arms on the table. "I'm sorry about that. I mean it. I should have called."

She leaned forward and placed a hand on his forearm. "We were worried sick, obviously, but more importantly we want to be there for you for *any* reason. Okay?"

He nodded.

"You have to let your family be there for you. Good or bad," she said, and then leaned back in her seat. "I hate to ask, but do you have a plan for what's next?"

My ears perked up.

"No, not really. Jess and I are going to meet back up with her family, and I want to make sure she's taken care of and . . ." His voice trailed off for a second. "And wherever she decides to go is where you'll find me."

Chapter 30

The next morning I woke up and found Caroline struggling with the state-of-the-art coffeemaker mounted on the wall of the hotel room. Grant was still asleep, so I lightly closed the door behind me. The suite at the Mandarin Oriental Miami had two bedrooms—one for us, and the second for Caroline and Allen, neither of whom had ever stayed in anything nicer than a DoubleTree. The décor was a modern Art Deco style, and the room overlooked the waters of Brickell Key.

"I was trying to make some coffee and wait out on the veranda for everyone to get up, but this looks like something out of *Star Wars*," Caroline said.

"Then I'm sure Allen will know how to use it," I joked, and she smiled in agreement. "I think it's an espresso machine. We can just order a couple pots of coffee."

"This is very indulgent. Grant didn't have to do this for us."

"He has connections here with these hotels. He used to work in the travel business for many years and still does at times, so he gets to stay for free or cheap. I think."

She looked at me, waiting for more details about him, but I didn't have many.

"Shall we sit outside?" she asked.

"Sure," I said, and ordered some room service before quietly sliding the glass doors open and walking out onto the marble tiles that made up the floor of the patio. "Would you care for the loveseat or the oversized beanbag of awesomeness?" I asked.

"I'll take the loveseat," she said, and I fell into a bright orange beanbag chair the size of a Volkswagen Beetle.

We sat in silence for a moment, pretending to enjoy the view, before I finally spoke. "What do you want to know?"

She cleared her throat. "Allen said I shouldn't push you or be too nosy, but I lose sleep at night thinking about what you went through and what your plans are from here." She met my eyes. "I think it's time you come home."

"I made it back safely. Isn't that what matters?"

"Yes, but I'm just sick about what you all had to endure. I keep imagining the worst, and I just want to make sure you get the help you need from here on out . . . if in fact you need help. I mean, what sort of medical treatment were you given? Did you talk with a psychiatrist? Were any of these men captured, and what's being done to them?" She paused to read my face. "Am I terrible for wanting to know these things?"

I shook my head.

"And, Jessica . . ." She sat on the edge of her seat and leaned in. "I can tell you're head over heels in love with this man. Does he feel the same about you? What are his intentions? Where was his family today?"

The coffee could not have arrived fast enough.

I pressed my palms into my thighs and lowered my eyes for a moment. "I think you know I'm not coming home with you," I said, and then looked at her.

She crossed her arms. "Where are you going then? Back to Phuket?"

"Yes. At first anyway. I mean, I have a life there, and that was my plan all along. To crew for Grant for a month and then fly back to Phuket. I have two jobs that I love and friends. Not to mention everything that I own. I can't very well abandon the place, nor do I want to."

She just stared at me.

"As far as me being in love with him—yes, I am, and 'head over heels' is putting it mildly." I sank lower into my chair.

Caroline sighed.

"Please don't be upset," I said. "We did suffer through an unspeakable ordeal, but we made it out alive, Grant and I, and I wasn't hurt too badly. Or raped. I know that's what you're thinking. The most I'm suffering is the loss of Quinn." I shook my head. "He was so fantastic, Caroline, I mean it. Like, just truly one of the most genuine people I've ever met. And while I didn't know him very long, I just can't get past how unfair it is to him and everyone who loved him."

"I've said many prayers for his family and will continue to do so."

"Thank you."

She uncrossed her arms and leaned forward. "I know you're a grown woman and you don't want or need your big sister telling you what to do, but I just worry about you." She managed a smile. "Would I love to have you home working for Allen at the bank, or at one of the local schools again? Yes, I would, but I'm not as naïve as you think I am, and I know that's not an option for you."

"I appreciate that."

"Good, and I would appreciate you doing your best to stay safe. That's all I'm asking." She paused. "I'm going to marry Allen."

My eyes went wide, and I had to force myself from blurting out my first instinct, which was to talk her out of it. Then I realized this was what Caroline wanted.

"If you're happy, then I'm happy. And if Allen makes you happy . . . then I love him more than you know," I said, and she smiled. "Can I tell you something?"

"Of course."

"Promise not to read too much into it or think that I've lost my mind more than you already think I have."

"I promise."

"Mom was with me on the boat." I paused. "Young, exuberant, New York honeymoon Mom."

Caroline blinked but said nothing.

I tugged my earlobe and looked away from her. "If I'm being honest with you and myself, I thought I was going to die. Maybe one day—if you want—I will tell you the details of what happened, but it won't be anytime soon. That being said, there was a moment, maybe more than one, where I was convinced I was going to take my last breath on that boat. And in those moments, Mom came to me." I brushed the hair from my face. "She didn't speak . . . but she *told* me she loved me and that she was proud of me."

Caroline's eyes were brimming with tears when I looked back at her.

"She'd never told me that before," I added.

A second later the sliding glass door opened, and Grant was standing there.

"Looks like your coffee is here," he said. "Am I interrupting?"

"No, I'm so sorry. I didn't mean for you to wake up," I said, and stood. "We should have listened for the door."

"It's fine. I was up and happy to see a fresh pot."

The four of us had coffee together before Caroline and Allen had to leave. I helped her pack up her things and then we walked them down to the lobby to get a cab.

"Thank you, Grant, for your generous hospitality and for taking care of Jessica," Caroline said, and then gave him a hug.

"Both are my pleasure."

Saying good-bye to my sister was never easy, especially when I didn't know when I'd see her again. We hugged for a long time, and it felt really good.

"If you see Mom again, tell her I miss her terribly," Caroline told me.

That night Grant and I drove his rental car to a restaurant called Michael's Genuine, located in the Miami Design District.

"I don't come to Miami all that often, but when I do, I come here," Grant told me.

We sat outdoors on the patio, which was sandwiched between some retail shops. The air was warm, and the food was made with fresh and simple ingredients but prepared with a twist of the eclectic. I ordered the wood-roasted, double-yolk farm egg, which came in a white ceramic ramekin with cave-aged Gruyère cheese, roasted tomatoes, and chives. I used the sourdough crostini that came with it to pop open the egg yolks, and the taste was unlike anything I'd ever experienced.

"I'm going to need four more of these," I said, and then closed my eyes in hopes of reliving the taste.

Grant was devouring his steamed mussels. He paused to wipe his mouth with a white linen napkin. "I'm so glad you got to see your sister."

"Me too. Thank you for taking such good care of them."

"Of course."

I took another bite of the gooey, drippy, warm, cheesy deliciousness that was in front of me and then sipped my wine, wishing the ramekin were twice as large. Once I was through, I sat back in my chair and drained the rest of my glass.

"I guess we need to talk," I said, causing Grant to raise an eyebrow. "Most dreaded words ever, right?"

"Not coming from you, no."

I placed my palms on the edge of the table. "I hate to ask, but have you made any decisions about what your plans are after Quinn's funeral?"

Grant placed his tablespoon next to the bowl of mussels and then dunked a chunk of French bread into the broth. I watched him chew for a moment before he sat back in his seat.

"My main priority is seeing you safely back to Phuket—if that's what you want—and then trying to get ahold of *Imagine*. I know the boat is in custody, and they'll want me to retrieve it at some point."

"Do you think you'll be able to sail her again, with everything that happened?"

He lowered his gaze for a moment and then made eye contact with me. "I do."

I nodded slightly.

"I understand if that sounds strange or callous to you," he said, "but I've thought about it many times, and I refuse to let those men take what is mine. And I don't even mean the boat. I mean the journey and the memories and the time I had with my nephews and with Quinn. That vessel is my life. She's all I have in this world. She's been my sole purpose—my home, my everything—and I intend on reclaiming her and making *Imagine* a happy place again. I'm determined to do that."

I glanced at the ground. He hadn't counted me amongst the things in his world.

"Are you upset?" he asked.

I looked up at him and tried to read his eyes. Could I ever compete with his dreams for himself? No one could've competed with mine, but mine had changed to include him. I just didn't know if his would ever change to include me.

"I'm not upset," I said. "And the fact that you want to live out your goals doesn't sound strange to me at all." I paused to take a breath. "I'm just not sure I'd ever be able to step aboard that boat again, but I'm glad you're committed to doing the right thing by her. You both deserve it."

Grant leaned forward, slid his fingers between mine, and gently squeezed my hand. "I guess we need to talk about us now."

I smiled, lips closed.

He continued. "I'm going to finish my trip. It's a promise I made to myself, and I have to do it. That being said, I would love for you to come with me if you want." He lowered his chin to study my response, which was nonexistent. "However, you have a life that you love in Phuket—you've told me so yourself many times—and I don't want to be the one to take you away from it if that's not in the cards for you. I've been a nomad for years now with no one to answer to, and really no one to look after." He stopped for a moment and gently shook his head. "And look what's happened to those I have." He exhaled. "Meeting you has changed me from the inside out, and I'll never forget what you've done for me. You cleared the haze and reminded my heart what it's like to ache in a good way. But I don't know if I'm at a point where I'd be comfortable uprooting you from your life."

I nodded.

"What are your thoughts on all this, Jess?"

I sniffed out a small laugh through my nostrils. "When we were on the boat in the midst of everything horrible, all I thought of was you. I don't remember anything else in my life mattering to me. My friends, my family, my jobs—none of it mattered. My prayers were for us, for our safety, and for a future together. You were and are all that was on my mind."

He squeezed my hand again.

"The waitress better not dare show her face right now," I said, rolling my eyes.

Grant smiled.

"Anyway, I'm sorry if I'm breaking every rule in the 'play hard to get' handbook, but I'm crazy about you, and I think you know that. Also, I don't think I'm a complete love-struck fool when I say that I think you care about me too." I looked up for his confirmation, and he nodded, thank God. "But yes, you're right. I do want to return to Phuket. My life is there, and that was my original plan."

"Plans can change," he interjected.

"They can, but I'm committed to the school through the end of June, and I owe them that. They've been exceptionally accommodating to me, and so has Niran. It's not in my nature to shirk my duties."

"I like that about you."

The waitress finally approached the table, and thankfully Grant ordered us some more wine.

"Can I ask you something?" I said.

"Shoot."

"What did Marie say to you?"

"About what?"

"About us. Did she say anything about you and me being together?"

He shook his head no. "Why do you ask?"

I shrugged. "I just felt awkward for some reason, holding hands in front of her. I don't know why."

"She and everyone else in my family just want me to be happy." He sighed. "I can't begin to describe what I went through both physically and emotionally when Jane died. Maybe I should've gone into therapy, maybe I'll write a book one day, or maybe I will sail around the world, accomplish my goal, and move on with my life. But seeing Marie and talking with my family and friends is still too hard. Even after all these years. It forces me to remember the worst of it, because those are the people that were with me during my darkest days. To call it a personal hell does not even scratch the surface of how awful it was. They saw me at my weakest, rawest state, and I still see that reflection in their eyes." He leaned forward. "When it's just someone asking me about Jane, I have no problem talking about her and remembering who she was. The real Jane, not the cancer Jane. But when I see my family, all I think of is Cancer Jane, and I hate it."

When I stared into his eyes, I understood everything. All he wanted to do was to hold on to the good. Didn't we all? Every memory that came to me during the worst moments of my life was one of comfort and simple pleasures. Grant was no different. And while time healed most wounds, it didn't erase memories. Maybe he wanted Marie to know he was happy again.

"I hope I've been able to make you happy."

"You have."

Chapter 31

A week later we boarded a flight from Miami to New York and sprinted to meet our connection, and then boarded a second flight that day to Dubai in the United Arab Emirates.

"This doesn't count as my trip to New York," I said breathlessly as I ran with my backpack over my shoulders.

Once we arrived in Dubai, our sightseeing was cut short there as well, and we slept on the floor of the airport for four hours before catching a flight to Muscat, Oman, where Grant had arranged for *Imagine* to be towed. Before heading to the marina, we checked into the Grand Hyatt and both slept for ten hours straight. It was a "grand" hotel and would be Grant's home for the next month.

The next morning we grabbed breakfast in the lobby and took a taxi to Marina Bandar Al Rowdha. As soon as the man at the front desk checked our credentials, we were led down a long dock to Slip 15.

And there she was, shrouded in tarp.

Around us, the marina was bustling. Mostly with men walking fast and furiously, tending to their cell phones and chatting with other boaters. Repairs were being made to a boat in the slip next to *Imagine* as Arabic music played from a radio on the dock. Each of the locals going about their business as the mystery boat amongst them stood proud yet sheltered. If they only knew the battering she endured and how she vowed not to go down without a fight. A few war wounds were visible, scratches and scars from where the skiffs had slammed into her side: a broken handrail that dangled precariously from below the edge of the tarp, and a few barnacles littering her once-pristine hull. Grant took my hand as two of the men with us began to remove her canvas veil. I swallowed hard as bullet holes and disarray from the night of our rescue became instantly visible. Grant let go of me and hurried aboard, then turned and extended a hand to me. I stood on the dock and glanced at him, frozen with trepidation.

Grant lowered his arm. "You don't have to come aboard, Jess. I mean it."

"I want to."

"Are you sure?" he asked.

I nodded and reached for his hand and came aboard the scene of the crime. Cushions were overturned and covered with dirt. Loose papers were strewn about the cockpit, along with empty plastic cups, and cigarette butts littered the floor.

Emma was long gone.

I paused at the top of the stairs that led to the salon and bent to lower my head. Below deck was the harshest evidence of the ransacking, and I had to cover my nose and mouth just to take a peek. The carpet had been removed, but there were still traces of blood and urine and food. The table was off its hinges, tilting to one side, and the couch had been slashed in no less than four places.

And then I saw it.

A tiny glimmer in the corner, wedged between the desk and the edge of the table: my gold Buddha.

I stood and walked back down to the stern of the boat and took a deep breath. Grant was talking with the two men on the bow, pointing at the masts. I crossed my arms and closed my eyes.

He came up from behind me and asked, "You okay?"

"My safe-travels Buddha is down there. He survived."

"So did we." He rubbed my arm. "Would you like me to get him for you?"

I nodded.

Grant walked down the stairs and came back immediately with the Buddha and handed it to me. He was unscathed. His delighted, exuberant smile made me long to see the Knights and Niran and Sophie.

I stepped off the boat onto the dock and had a seat with my legs dangling over the water. There was a breeze hitting the side of my face, so I turned to face it in an effort to dry my eyes. I really didn't want to cry. I wanted to be strong for Grant and *Imagine*. She'd been stripped of her beauty, brutally violated and left vulnerable, yet remained standing. I glanced at the water lapping at her hull and was able to find solace in the fact that she would be restored and live to feel the wind in her sails again.

Grant joined me fifteen minutes later. "Let's head out. They're going to assemble a team for me, and I'll come back in a couple days to go through the details with them then. In the meantime, these guys are going to get a cleaning crew in here and take care of that first."

I stood and embraced him. He rubbed my back and held me tight. I felt his chest expand and release as he slowly exhaled.

"I'm glad I came with you," I said as I pulled away.

"Are you?"

I nodded.

"They're going to do their best to salvage our belongings, but I really won't know what condition they're in until next week."

"That's fine."

Grant took my hand, and we went back to the hotel, where we ate dinner in the room, and afterward we went to bed.

He pulled me on top of him as we lay there and held me close to his bare chest with my ear pressed against his beating heart.

"How long did they say the repairs would take?"

"A little over a month."

"Will you need to be here the whole time?"

"Yes."

"I'm going to miss you like crazy," I said, lifting my head.

"I'm going to miss you too." Grant cradled the sides of my face with his hands and pulled my mouth to his. We kissed like it would be our last, needy and ravenous, and then he ran his hand up and down my back.

"I hate to leave you," I said.

"I'll be fine, and you need to get back."

"Who is going to make me feel this good while you're away?"

"Hopefully no one," he said, and covered our stacked bodies with the thin white bedsheet.

It took me hours to fall asleep that night. Not knowing when I would see him again left my emotions shattered. I didn't want to put any pressure on him, but the anxiety of losing him for good was nearly impossible to endure.

I think it was just past midnight when I closed my eyes and felt myself drifting off. An hour later I awoke to Grant screaming. Deep, frantic, panicked sounds like nothing I'd ever heard.

Chapter 32

Grant!" I said, shaking him. "Grant, wake up. Grant, it's okay!"

His chest and face were covered in sweat, and his hands were trembling when his eyes opened in one swift move and stayed wide as he looked right through me like I was a stranger.

"Grant . . . you're okay. It was just a dream."

He sat up and slowly glanced around the room.

"We're in the hotel. Everything's fine," I said.

He swung his legs over the bed and hunched over, his head in his hands. I moved to place a hand on his shoulder, but he brushed me off. After a few minutes, he stood and went to the bathroom and closed the door.

I don't think I did so much as blink until he emerged.

"Are you all right?" I asked.

He stood leaning against the doorframe, wiping the back of his neck with a hand towel. "I can't do this."

I felt my heartbeat come to a screeching halt. "Do what?"

"I can't be responsible for anyone anymore." His tone was almost robotic.

"You're not responsible for me."

He shook his head. "I would never forgive myself if something happened to you. I just couldn't take it."

I swallowed. "Nothing is going to happen to me." I sat up on my knees in the bed and held the sheet to my chest. "Come back to bed. You had a horrible nightmare. I have them all the time, but look how far we've—"

"I can't afford to get close to another person right now!" His voice was raised.

I looked down at the mattress and cocked my head to the side before looking at him square in the eyes. "Well, maybe you should have thought of that weeks ago. Isn't it a little late for that?"

He tossed the towel on the bed and paced the floor, pulling at his hair.

"It was hard for you today, seeing your boat. I knew it would be. But you don't have to do this to us. You said yourself that you refused to let those men win and take away the things you care about."

He sat on an armchair in the corner. "But they did."

"I'm still here."

He lowered his head and wrapped his hands behind his neck. I could feel my insides crumbling into ash.

"It was just a nightmare," I whispered.

"They're never just nightmares. They're products of my reality, and I'm sick of them. The minute I think they're gone for good, something else happens to awaken the beast." He looked up at me. "My heart won't survive the next something."

I don't know if feeling vulnerable is anyone's strong suit, but it certainly wasn't mine. His resolute demeanor, and the lack of uncertainty in his voice, left me weak. I just kept repeating in my head, *This can't be happening.*

"So this is it?" I asked. "You put me on a plane tomorrow and just move along? Back to our old routines like nothing ever happened?" I shook my head. "How do you expect me to do that?"

"I don't know."

"I think you're more afraid of getting close to someone than you are of losing them."

"Maybe I am."

"Look, Grant, I would never for one second pretend I know what you went through with your wife—I promise you that. But I read her letter, and you said yourself that she wants you to be happy, and I know I can make you happy."

"You don't know that."

"Yes, I do, because I'm not going to let you play the victim for the rest of your life." I sighed. "And Quinn, although I only knew him for a short time, I felt like I knew him forever. Everyone did. I wish I had the right words to say to make things better, but I don't. All we can do is be there for each other." I scooted to the edge of the bed. "I can't stop you from breaking things off with me, but the least I can do is fight for us. If you made your mind up after ten minutes in the bathroom, then so be it. But consider how far we've come and how happy we make each other. It would be a shame to throw it all away on account of a few sleepless nights."

He considered what I said. "My gut is telling me I need to be alone. I deserve to be alone."

My heart was crushed, but my head was fuming. I didn't want to be angry with him, because I felt bad for everything he'd been through, but it killed me to see someone pushing people away when they needed them the most.

"I'm sure I'll regret this," he said.

"You will."

"But I won't regret keeping you safe."

"You can't protect me or anyone else, and you certainly can't protect your heart. Pushing people away, the ones who love you the most, isn't going to bring you any less heartache. Until you realize that, the nightmares will never stop." I laid my head on the pillow and closed my eyes before the tears could escape. "Good night, Grant."

Is there a Buddha to mend a broken heart?

Chapter 33

I packed my few belongings amongst awkward small talk with Grant the next morning, and after we'd both had our coffee he took me to the airport to catch a flight to Phuket. He stepped out of the taxi to grab my backpack from the trunk and then stood with me on the curb. We stared at each other for a long moment before I leaned in and hugged him. I took a deep, long inhale through my nose to capture his scent and then pulled away.

"Good-bye, Grant."

I was determined to stay strong in front of him.

When I woke that morning, I thought about my mother and the contrast between her as a beautiful young newlywed so full of life and the God-fearing, angry introvert I knew. At some point in her life, she must have been at a crossroads and chosen the wrong path. Maybe people tried to talk her out of it; maybe they didn't. Either way, she stayed with what she knew, what she thought would keep her safe and protected, yet it held her captive and robbed her of loving relationships with her children and true happiness.

Growing up, the Serenity Prayer was printed on a large wooden cross that hung above the breakfast table in our kitchen:

> *God, grant me the serenity to accept the things I cannot change,*

The courage to change the things I can,
And the wisdom to know the difference.

It occurred to me that morning that she hung the prayer there for me.

I knew that my relationship with Grant would never survive unless he faced and conquered his demons. That I would never be able to make him whole unless he was willing to accept what he couldn't change, and choose the path to happiness.

"I'm going to miss you," he said.

"It's your choice."

"I love you, Jess, and I'm so sorry. You have no idea how much." His eyes were intense. "I should have told you that before, but I'm telling you now. It pains me to let you go, but I know it's the right thing to do."

"Please don't."

He sighed. "Will you be okay?"

I nodded and lifted my backpack onto my shoulder.

⸺◆◆⸺

When I landed in Phuket, Sophie was waiting for me at the gate. We hugged and cried a little, and seeing a familiar face was exactly what I needed. Oddly enough, arriving in Phuket that time wasn't much different than when I came there six months earlier. My emotions were fragile, and I was nervous and anxious for the future, but in a totally different way.

"God, I missed you something fierce," she said with her arm around my shoulders as we walked.

"I missed you too."

Sophie knew everything that had happened to me, aside from my own personal nightmare in the hotel room with Grant the night before. I e-mailed her and Skylar and Mrs. Knight from Miami, updating them on most of the details from our ordeal. But I'd sent Sophie a separate note with the details on Grant.

"Niran has a huge welcome-back party planned for you tonight."

"He does?"

"Of course he does. Are you up for it?"

"I really don't know."

She stopped walking and stood in front of me. "Darling, you just say the word. None of us have recovered from hearing your story. Shit, I cried for three days straight over Quinn." She shook her head and placed her hand to her heart. "That frisky little bugger. Damn shame, I tell you. Damn shame."

I nodded.

"So if you're not up for a party, I will call it off this instant."

"It's fine. I'm really looking forward to seeing everyone."

"You sure?"

"Yes."

"What about lover boy? What's his plan? Is he cleaning things up, or getting on with a new boat?"

I threw my hands up. "I think we're done."

She drew her head back. "Done with what?"

"With each other. He told me last night that he can't afford to get close to anyone else. That he feels responsible for what happened to Quinn and maybe in some way his wife. I guess he's scared."

She shook her head in disbelief. "Scared of what?"

"Losing someone else."

"That's bollocks!"

"I know, but it's the truth."

She turned and we kept walking. "After everything that went down, I don't know what to say."

"Neither do I."

Sophie dropped me off at home, and for a moment I felt like the naïve girl who stepped out of the taxi with only American money just months ago.

Mrs. Knight was waiting for me just inside the door and embraced me when I walked in. I was touched by how moved she was when she saw me.

"Niran is throwing me a little welcome-home party at the bar tonight. I would love to have you both join me. Do you think you'd be up for it?" I asked her. Mr. Knight rarely left his beloved Barcalounger on the back porch.

"We wouldn't miss it," she said. "Mr. Knight is on the porch. I know he's very eager to see you."

"And I him." I left my bags in the foyer and walked to the back of the house. "Please don't get up," I said as he braced himself on the armrests and began to stand.

"My dear, I'm not too old to stand up for my favorite girl." We hugged. "You gave us quite a scare. Please have a seat."

"I'm sorry I worried you both. It was . . ." I paused and looked away for a second. "I really have no words. It was awful. I'm just grateful to be back in one piece."

"We're very sorry about your friend."

"Me too."

He leaned back. "What about the other man? Sophie told us that you and he are an item."

I smiled at his terminology. "Grant. Yes, we were. But he sort of ended things with me last night."

Mr. Knight furrowed his brow. "Are you upset by that?"

"I am, but I'll be fine. He's a good man. A really good man, and I wish him the best. I may or may not have mentioned to you that he'd lost his wife a few years ago and this trip . . . This journey he's on is something he has to complete for himself. I was just a small part of it."

He stared at me. "Do you love him?"

"I do."

"Has he hurt you?"

His question caught me off guard. I knew he wasn't referring to physical pain. He was asking about my heart. Was it ripped apart and left to heal with no bandage? Yes. Did my stomach turn when I thought of Grant—which was every second? Yes. Did he hurt me? It felt unfair to say yes when he'd taught me so much about love in such a short time. There are certain things in life that must be experienced in order to fully understand them, and falling in love and heartbreak are two of them. No one can amply describe what it is to love someone unconditionally and then lose them in an instant. He didn't hurt me on purpose, but being separated from him did bring me immeasurable pain.

I looked up at Mr. Knight, married for fifty years to his high school sweetheart. "I wish things could have been different, but I'll be okay."

I retreated to my room and was overcome with emotion. It smelled like home, and there was an embracing calm in the air. My tiny corner of the world where so much had happened yet so little had changed. I closed the door and lay down on the bed, where I prepared for tears that never came. Where I normally would've cried— over the boat, the trip, the attack, Quinn, Grant, all of it—I didn't shed a single tear, because it seemed juvenile and unnecessary.

Everything felt right, but it would be forever wrong without Grant, and I feared what was to come. I knew this was going to wound me in ways that would take months, maybe years to recover from. I'd fallen hard and fast for him and experienced emotions I'd never known. I knew the withdrawal would be the hardest part, and I dreaded it. Leaving Caroline was initially hard, but she was family— and even if we were separated by distance, we would always be close. But tethering my affections to a drifter like Grant was much different than anything my adventurous heart had ever *imagine*d.

When I walked onto the back patio of the bar that night, I was greeted by a twenty-foot banner that read "Jessica Lives!"

Niran was wearing a hot pink tunic with white linen pants and sipping a cosmopolitan. "You miss Niran?"

"Very much." We hugged. "You miss Jessica?"

"Very much, yes. My place not the same without my girls."

"Thank you. It's good to be back."

"It is very sad about Quinn. He was really good guy, like me."

"Yes, he was."

"You have sex with the other one?"

His question made me laugh really hard for the first time in a long time.

Chapter 34

"Good morning, class. Please take your seats."

It had been three weeks since my return, and things were eerily back to normal. There's no rulebook for how to deal with tragedy and live through the aftermath. No etiquette for how long you're supposed to carry survivor's guilt, so I did the best I could with what I had, which was my work and my friends. My heartbreak over Grant had to take a backseat to dealing with everything else.

Once I was back in my comfort zone, I started to have anxiety about the pirates. I grew wearier of my surroundings and of perfect strangers. It was natural, I was told, and all I could do was manage it to the best of my ability. Skylar was given news that there was a school in London that she could be transferred to, so she'd promoted Sophie to the director job. I asked to be relieved of my assistant duties when I came back to school, preferring to focus on teaching.

I missed being with the kids. My first day back, Alak embraced me and held on for dear life.

"Missed you, Miss Jessica," he whispered.

I pulled back and wiped his tears with my hand. "I missed you too, little man. And guess what?"

"What?"

"I have tons of laundry to do!"

He smiled. "The Laundry Kitties are really hungry."

"I bet they are, and I'm going to bring, like, ten cans of tuna with me. Will you meet me at the 'Mat on Sunday?"

He nodded with great purpose.

I'd moved on, but I thought about Grant every day. That night, I went home and wrote him an e-mail.

Hi Grant,

I just wanted you to know that all is well with me. I'm back to work at the bar and the school like nothing ever happened. I think about you all the time, but I'm determined to respect your wishes. I just hope that you will keep in touch and let me know how you're doing. I miss you, and I am safe.

Then I deleted it and started over.

Why was I bothering with niceties? I'd spent my entire youth placating people and smoothing feathers. Why on earth was I still doing it? I left that life behind. I moved to Thailand to do what I wanted and to get away from appeasing everyone else. Had I not learned anything? I was slipping back into familiar habits and letting people decide what was best for me. I needed to put a stop to it once and for all.

I adjusted my shoulders and typed a new e-mail to Grant. It read:

You're a coward.

And then I hit Send.

A week later, Sophie and I were sitting in the school office hours after classes had ended when one of the student's parents came in, outraged. Apparently, six-year-old Marina got on the bus but fell asleep in the backseat and never got off at her stop. I excused myself to my classroom and left Sophie to her coveted director duties.

I was placing all the chairs upside down on the tabletops when I heard a man's voice behind me.

"Excuse me."

I turned to find Mr. Knight standing there.

"Mr. Knight, hello! Please come in." I gestured with my hand.

"Hello, dear. What a darling classroom this is."

"Thank you." I placed my hands on my hips. "Is everything all right? To what do I owe this pleasure?"

He took a couple steps forward. "Well, you see, something came for you at the house, and I thought I'd better bring it to you right away."

"Oh?"

Mr. Knight turned around, and Grant appeared in the doorway. My hand flew to my mouth.

"Here it is," Mr. Knight said, oddly amused, and then took a step forward and whispered in my ear. "I'm not too old to stand up for my favorite girl." He winked at me. "I'll leave the two of you alone now."

My eyes were glued to Grant. He stared at me apprehensively, and I realized my body had frozen. I blinked and then lifted my chin.

"Hi," he said.

"Hi."

"It's getting late, so I stopped by your house. I thought you'd be home by now."

"Sophie and I had some work to do."

My insides were drawn to him like a magnet. I had to struggle to keep my feet firmly planted and not run into his arms. I wasn't a game player; I hadn't enough experience with relationships to know how to play it cool and act indifferent. All I knew was that the man I'd fallen in love with was standing a few feet from my reach, and I wanted to touch him. I had no desire to play coy, but I knew I had to, and I hated it.

"Can I come in?" he asked. His voice made me shiver.

"Yes, of course."

Grant walked toward me and left little space between us. I couldn't breathe.

"How have you been?"

"Good," I said softly.

"I missed you."

"Is that why you're here?"

"Yes."

I looked up at him. "You're here because you missed me?"

He loosely took both my hands in his and I let him. To this day I don't know how I held myself together in that moment.

"I'm here because you were right. I'm tired of living with regret." He lowered his head. "And I regret letting you go." He released my hands and sat on the edge of the desk.

"How's *Imagine*?"

"She's gone."

I gasped. "What happened?"

"You were right about her too. There were too many memories there. Many were great, but most were ones that I'd like to forget. I traded her in for someone new."

I smiled.

"I was hoping you and I could talk." He stood. "I have a room at the marina hotel. Will you meet me there tonight around eight?"

"Sure."

"Great. I'll see you then."

Chapter 35

I sat on a couch in Grant's hotel suite as he brought over two glasses of wine and joined me. He took a sip and leaned back, releasing a long breath through his nose.

I stared at him, speechless, yet with so much to say. But that time I wasn't going to wait for my questions to be answered or my sentiments to be reciprocated. He needed to make the first move.

"Thank you for your e-mail," he said.

I glanced down for a second and couldn't help the corners of my mouth from turning upward. "Maybe it was a little harsh."

"It wasn't, and you were right. I was being a coward, and I have been for a long time. I think it took me spending time with *Imagine* to come to the realization that like her I was damaged. But where she was beyond repair, I'm not." His eyes narrowed. "I saw myself in her, beaten and broken, and although she couldn't be fixed, I can be. I'm convinced of it now." He sat forward and rested his elbows on his knees but kept his eyes on mine. "I love you."

My heart leapt.

"And I don't want to waste any more time," he said. "I'm pushing forty, and we love each other, so why wait to be together? I knew what I had with Jane was something special, and it was gone too soon." He paused and shook his head. "And to think you almost were too. I'm smart enough to know that what we have is also extraordinary. The fact that you've fallen for me despite everything we've been through and everything I've put you through . . . the fact that you still want me is a gift. You are a gift, and I don't want to be scared anymore. I have no intention of losing you again. Certainly not on my account." He came closer to me. "It doesn't have to be today or even tomorrow, but I'm determined to spend a lifetime with you if you'll let me."

I looked away from him for a moment, out a window that overlooked the water. He'd chosen the right path. I turned my attention back to him. He wasn't anxious or eager or overzealous. He was calm and strong and confident. As always.

"I think you know how much I'd love to spend my life with you," I said, and he leaned in and kissed me. "I hoped you'd come around, of course, but more importantly I wanted you to realize that you deserve good things and good people in your life."

He nodded and sat back. "Thank you. I know, and guess what?"

"What?" I asked.

"My parents and my sister are coming to Phuket. My nephews too."

"They are?"

"Yes. I called them a week ago and invited them out here. So you should know you've made many people very happy, not just me."

I smiled. "That's wonderful news."

"It is, and I can't wait to see them. It's been way too long." He reached for my hand. "And they can't wait to meet you."

"You told them about me?"

"Of course I did. What kind of a creep do you think I am? If I'm going to introduce my family to the woman I'm going to marry, I'm certainly not going to treat it like a dirty little secret."

My eyes went wide. "What if I'd rejected you?"

"You wouldn't."

I tilted my head and raised a brow.

"So, Jessica, will you marry me one day?" He knelt before me. "Soon?"

"I will."

Chapter 36

Four months later

August 6, 2011, a federal jury in Florida convicted three Somalis on murder, piracy, and other charges stemming from our attack. All three faced potential death sentences. Bridget's and Quinn's families were on hand for the trial. The other ten pirates who surrendered pleaded guilty to piracy and were each given mandatory life sentences.

Soon after he returned to Phuket, Grant rented a home on the beach, and I moved in with him, but not before Mr. Knight drilled him with questions regarding his intentions. So I left my coral walls and limited pantry space and unpacked my things into a house with a walk-in closet, king-sized bed, and built-in washer and dryer. Alak would be coming to my place to do his laundry from then on, and for his first visit I had a surprise for him.

I met him out front as he laid his bike on the ground.

"I want to show you something. Come with me," I said, taking his hand.

We walked around to the back patio, where there was a large cardboard box, open on top. "Take a look inside."

He knelt beside it. "Kittens!"

"Grant and I found them the other day down by the beach. We think they're a few months old, because they're not super tiny, so we're going to keep them. Would you like to help me name them?"

He nodded.

"Any thoughts?" I asked. "They're both boys like you."

He thought for a moment. "Maybe I should get to know them first."

I placed my hands on my hips. "I think that's a great idea. See what their personalities are like before making such a big decision."

He sat down as the cats hopped out and climbed all over him, all three of them huggers. I watched as he held them close in his lap, and then I ran inside when I heard the phone ring. "Hello?"

"Where you?" Niran said. "You suppose to be here now. Decoration is waiting on you. Lots of work to be done."

I glanced at the clock on the microwave. "I'm so sorry, I'm on my way!"

That summer, Sophie had met a man. He was from Australia and had come to the bar one night looking for her. His name was Jack Taylor, and he was a friend of a friend, who, when he found out Jack was traveling to Phuket, gave him Sophie's name and told him to look her up. And look her up he did. Jack was a former rugby player. He was six foot five, two hundred pounds of solid muscle, and when he walked into The Islander looking for Sophie, it was like Russell Crowe walking into the Coliseum in *Gladiator*. He conquered her heart and convinced her to move back to Australia with him.

Needless to say, as sad as Niran was to lose her, he was always eager for a reason to throw a party. That evening he'd planned an elaborate going-away bash for Sophie and invited everyone we knew on the island, even a handful of our students and their parents. Grant went to the flower market for us and purchased handmade bouquets for each of the tables, and then helped me and the rest of the staff hang hundreds of additional strands of lights on the trees and the bar. Once the restaurant was decorated, Alak and some of his friends came by to assemble paper lanterns just like we had on New Year's Eve in Patong. Sophie had loved them so much, and I couldn't wait to surprise her with them.

As it turned out, I was the one who was most surprised when a half hour before the party was to begin, there was a tap on my shoulder. When I turned around, my sister Caroline was standing before me. She and I screamed so loudly that we frightened everyone nearby and ourselves. I could hardly breathe.

"What are you doing here? I must be hallucinating!"

She cried tears of joy and hugged me tight. "I can hardly believe it myself!"

I just kept shaking my head back and forth and finally looked over her shoulder at Grant. "How on earth did you keep this from me?"

He shrugged. "I have my ways."

I looked at my sister and put my arms on her shoulders. "Oh. My. God. You're here! You're in Thailand. I'm . . . I'm . . . I don't know what to say. Was your flight okay? When did you get here? Do you need anything?"

"Allen and I arrived a day ago. We've been at the hotel adjusting to the time difference and eager to see you."

"I can't believe he kept this from me. I can't believe you're here!"

"Well, I certainly wasn't going to miss your wedding."

I lifted my head and locked eyes with Grant. "My wedding?" I laughed out loud and then ran to him. "Are you telling me I've just spent the afternoon decorating this place for my own wedding?"

He shrugged and pulled me close and kissed me. Grant was all I'd ever dreamed of. From the moment he stole my heart, I knew I would never be the same. I stood and wrapped my arms around him and buried my head in the base of his chest, and he gently caressed my hair.

"I love you, Jessica."

"I love you too."

"May I borrow the bride?" Caroline asked, and then led me around back to Niran's office, where Sophie was waiting for me with three white sundresses.

"All right, love, what's it going to be? Sexy, sassy, or sweet?" She held them up one at a time.

But before I could respond, Niran—who'd changed into a gold lamé robe and rhinestone crown—walked in and lifted me off my feet. "You my bride today!"

Sophie rolled her eyes.

"I take good care of my girl," he said.

"Thank you, Niran."

"I see you down by the water when you're ready." He patted my head and left.

I chose the sweet dress, which had a halter-style neckline and came just above the knees. Caroline pulled my hair into a low bun and pinned white orchids into it.

"He's a wonderful man," she said to me.

I nodded. "He really is."

"I'm so happy for you, sweetheart. You've grown into such an incredible young woman. Mom would be so proud."

I smiled and gave her a hug. "I think she would be."

Once I was dressed, Sophie and Caroline walked me down to the small pier that belonged to the restaurant, where Grant and Niran and a few other guests were waiting just after sunset. My head was spinning, and Grant was as relaxed and poised as ever. He'd changed into a white linen dress shirt and khaki shorts.

"Come, come," Niran said, and Grant took my hands in his as we faced each other. "We gather today for wedding . . . and little bit for going-away party." He paused. "But mostly for wedding. Be sure to celebrate with many drinks and food," he told the small crowd that had followed us down there.

Then he instructed us to kneel before him, and he placed a garland of flowers around both our necks. I'd seen him officiate many weddings before, and if it were an American couple like us, he'd read standard American vows but incorporate a few Thai traditions. He reached inside his robe and pulled out a small laminated card.

"Do you, Mr. Grant Flynn, take Miss Jessica Gregory to be you wife? To have and to hold from this day forward, for better or for worse, for richer, for poorer, in sickness and in health, to love and to cherish until death?"

I raised my brows and smirked.

"I do," he said.

"And little Miss Jessica, do you take Mr. Grant to be you husband? To have and to hold from this day forward, for better or for worse, for richer . . ." He leaned toward me and whispered, "I leave out the poorer." He winked. "In sickness and in health, to love and to cherish until death."

"I do."

"Okay, very nice," he said, and then waved to Alak, who brought forth a large conch shell filled with holy water for one of Thailand's most renowned wedding blessings, the water pouring. Niran asked us to place our hands in front of us, palms together, and each one of our friends and family took turns pouring a trickle of water over our hands from the base of the thumb to the tips of our fingers.

"By the power of Niran, I now pronounce you husband and the wife." He lifted his arms. "You kiss bride now!"

We stood and locked lips, and everyone cheered. Tears were spilling out of my eyes as Grant embraced me. Maybe he would keep my heart safe after all.

He released his grip and gestured with his head toward the sky, where dozens of glowing lanterns slowly rose from the water's edge.

"Next to you, it's the second most beautiful thing I've ever seen," he whispered in my ear.

It was close to midnight when the majority of the crowd had filtered out. Sophie and Jack went home early to spend some time alone because Jack had to head back to Australia two weeks early without her.

Caroline and Allen were wide awake and both a little tipsy, something I'd never seen before but quite enjoyed.

"This was just the loveliest thing in the whole world, Jess. I can't believe my baby sister is married."

"I can't believe you're standing here saying those words to me."

Grant squeezed my hand.

"So," she said, "where would you like to have your honeymoon?"

Grant turned to me. "We obviously hadn't discussed that. What do you think, Jess? Fiji? Maldives? Maybe New Zealand?"

Caroline was ripe with excitement and awaiting my answer.

I looked up into Grant's eyes and shook my head. "How about New York?"

Chapter 37

Grant and I stole a moment alone and walked up the lit path to a terrace that overlooked the water.

"I have a gift for you," he said.

"You do?"

"Yes. It's back at the marina." He lowered his chin. "Can you meet me there in fifteen minutes?"

I crossed my arms. "What have you done?"

"You'll have to come see for yourself."

"Where should I meet you?"

"On G Dock."

I brought my hand to my heart.

He stepped forward and wrapped his arms around my waist. "I told you I traded *Imagine* in for someone else. You didn't think I meant you, did you?" He smirked.

I smiled and slowly shook my head. "I can't wait to meet her."

"I was hoping you'd say that." He dropped his arms, kissed me, and started to walk away.

"Wait! How will I know which boat it is?" I shouted after him.

"You'll know," he said without breaking his stride.

I quickly changed back into shorts and a tank top, hopped on my bike, and rode the ten-minute ride to the marina. I walked around the side of the main building to the back, where the docks were lined up alphabetically, and located G Dock. My heart was beating out of my chest. I pressed open the gate and made my way down the brightly lit dock past the first few boats—all were cabin cruisers, no sailboats—and read the names as I moved forward.

Ragtime.
Miss Kim.
Bad Latitude.
Lyndi R.
Second Wind.
Deck the Hulls.

And then I saw it. My chest tightened, and my eyes filled with tears, but I was grinning from ear to ear.

The Mighty Quinn.

Grant appeared from below and stood facing me on the stern. "What do you think?"

I took a deep breath before answering. "He's magnificent."

Grant stepped forward and extended his hand.

Epilogue

One year later

Jessica had asked me to grab a few things from the boat, so I hopped in our rental car and drove back to the marina on the Fiumicino River. No matter how many times I'd been there, I would never get accustomed to driving through the streets of Rome.

Once aboard, I grabbed a small duffel bag and filled it with pajamas, T-shirts, underwear, and a few toiletries. The past two days had been harrowing. I tossed the duffel on deck and sat down with a beer and a pad of paper. We'd been told we'd have to stay in Italy for at least eight weeks, we just didn't think Jessica would go into labor so soon.

She and I had been sharing a triple fudge gelato at the base of the Spanish Steps when it happened. She dropped the ice cream and clutched her stomach. "I think my water just broke." Our eyes locked.

"Well, our spoon certainly did," I noted.

I ushered her into a cab with an Italian driver, who couldn't have been happier to deliver us to the nearest hospital. He clapped and waved his arms around, recounting the births of his twelve grandchildren for us. Jessica silently begged me to ask him for silence, but I couldn't bring myself to do it. I held her in my arms and comforted my wife until we arrived.

Forty-eight hours later, Sophia Caroline Flynn was born.

I took a sip of my beer and began to write. The words I was putting down on paper came to me the moment I saw my daughter's face, and they needed to be told. I'd never been presented with such beauty before. She and Jessica would forever have my heart.

Once I was through with the letter, I folded it into an envelope, placed it in the duffel, and said a prayer for my life before getting back into Roman traffic.

My girls were awake when I returned.

"Hey," Jessica said, "we missed you."

I placed the bag on the end table and took the letter out.

"Is that your note?" she asked me.

I nodded.

"Can I read it?"

"Of course you can."

Jessica handed me our child, and I handed her the letter.

Dear Sophia,

Welcome to this crazy world of ours. I sure hope you like to travel, because your mom and I haven't planted roots anywhere in almost two years. Scratch that . . . I just hope you like boats.

Thankfully, it's been a long time since I've been to a hospital, and this time I couldn't be happier for the reason that brought me back to one. In fact, sitting next to a hospital bed for two days awaiting your arrival made me think of someone else. Someone I loved once, and someone who led me to your mom.

Jessica paused to look up at me, and I leaned in and gave her a kiss.

I want you to know how much your mom and I love each other, and how much we love you. How much we've talked about your arrival, and how eager we are to get to know you better. We can't wait to hear the sound of your voice. We can't wait to see if you'll like dresses or jeans, or prefer blue to pink. We can't wait to show you the water and our world, and we can't wait to see what an amazing woman you'll become. We've imagined all of it.

Mom and I want you to know that you can do anything with your life. That we will take care of you and teach you everything we know and give you every opportunity to follow your dreams. Imagine us smiling and cheering you on every step of the way.

As for what you do afterward . . . we can only imagine.

A Note from the Author

This book was inspired by two truly unimaginable stories. The first one begins with following your dreams—and we can all take a lesson from Jane and Marc Adams, friends of mine from college who purchased a sailboat, took their three young kids (Caroline, Grant, and Noah) out of school, and sailed around the world on a boat named *Imagine*. They set sail from Monroe Harbor in Chicago, Illinois, in August of 2008 on course for an adventure of a lifetime.

Jane, a nuclear pharmacist, and Marc, who works in consulting sales, both put their careers on hold and chose to educate their children through homeschooling and firsthand experiences. Nearly four years, forty thousand miles, and forty-two countries later, they returned to their Chicago home, their schools, and their careers with a new perspective on life. They lived their dream.

I highly encourage you to read more about their family and their incredible journey at www.sail*imagine*.com.

The second story is extraordinarily moving and astonishing, yet sadly doesn't end with a safe return. On February 18, 2011, a sailboat by the name of *Quest* carrying two American retired couples—one of which ran a Bible ministry and had been distributing Bibles to schools and churches in remote villages in places, including the Fiji Islands, New Zealand, and French Polynesia—was hijacked in the

Arabian Sea off the coast of Oman. Their boat was boarded by nine-teen Somali pirates, who held them captive for five days until finally killing all four Americans below deck without warning. During the days they were being held, the naval ship USS *Sterett* was trailing their boat, and two of the hijackers were taken aboard the USS *Sterett* to begin negotiations for the release of the Americans, but during that time something went very wrong.

Below is an excerpt from a February 22, 2011, Fox News article.

The yacht Quest *was hijacked on Friday off the coast of Oman, and US forces had been closely monitoring the vessel.*

Unlike most pirate incidents, these pirates boarded the Quest *directly from their mother ship, rather than using faster skiffs. The mother ship remains free.*

Vice Admiral Mark Fox, commander of Centcom's naval forces, explained the timeline of events during a press briefing with Pentagon reporters. According to Fox, there was "absolutely no warning" before the hostage situation turned deadly.

On Monday two pirates boarded the USS Sterett *(one of four US naval ships monitoring the situation) to conduct negotiations for the release of the American hostages. They stayed on board overnight and it's unclear if any ransom was offered before the killing took place.*

At 8:00 a.m. local time Tuesday morning a rocket-pro-pelled grenade was fired at the Sterett *from pirates on board the* Quest. *The shot missed, but immediately after gunfire erupted inside the cabin of the* Quest.

"Several pirates appeared on deck and moved up to the bow with their hands in the air in surrender," Fox said. That's when US Special Operations Forces (SOF) approached on small boats and boarded the yacht.

When SOF soldiers—from a classified Navy SEALs unit—reached the yacht, they found two pirates had already been killed by small-arms fire. As they went below deck, there was an exchange of fire that killed one pirate. The other pirate was killed by an SOF member who used a knife in close combat, Vice Admiral Fox said.

The SOF found some of the Americans still alive, but all four soon died of their wounds. Vice Admiral Fox called it the deadliest pirate incident to date.

This was the same week that my friends Jane and Marc and their family were also making their way across the Indian Ocean. Needless to say, it was a harrowing, frightening, and challenging time for them.

For me, the story of the *Quest* was both deplorable and intriguing. After reading about it on Jane and Marc's blog and then hearing about it on the news, I couldn't stop thinking about the conditions the Americans on board had to endure. No one will ever know for sure, but I can only hope they were treated with a modicum of respect and that their families can find solace in the fact they were doing what they loved.

It's important for me to address one lingering question that I know many readers will have: Why do boaters sail this passage if these dangers exist? So I've asked Jane and Marc to answer it for me. Here is their answer.

We realize that there are a lot of people wondering why reasonably intelligent people would actually sail through these waters and do this not because they have to, but because they want to. As with all of the decisions regarding this passage, each captain and crew has its own reasons for what course it chooses. We were fully aware of the dangers in the Indian Ocean at the time, and we evaluated all of the alternatives available to us to avoid the piracy.

First of all, we were unarmed. Although there was indeed

a small handful of boats who were armed with a handgun or shotgun, in reality even if we were armed we would be no match if confronted by skiffs full of pirates with fully automatic AK-47s and RPGs.

We knew we were on our own, and could not rely on US or other military support. It's a massive ocean, and impossible for the military to patrol. The US & UK military agencies that we were in daily communication with months before our passage and while crossing the Indian Ocean, cautioned all sailboats and recommended they not sail this passage. It was simply too dangerous in their view.

We were close to abandoning our dreams of continuing our cruising life and sailing around the world, and even looked at selling Imagine in Southeast Asia or Australia. We considered sailing east back through the Philippines, Japan, and the Aleutian Islands of Alaska to get back to the west coast of the United States, but that 4,000-mile passage across some of the most treacherous waters was not appealing. We evaluated changing our course to go south around South Africa and back up the South Atlantic, but the sailing conditions along that route too are extremely poor, and it is also fraught with piracy.

For months we tried to organize a transport ship (transport ships carry yachts across the Indian Ocean on into the Mediterranean), but at the time no ship was available. Months later, we did learn of a transport ship that was newly launched which ended up carrying over thirty sailboats safely from the Maldives to Turkey. For many cruisers, however, the cost was too expensive, since it exceeded their entire cruising budget for a year.

For our friends from Europe, this route was about their only way to get home. Some felt that the safety of a convoy was enough to get them through the scariest waters. A few even felt

*that the risks were overblown, and they believed wholehearted-
edly that yachts would not be of interest to the pirates. In contrast, many others believed that the best approach was to go
alone, fast and stealthy. It is a vast ocean out there, and what
are the chances that a pirate is going to come across them?*

*And shockingly, there were also those that just didn't know
about the increased danger of piracy in the Indian Ocean. And
we can't say anyone was so bold as to think they were invincible or immune to the dangers, but there were a few who either
concealed their fears better than us or were far braver than
we were.*

*As for our decision . . . rather than crossing through the
center of the Indian Ocean—the traditional sailing route—
based on the locations of the known piracy attacks and our
boats' ability to motor long distances, we chose to sail along
the coast of India. We kept close to the Indian shore, sailing far
north of the northernmost known piracy attack toward Paki-
stan, en route to Muscat, Oman. This was a difficult 1,500-
mile detour that most boats could not attempt, motor-sailing
into headwinds. But* Imagine *could, and Muscat was a safe
and welcoming home for Jane and the kids for four weeks as
I continued on with my two crew members, Mike and Kier-
an, through the Gulf of Aden into the Red Sea. Once safely
through to Egypt, Jane and the kids flew to meet us and were
reunited with* Imagine *and me.*

*The day I left Jane and the kids behind in Oman was the
day we heard the news that the crew aboard* Quest *had been
killed.*

Acknowledgments

T he words "thank you" can hardly express the awe and gratitude I have for Jane, Marc, Caroline, Grant, and Noah Adams. Without their unimaginable journey and courage to follow their dreams, this story would not exist. Jane and Marc spent countless hours with me reliving their travels and telling me stories of the countries they visited, as I would take notes and live vicariously through them, seething with jealousy. They have also each read this manuscript almost as many times as I have over the past year. Love you guys!

During the course of writing this book, I was also blessed to find a partner in crime in editor Madison Seidler. Madison, thank you for your encouragement, your texts, your generosity, and most of all your insight. You have a true gift when it comes to knowing what appeals to readers, and I thank you for that and so much more.

Next, a huge, mega thank-you to my beta readers. I cannot stress how much I rely on them and how much their opinions mean to me. Meg Costigan, Tammy Langas, Iris Martin, Kelly Konrad, Beth Suit, Wendy Wilken, Rebecca Berto, Amanda Clark, Nicole Angle, Angela Schillaci, Liis McKinstry, and of course, my mother-in-law and my mom, who are my biggest and most vocal fans/critics.

I was also fortunate enough to have some amazing naval contacts, who helped me navigate my way through the chapters dealing with the rescue and the protocol on board an aircraft carrier. They are Becki Moran, Spencer Langley, and Justin Krit. Thank you for your service and for your invaluable help with this book.

Lastly, I would like to extend my gratitude to those I affectionately refer to as Team Dina.

My agent, Deborah Schneider, thank you for telling me I'm a better writer than I think I am. I needed that.

My developmental editor on this book, Andrea Hurst, thank you for enjoying this story as much as I do, and for making it better than it was.

My publishing family at Lake Union Publishing. Many, many thanks for your continued support, your enthusiasm for this book, and your belief in me.

It takes a village . . .

ABOUT THE AUTHOR

DINA SILVER is an author, a wine drinker, and an excellent parallel parker. She lives with her husband, son, and twenty-pound tabby cat in suburban Chicago. She'd prefer to live somewhere where it's warm year-round, but then she'd never stay home and write anything. For more information about Dina and her other books, visit www.dinasilver.com.

ROBIN MILLER